SKIN AND BONE

DS VICKY DODDS 3

ED JAMES

OTHER BOOKS BY ED JAMES

SCOTT CULLEN MYSTERIES SERIES

Eight novels featuring a detective eager to climb the career ladder, covering Edinburgh and its surrounding counties, and further across Scotland.

1. GHOST IN THE MACHINE
2. DEVIL IN THE DETAIL
3. FIRE IN THE BLOOD
4. STAB IN THE DARK
5. COPS & ROBBERS
6. LIARS & THIEVES
7. COWBOYS & INDIANS
8. HEROES & VILLAINS

CULLEN & BAIN SERIES

Four novellas spinning off from the main Cullen series covering the events of the global pandemic in 2020.

1. CITY OF THE DEAD
2. WORLD'S END
3. HELL'S KITCHEN
4. GORE GLEN

CRAIG HUNTER SERIES

A spin-off series from the Cullen series, with Hunter first featuring in the fifth book, starring an ex-squaddie cop struggling with PTSD, investigating crimes in Scotland and further afield.

1. MISSING

2. HUNTED
3. THE BLACK ISLE

DS VICKY DODDS SERIES

Gritty crime novels set in Dundee and Tayside, featuring a DS juggling being a cop and a single mother.

1. BLOOD & GUTS (a new prequel coming soon)
2. TOOTH & CLAW
3. FLESH & BLOOD
4. SKIN & BONE (coming 1st May 2021)

DI SIMON FENCHURCH SERIES

Set in East London, will Fenchurch ever find what happened to his daughter, missing for the last ten years?

1. THE HOPE THAT KILLS
2. WORTH KILLING FOR
3. WHAT DOESN'T KILL YOU
4. IN FOR THE KILL
5. KILL WITH KINDNESS
6. KILL THE MESSENGER
7. DEAD MAN'S SHOES

Other Books

Other crime novels, with Senseless set in southern England, and the other three set in Seattle, Washington.

- SENSELESS
- TELL ME LIES
- GONE IN SECONDS
- BEFORE SHE WAKES

PROLOGUE

Where the hell was she?

Noel swung around a full three-sixty and took in the square. That sandwich shop that did the "belly buster". That restaurant his old man said he took birds to, not far from where the old wanker worked.

He checked his watch – five past ten – and a bead of sweat trickled down his back. Skipping school for this, it better be worth it. He had that knot in his stomach, like someone was making scones out of his guts. If he was spotted by someone, he'd be deep shit.

'Dax!'

Noel swung around to his six – that's what they called right behind you in that game – and saw her.

Over the wet road by that pub, the February morning light caught her, a ray of sunshine like God was pointing at her, like he was parting the rainclouds just for her. Not that Noel believed in God, mind. He stuffed his hands in his pockets and nodded at her, trying to act all cool. Not approaching her just yet. Let *her* sweat for a bit.

She was frowning at him. 'Dax, you okay?'

He couldn't help but grin. 'Aye, I'm good.' He knew they were going to do it again, and his heart was racing at the prospect. Jesus, she was *gorgeous*. His fingers ran across the condoms in his pocket, the sharp foil edge, the round shape in outline. He set off towards her, but had to stop on the edge of the road. Thick traffic, cars and vans on this back road, a rat run behind the Caird Hall, and one of the few places you could park in the city centre, or so his old man told him. He made a face at her about the traffic.

She didn't seem to find it funny, just stood there, hugging her bag tighter. Then she checked her own watch.

Noel scanned along the street, trying to spot a break in the traffic, somewhere he could dart across to her side.

He didn't spot the van stopping behind him, and didn't hear the door sliding or the two men jumping out, didn't see them until they were on him, grabbing his arms, smothering his face. He raised his arm to wave at her, but it was like he was drowning in the sea and she just couldn't see him. He tried to shout, but fabric bit into his lips. Something covered his eyes and it all went dark.

A punch in the side that felt like it had burst his kidney and he was lifted off his feet. He fell and his back hit something hard. Something ground shut behind. Then two thumps.

Noel was pushed forward and hit his shoulder off something hard and cold. Then he was jerked to the side, hard enough for the prick behind him to let Noel's mouth go for a few seconds, long enough to let Noel speak. 'What are you—'

'Shut up.'

But the bag was off Noel's head. Not that it was much lighter. He could see two shapes near him. A shaft of light burst out of the right.

'Get my torch.'

A light clicked on and pointed down at Noel's hands. Two big hairy shovels held his forearms for his mate to start binding them. The torchlight climbed his torso. Adidas tracksuit, Nike jacket. And a balaclava, though it was so dark in here that Noel couldn't see anything other than that shape.

'Ow!'

The prick was holding Noel's wrists super-tight. The pain was bittersweet even when he let go.

Noel tried to move his arms, but they were tied together now. Zip ties, like in the game. He had an idea, though. One way to screw them over. He slipped his watch off and found the prong of the buckle. Felt sharp against his thumb. Right. Here goes.

He could see just enough of his wrist to get it working and started cutting the edge against his skin.

But he needed to distract them.

'Who are you?'

'Kid. Shut up and you *might* live.' The prick's beery voice was from way out of town, way out of this country. English, maybe Liverpool or Manchester.

Aye, Manchester.

Like that guy on the telly, the ex-player on Sky, who Noel's old man said was smart, the one who Noel kept forgetting the name of. 'What have you been saying, Noel?'

'Don't call me that.'

'What's wrong with Noel, eh? Your old man a fan of Mr Blobby?'

'Oasis, but I hate them. People call me Dax.'

'Dax, eh? Like that bird in *Star Trek*?'

Noel shrugged, but it was working. He was on the fourth symbol and it was working really nicely. 'It's a nickname.'

'Huh. Takes all sorts these days, doesn't it?' A guttural laugh rattled Noel's good ear. 'Hey, Our Kid, remember when we saw Oasis at Maine Road, eh?'

The one who bound Noel's hands looked up, rolling his eyes in the gaps in his balaclava. 'Shut up, Sid.'

'Dickhead. Told you not to say my name.'

'Shit, yeah. Sorry.'

'Noel here won't remember our names, would he?'

Noel shook his head. Just three left to go, but blood was dripping down to his fingers now. 'No way. Let me go and I'll not say anything.'

'What the hell are you doing?' The prick behind him rolled his sleeves right up to the bicep. 'You a self-harmer, son?'

Noel clutched his watch in his palm, hiding it from the dickhead. 'You wouldn't understand.'

'Our Kid here used to cut himself, until his old man booted the living daylights out of him. That learned him, eh?'

'Shut up, Sid.'

'I told you, man.' He walked over to the other one and it seemed like they locked foreheads. 'No names.'

Noel let his watch go again and started scratching. The last three. There. Done.

Our Kid grinned, a gold tooth catching the sharp torchlight. 'He won't remember much after we're finished, eh?'

Sid the Prick laughed. 'Very true, our kid, very true.'

No two ways about it, Noel was in the shit here.

This wasn't a joke.

This was real.

Warm wet liquid trickled down his leg.

He was pissing himself. Literally pissing himself. He needed to get out of here. Now. No messing about. He needed a plan.

He looked at the one holding the torch. 'You Man Utd?'

'Our Kid is. I'm City.'

'My old man played for Man U in the eighties.'

'Yeah?'

'Swear.'

'Sounds like bollocks to me, Our Kid. What do you think?'

'I think this little sod's doing whatever he can to get out of this, isn't he?'

'I swear, if you let me go, I won't tell anyone.'

The torch shone in Noel's eyes. 'That's the problem, you little sod. What you've been telling everyone.'

'I swear, I've told nobody nothing.'

'No, you lying shit. You've been talking. We know. We've heard. Now, who the hell are you talking to?'

'Nobody!'

'Son, if you tell us, we might let you go.'

'I haven't told anyone.'

'Okay, but the alternative here is that we're going to set you on fire. You ever smelled burning human flesh? It's like pork. Like someone's making bacon, know what I mean?'

'Please. I haven't done anything!'

Something splashed over Noel's head, cold and stinging. It absolutely reeked. Noel got some in his mouth, it tasted so bitter. 'What the hell's that?'

'It's petrol, you little dickhead.'

The fuel stung his fresh wound, like he'd touched the hot stovetop. 'Don't set me on—'

Sid the Prick laughed, cutting Noel off. 'Don't sweat it, you little punk. This is just a warning.'

'This is like a game.'

'Kid, this ain't a game. It's for real and you'll know it's for real when we say that if you don't keep your frigging mouth shut, next time you will be set on fire.'

Noel laughed, trying to take control of the situation. 'Frigging? What's wrong with swearing?'

'It's not big, hard or clever, sunshine.'

'Frigging is still swearing.'

Sid barked out laughter. 'You hear this, Our Kid?'

'It's for female masturbation.'

Sid shook his head. 'This little sod thinks he can— FUCK!'

Noel drove the back of his head into Sid's nose. Made it feel like he'd split it open. But he had no time. He lashed his head forward this time, at the spot just above where Our Kid's gold tooth had been, and cracked into his jaw.

Our Kid squealed in pain.

Both sides of Noel's head were on fire, but he was the only one standing. He picked up the torch and swung the light around the van. Empty, but the back was over there. He charged over and reached with his fingers until he found the door handle. Just a catch, one of those thick ones that took a lot of effort. He put his elbow into it and fumbled it open.

The wind almost blew him over, almost tugged him down to

the road. Bright sunlight burst into the back of the van. They were moving, away from Dundee, heading south on the Tay Road Bridge towards Fife.

Shit. This was serious. Noel had to jump. But he couldn't jump. Couldn't he?

Behind him, the two idiots were still moaning but Sid was pushing up to standing. He reached into his pocket and pulled out a pistol.

As he raised it up to head height, Noel jumped forward out of the van onto the carriageway. He slid and rolled and tumbled and his body screamed out in pain. His trousers tore and his skin shredded, and it felt like a sander was pressed against his cheek. His palms felt torn open and his wrist scars were on fire again, petrol mixing with blood.

But he was out, he was free.

The van sped away from him.

Noel hauled himself up to standing, but he was sure he'd broken a leg and an arm. He was standing on a bridge over the Tay, wind lashing him, cars flashing past on the other side of the road. He needed a plan and fast.

He needed to get back to Dundee.

No, he needed *help*.

Cars were hurtling towards him in both lanes. Flashing their lights like Noel couldn't see them.

If he got to the walkway in the middle, he could flag someone down. Maybe a cop, but probably just someone. Anyone. Just not gangsters from Manchester who were trying TO SET HIM ON FIRE.

Noel set off towards the middle.

Honking horns.

Squealing brakes.

Broken bones that were too slow.

Noel jerked himself backwards, away from the road and up onto the narrow pavement hanging over the river.

The cars whooshed past and he tried to move his hands to grip the barrier, but they were round his front and tied together.

Another gap. He had to move!

He tried to run but the honking horns stopped him. He stepped back again, trying to brace himself against the slipstream.

He twisted round and grabbed the cold metal, facing onto the carriageway. His slippery fingers gave way and fell forward onto the carriageway and lay there, trapped by his bound wrists.

A car was closing in on him, flashing its headlights. Another two were hurtling his way, followed by a bus.

He tried to get up, but he kept slipping. He rolled over and got his left knee on the ground, then his right, and somehow he pushed up to standing. He stepped back up onto the small pavement, no further forward.

The car whizzed past him, the horn a long smear of sound.

He was okay. He'd survived. He was free, but nobody was stopping and the van would be back, wouldn't it?

It'd turn around at the roundabout, then come down the other carriageway and Sid or Our Kid would jump out, dash across the central walkway, then they'd have him again. And there was another guy, someone driving – maybe he had a gun? But maybe this time they'd actually set fire to him. Or just shoot him with that gun.

No, he needed help.

Police.

Another car shot towards him, flashing headlights and hitting the horn.

They zipped past.

He was okay, still standing.

The horn got louder, like it was being held down.

The bus hurtled past him, slapping a massive wall of air towards him, pushing him back. He tried to brace himself again, but he slid and slipped against the barrier.

Another horn, loud as hell this time.

He looked back the way, away from Dundee, and his eyes widened.

The van was reversing at him, full speed, that loud whirr. It shot past the bus and kept going, aiming for him.

He had one move here. He clambered up onto the railing, bum first, then planting both feet. Then standing.

The van slammed towards him. Another car hammered its horn.

Noel slipped and rolled over.

The sky spun around until the dirty, foaming wash of the Tay hurtled towards him.

DAY 1

Tuesday
25th February 2020

1

Vicky looked out of the wide window across the narrow concrete path. The murky grey-brown river foamed between the two bridges, though they were nearer to the Tay Bridge, with another train easing south. She enjoyed that moment just to herself, the bitter tang of her tea still on her lips, the rich roast of the coffee brewing behind the counter, the loud chatter rattling around the room.

Bliss.

Another queue of school kids stood behind a rope, readying themselves for a morning in the V&A museum. Vicky's mum hadn't shut up about it while it was being planned and built, but hadn't bothered to visit in the eighteen months since it opened. The kids reminded Vicky of herself on any number of similar trips, all the school politics that would play out, all the games, all the teasing, all the bitter rivalries. And she could never remember anything about the actual thing they were visiting, just the kids and their antics.

Vicky headed back to their table and sat next to Rob, kissing him lightly on the cheek and grabbing his hand, twisting her foot around his. She leaned in and whispered, 'Thank you for this. Makes my birthday feel special.'

Rob smiled back at her. 'Next year will be more special, believe me.'

'Don't remind me.' Vicky winced. She held her teacup over her empty plate, just a smear of tomato ketchup left from her brunch. 'Thirty-nine still feels young, forty... doesn't.'

'You still have a few years on me, baby.'

Vicky laughed at the pet name. She'd never thought she was one for being so soppy, but here she was. So deeply in love. She looked around the table at her parents, arguing over something stupid. At her daughter and Rob's son, who had blended into being brother and sister. It felt like a life.

Vicky leaned back to Rob. 'But seriously, thank you for organising this.'

'It's important that you feel as lovely as you make me feel.'

'Thank you.' That tangle of love tickled at the back of her throat.

Rob checked his watch. 'Anyway, we'd better get along to the exhibition. A ton of school trips today, so we want to beat that rush.'

'There's one just going in.'

'See what I mean? We need to hurry.' Rob stood up and winked. 'I'll just go to the gents.' But he set off towards the till.

Vicky's mother was keeping an eagle eye on him. Even had her glasses on. Her mouth fell open to an O and she shot to her feet. 'Robert!' She raced across the restaurant as fast as her seventy-year-old legs could carry her. 'Don't you dare!'

Bella was looking over to the hubbub at the counter. Her hair definitely needed a cut; it was coiled over her shoulder like a pet snake and ran right down to her waist. 'Where's Granny going?'

Vicky leaned forward to Bella and gave a crafty wink. 'Granny doesn't like other people paying.'

Bella's face twisted into a frown. 'Why not?'

'I honestly have no idea.' Vicky smiled at her daughter. 'It's a Dundee thing, maybe.'

'No, you see it all over Scotland. It's one-upmanship... I don't want to pay but owing you is worse.' Dad sipped from his white coffee mug. His third of their brunch, so he'd be... Christ, he'd be havering all morning. At a hundred miles an hour. 'I don't get it either, Bella.'

'*My* granny doesn't do it.' Jamie was staring into his Nintendo console, his thick glasses reflecting the bright cartoon world. His hair needed to grow, if anything, but he liked it really short, just like his father. 'She lets Dad pay for everything.'

Bella stuck out her tongue, even though he wasn't looking at her. 'Your granny smells.'

Jamie shrugged. 'That's not her fault.'

Dad laughed, but caught himself. 'That's not very kind, Bella.'

Vicky gave her a stern look. 'No, it's not.'

Bella stuck her lip out. 'It's true, though.'

'Hey, Bella! Happy birthday!'

All of Vicky's instincts kicked in. She shot to her feet to race around the table to grab his wrist and keep him away from her child. Then she stopped dead.

Alan stood there, almost dwarfed by the giant wrapped gift he held out for his daughter. His head was shaved, but his sideburns had spread into a beard, making him look like a slightly pink tennis ball with features crudely drawn on.

Vicky yanked him away from the table and kept a tight grip on his arm. 'What the hell are you doing here?'

'Hey, Vicks.' Like always, he avoided the question. 'You're looking well. Very good, actually.'

'Alan. Quit it. Why are you here?'

He ignored her, keeping his focus on his daughter. 'Hey, Bells, I—'

Vicky stood between them, blocking him from getting at Bella. Just as well she was taller than him. 'How the hell did you find out about this?'

Alan smirked at her, then nodded over to the till. 'Your new lad should be careful what he shares on Schoolbook.'

Vicky glanced to where Mum was trying to slap Rob's card out of his hand. She looked back, but Alan was gone.

'Can't stay, Bells, but I brought you a pressie.' Alan put the package in front of their daughter.

She squealed with delight and started tearing at the paper.

Vicky got in close to Alan. 'It's not her birthday, you idiot, it's *mine.*'

'Oh.' Alan tried to smile, but his cheeks weren't having any of it. 'Right.'

Vicky shook her head at him, her ponytail swishing through the air. 'Don't even know your own daughter's birthday.'

'Aye, not exactly my fault, is it? Didn't even know I had a kid.' He made for Bella again.

Dad was scowling at Alan, hands resting on his belly. 'Son, you should clear off if you know what's good for you.'

'Aye, aye.' Just one look from him to get through to Alan. Then again, he'd seen what Vicky's father was capable of. 'I'll see you around, then.' He set off back through the restaurant, hands in pockets.

Vicky gave her dad a stern look to keep an eye on the kids, then set off after Alan at double speed. She grabbed him by the now-empty queue. 'You brought Bella a gift, when what she needs is a father.'

'Your new lad seems to think that's his role.'

'Aye. And he's doing a really good job, as it happens. Same with me and Jamie. Rob and I care about each other and about our children.'

'I'm very pleased for you, Vicks. Honest.'

She prodded his sternum. 'If you're going to be in her life, then do it. Be present. Be with her. Be her dad. But if you just like the idea of it, not the reality, then you can piss off.'

He stared deep into her eyes for a few seconds, then down at his shoes, that smirk back on his face. 'Rightio.'

She'd seen that before, the wounded swan act. But he could certainly hiss and batter with his wings. So she poked him again. 'And stop suing me.'

He looked back up at her. 'Why?'

'I know why you're doing it. You just enjoy seeing me squirm.'

'Getting a lot of pleasure out of it, Vicks.' With one last smile, Alan sloped off out of the restaurant.

Vicky made to go, but a hand grabbed her shoulder.

'Leave it.'

Vicky looked round at Dad and locked eyes with him, and she just let it all out. Tears started filling her eyes, that bitter taste in her mouth, and the rancid heat in her armpits, the trickle of sweat crawling down her back. 'I can handle all the stress of my job, but can I handle that worm? No.'

'Of course you can.' Dad wrapped Vicky into a hug and held her there. 'He's a worm, that one. You got that right. And you can handle your job. But you're handling him.'

'I just don't think I can fight off the legal stuff, Dad. What if he gets joint custody?'

Dad let her go and focused hard on her. 'You can and you will. We just need time to sit down and discuss it. Okay?'

'It's not that, it's...' Vicky felt a deep sigh rattle her throat, right where the tears pooled when they didn't slide down her cheeks and ruin her crude make-up. 'It's just...'

'Go on?'

'Rob doesn't want me to fight it off.'

Dad looked over to the tills. 'Seriously?'

'Right. He wants me to... What does he call it? Oh aye, "negotiate back support and workable access rules to provide a meaningful contribution to Bella's life". I mean...'

'Aye. Well. I can see the logic in that. Bella's half Alan's, right?'

'Right.' As much as she didn't want to admit it, it was the truth. Even if he had none of his time, Bella had half of Alan's DNA.

'Come on.' Vicky patted Dad's arm then walked back to their table. 'You shouldn't have left the kids alone.'

'The boy's lost in that game and Bella's all over that present. And your mother was heading back, anyway.'

Mum was putting her purse away with a sour look on her face, aimed at Rob. Proved Dad's point of it being a show, at least to be seen trying to pay and then *having to*.

'What?' Jamie was peeking inside Bella's box. 'How does *she* get a Switch too?'

'Because I'm worth it.' Bella stuck her tongue out again and this time he noticed it. 'You'll not be able to beat me.'

'Always can, always will.'

Dad sat down again and leaned across the table to Jamie. 'Your Uncle Andrew was always on at us to get him the latest this, that or the other thing. Usually Nintendo.'

'Nintendo is the *best*.' Jamie went back to focusing on the screen instead of the human beings around him.

Vicky sat next to Rob and leaned in to talk to him. 'I can't believe you thought it'd be good to involve him in our life.'

'Eh?'

'Alan. He's making my life hell trying to get access to Bella.'

'Aye.'

'That's it?' Vicky shifted round to stare hard at him.

Rob had gone all white and was shaking his head at something. Whatever it was, it was on his phone, giving it much more attention than Vicky.

'What's up?'

Rob put his mobile down on the table and let out a slow breath. 'When I went to pay, my card got declined.'

'Wait, what?'

'Your *mother* had to pay. My credit card is maxed out.'

'What? How can it be?'

Rob stabbed a finger off his phone's screen. 'I'm checking the statement just now.'

'Is it our holiday, because we can cancel and get—'

'No, it's not that. That part's fine, we'll pay that off. It's not that — Jamie!' His eyes shot across the table.

The boy didn't look up from his Nintendo. 'What?'

'What the hell have you been buying?'

'Nothing?' Still didn't look up.

Rob held up the mobile. 'Doesn't look like that to me. An Xbox transaction for eleven hundred quid!'

'Wasn't me.'

'Was it Bella? Because she doesn't play on it.'

'Wasn't me.'

'Quit denying it, son. And look at me when I'm talking to you.'

'But I'm just at the—'

Rob snatched the console out of his hands. 'What have you been buying?'

'Nothing. I swear.'

'Have you heard of something called *Indignity Online*?'

'Right?'

'And you have been playing it?'

'So?'

'And you haven't bought anything in that?'

'Well, I mean me and Brendan were playing and got some clothes for our guys and a new car and a helicopter.'

Rob put the Nintendo down by his empty plate, face down. 'Did these clothes and that car have any monetary value attached to them?'

'I don't know. Maybe. I clicked buy and it did. It's just pretend.'

Rob pinched his nose. 'It's not pretend...'

Vicky leaned in. 'What's up?'

'The wee sod's spent eleven hundred quid on virtual clothes and cars and helicopters.'

'How can that happen? I thought you had—'

'I *did*.' Rob gritted his teeth. He picked up his phone. 'I'm going to speak to the company and find out.'

'You can wait until later, right?'

'No. If I can't pay for this meal, I can't pay for our tickets for the museum, I can't get our lunch or petrol to get home and I can't—'

Vicky's mobile blasted out her old phone ringtone. She checked the display, expecting Alan.

Forrester calling...

Vicky wanted to throw the bastard thing in the Tay, but she got up. 'Back in a sec.' She walked back towards the door, answering the call as she went. 'What's up, sir?'

'Sorry, Doddsy, but I need you to come in to work.'

'On my birthday?'

Forrester sighed. 'It's not the big one, is it?'

'No, but we're just at the V&A and it's—'

'Well, I really need you to come in today. Just landed two cases in the last twenty minutes.'

Vicky didn't say anything in the hope that he'd shut up and go away.

'Pretty please with sugar on the top and chocolate diamonds?'

'Sir, I just can't—'

'Well, I hate to do this, Doddsy, but I'm ordering you to come in to work.'

2

Vicky indicated left for the spiralling road up to the Tay Road Bridge and hit a queue of cars honking their horns. A uniformed police officer made his way down the lane of traffic cones blocking the cars from the outside lane, then peered into the car in front of her, no doubt receiving a volley of abuse when he suggested heading to Fife via Perth and the treacherous road on the south bank of the Tay.

Vicky rolled her window down in advance, but caught a bitter fug of exhaust fumes. And driving rain, at the exact right angle to soak her thin blouse.

The uniform plodded towards her with a grim look on his face. 'Excuse me, but the bridge is—' He laughed. 'Oh, it's you.'

'Morning, Dumpy.' She held out her warrant card.

'I know who you are, Vicky. Just, nobody told us to expect you so quickly.'

'Can I get through?'

'Sure, sure.' He moved a few cones aside and beckoned her through.

Vicky drove on with a thumbs up, then hurtled up the carriageway towards the crime scene and the flashing blue lights.

Didn't take much effort to spot Forrester flapping around like police tape in the wind, though there was a good chance it could catch his long limbs and send him flying out towards the North Sea. His white mullet was catching the breeze too, just the right side of long to be allowable in a police force, even as a detective. Vicky pulled in at the end of the long line of traffic and killed the engine. She got out into the biting February air. At least the snow had gone, but it had retained the threat of sleet in the Arctic blast and her coat wasn't coping with it at all. She hugged it tight around her and jogged towards Forrester.

He was scowling at someone hidden behind a police meat wagon. 'Brian, Brian, Brian, come on.'

Vicky recognised the man in the uniform, even clocked the shiny superintendent's cap before she made an arse of herself for once. Brian Masson, head of Dundee Local Policing. A chubby wee guy with a moustache twenty years out of date. Even though it was after ten, the rest of his face looked like he hadn't shaved in days, but he had a fresh nick on his chin. 'I get where you're coming from, David, but seriously, we need us to get the traffic moving ASAP.'

'Way above my pay grade.' Forrester stepped closer to him. 'I'm here to find out what's happened to that laddie. If you've got another motivation, then you need to call up Carolyn Soutar. She's my boss and she's told me to find out—'

'Come on, can't we get one lane moving?'

'Nope. Forensics, Brian. Forensics.'

Masson raised his thick eyebrows. 'You're not going to change your mind, are you?'

'Nope.'

'Right, well. It's a shame.' Masson walked off, limping like he'd stood on a landmine. He nodded at Vicky as he passed. 'Sergeant.'

'Sir.' Vicky waved at Forrester to get his attention. 'David, you okay?'

Forrester looked around at her, but his smile was tempered with a snarl. 'That arsehole just doesn't change, does he?'

'What's up?'

'Piling pressure on me to open the bridge. Not my remit, Doddsy. But he still takes the bloody piss, doesn't he?'

Vicky had less than no idea what was going on here. Squad cars raced up the oncoming two lanes, flashing blues and twos. She focused on Forrester. 'What happened?'

'Trying to figure that out myself.'

'Better be important to make me cancel my birthday.'

'Aye, aye, you'll get two days back, don't you worry.' Forrester made a vain attempt at taming his hair, way past the point of being windblown. He frowned, like he was trying to collect his thoughts. 'Got a report of a kid taking a header off the side of the bridge.' He waved off to the Broughty Ferry side, past the industrial estates to the old castle on the beachfront. 'Coasties are out looking for him.'

Vicky's turn to frown. 'So why are the MIT involved? Why bring us out?'

'Because the laddie was either dumped from or jumped out of a moving van.'

'So someone had kidnapped him?'

'Maybe. Or they were chasing him. Got a report of some idiots wearing balaclavas. Oh, in the name of the wee man.'

Masson jogged back to them, lugging an iPad.

'Aye, and that arsehole Masson keeps on hammering the point about getting the traffic moving soon.' Forrester raised his eyebrows at Masson. 'Sorry, sir, swear I didn't see you there.'

'Well, I am an arsehole, hard to deny it.' Masson smiled. 'And we really have got to get the bridge open, even if most of that traffic is Fifers.'

Forrester laughed at that. 'Aye, even so. You speak to Carolyn?'

'Sure did. She's given you until eleven, then we clear the bridge.'

'Bloody hell.' Forrester looked out to sea. 'Any word on the victim's location?'

'Nope.' Masson looked back towards Dundee. 'Got cameras all over the bridge, so it should be a piece of piss to find out what happened.' He flipped open the iPad and stabbed a chubby finger off the screen. 'Okay, the plates are probably going to be wrong, but we've got it.' He held the screen out for them to both see. A gust of wind almost blew it out of his hands.

The display was split in half. The left showed the view from a traffic camera looking back towards the city, almost the exact same view Vicky saw now, meaning they were in the right spot to decipher what the hell had happened. Sure enough, a white van was hurtling towards the camera.

The right side showed the view towards Fife and Newport's grand houses. The back of the van was open and a kid stood in the open doorway, looked barely fifteen. On the next shot, he was looking behind himself, then the next he was flying through the air. Two men wearing balaclavas stood where he had, clutching air, then the van disappeared.

Vicky glanced at Forrester. 'Well, sir, there's your balaclavas.'

'Aye, aye.' But he was looking at the tablet like he'd never seen one before.

Masson adjusted the view back and the kid tumbled and rolled along the carriageway. Looked touch and go whether anyone could survive that. Then again, a van with three people in the back maybe wasn't travelling at anything like the fifty limit.

The kid stopped rolling. Then got up and looked around. Cars were hurtling towards him. He stepped onto the side pavement and swayed around in the wind. It looked like his hands were bound in front of him. He looked right at the camera and his face was all cut up and bloody.

A car whizzed past. It looked like he tried flagging down the next one but it shot past as well. Then a bus hurtled towards him.

Vicky almost couldn't watch.

But it went past too.

Then the van slammed back into the frame hurtling towards him. Noel jumped up, off the carriageway, onto the barrier. Then he slipped and plunged down into the sea.

Forrester let out a deep breath. 'Well, that's all there in Technicolor, isn't it? The kid was clearly trussed up and clearly dripping wet.'

'Dripping wet?' Vicky squinted at the screen and wound it

back to him standing on the pavement. The zoom didn't clarify much. 'You think he's wet?'

'Aye. It's not raining on there.' Forrester circled the kid. 'And he's being taken by those goons in balaclavas. Even if they didn't intend to kill him, it's still murder.'

'Death during the commission of a criminal act...' Masson folded his iPad away. 'Aye, he's right. Anyway, I'll see what I can do, but seriously, we need the bridge back by half eleven at the latest.'

'Appreciate it, you bloody arsehole.'

Masson pinched Forrester's cheeks. 'Takes one to know one.' He stuffed the iPad under his arm and marched off back to the slowly forming command centre, or at least where the cups of tea were.

Forrester walk over to the barrier, where a CSI was inspecting a pair of oily handprints. 'Doddsy, you're in charge here.'

Vicky followed him. 'Excuse me?'

'I know you don't want the hassle of being an Acting DI, but just be my eyes and ears on this.'

'Why, where will you be?'

'Some lassie's been kidnapped in town. Name of Ashlynn Thomas. DS MacDonald's looking into that for me. I'll sit across both, but I need you to act up. You okay with that?'

'Fine.'

'That's what I like to hear.' He walked off in Masson's wake. 'Hey, wait up!'

But Vicky wasn't fine. Maybe she *was* ready to do that Acting DI thing, but Forrester never thought she'd be ready, did he? Maybe if she had different parts between her legs she'd get the chance. And maybe MacDonald had got an Acting gig.

Sod all that.

No, some poor kid had taken a header off the bridge. She needed to find who'd done that to him. Focus on that and only that.

Christ, maybe he was alive.

Vicky peered down into the river. Almost at the Fife end, so over a mile from the Dundee side, and the bridge was much higher here. Meaning he was more likely to have died going in. But if he'd survived, staying alive was less likely the longer he was in the water.

And like anyone working by the water, she'd come up against suspicious suicides many times. And this was clearly a murder, or as near as damn it. Someone had done this to him. Let the coast-guards focus on finding and recovering the boy, she needed to do her part.

Vicky looked at the CSI, but kept her distance. 'You got any idea what that is?'

They looked over and Vicky recognised the face. Zoey MacDonald. Her figure had thickened a lot since Vicky had last seen her, no longer the skinny waif, but now a young mother struggling with a tough situation. 'Hey, Sarge, didn't see you there. I think it's petrol.'

'Petrol?' That got Vicky in the guts, like she'd swallowed half a gallon of the stuff. They'd been trying to set him on fire. 'Call me the second you know for sure, okay?'

'Will do.'

Vicky headed towards the huddle around the tea order.

DC Karen Woods was talking with her husband, Colin. She wore a business suit; he wore a short-sleeved summer uniform despite the biting wind. They shut up as Vicky approached. Colin slipped off with a cup of tea and Karen stepped forward. 'Hey, Vicks, surprised to see you here.'

'Forrester's orders.' That was all Vicky was giving her.

DC Stephen Considine appeared, clutching two teas. 'Here you go, Sarge. Saved one for you.'

'Thank you.' Vicky was so cold that she couldn't even give him hassle for sucking up to the boss. 'Okay, Karen, I need you to take a lead on speaking to witnesses.'

Considine cleared his throat. 'I've been all over that, Sarge.'

'And?'

He slurped tea. 'A bloke was driving back from walking his dog at Tentsmuir. He was the one who called it in. Saw it all unfold, but didn't get a chance to stop until he was over the other side.

Saw the kid jumping out. Saw people in balaclavas in the back. The kid ran off, but took a header off the bridge.'

Vicky didn't have the heart to say she'd already seen it. Would be like shouting at an eager puppy. 'Did they see what kind of van it was?'

'White, like a Transit or something?'

Vicky pointed along the bridge. 'Just need anything that we can use to identify it. Plates? Logo? Anything?'

'Nothing on the side. Lad said it was plain.'

'Well, we've got the CCTV, so get that van found.'

'Aye, aye.' Considine walked off, sipping tea through the lid.

Vicky looked back along the Tay towards Broughty Castle, where some boats were dancing about in the water.

Colin Woods ran back towards them. 'Vicky, that's the coastguards. The inshore lifeboat's got him, transferring to offshore for first aid.' He stood there, listening to his radio, staring into space.

Vicky sipped tea, but it felt like her insides were burning. Was the kid alive or—

Colin looked up at her. 'Shite, he's dead.'

3

Vicky hoped it would be an ambulance meeting them, but it was the pathologist's van.

Karen patted Vicky's arm. 'I'll go and have a word.'

'Thanks.' Vicky stood alone on the waterfront, sipping the last of her lukewarm tea. Even with sugar in it, she still needed it.

Behind her, the City Quay was basically dying on its arse, losing the effects of its redevelopment of twenty years ago. That Chinese buffet restaurant where her brother almost literally broke his stomach on the fourth plate. An outdoor shop. And... Aye, it was dying on its arse. Had to only be a matter of time before it was turned into posh flats like the rest of the buildings along the river. Some new one going up between the bridge and the V&A, similar to a block that opened a year ago.

The boat pulled up and two coastguards hopped onto the concrete and moored it. The older-looking of the two nodded over at Vicky. He was late fifties and had the deep winter tan of an Atlantic trawlerman, someone who spent all day outside. 'You Sergeant Dodds?'

'For my sins.'

'Any relation to George Dodds?'

'My dad, aye.'

'Well, tell him Big Shug says hi.'

'Sure.'

Big Shug folded his arms across his thick jacket and stood there. Didn't seem in any hurry to get the corpse out of his boat. 'You're lucky, doll. Laddie could've drifted for miles, but we found him dragged up against a buoy in the Middle Bank.' He casually thumbed out to sea like any of that would mean anything to Vicky.

'Mind if I see?'

Big Shug looked over at his mate, but he was laughing and joking with the pathology driver. Sometimes there was maybe a bit too much humour in gallows humour. 'On you go, doll.'

Any more and he was getting words, coastguard or not.

Vicky walked over to the edge and peered into the boat.

Up close, the kid looked even younger than on the video feed. Way too young to be dead. Still, he didn't look anywhere near as bad as Vicky had expected. Looked just like he was sleeping, though his neck was a bit crooked.

'Expected raw mince, didn't you, hen?' Big Shug laughed. 'No, you're thinking about how hitting the water's like hitting concrete, aye? Well, it is, just his neck took the brunt of it, got all buggered up on entry. That's what killed him.'

'Could he have survived?'

'Maybe if his wrists hadn't been bound, aye.' Big Shug got out an ancient phone, about five times thicker than anything you could buy in the shops. 'The pathologist's on her way but you or I could declare death, eh?'

Vicky gave him a polite smile. 'Any idea who he is?'

Big Shug pulled out an evidence bag containing a wallet. 'Assuming this is his, the kid's called Noel Russell. Middle name Liam. Why does that ring a bell?'

'The brothers in Oasis.' Vicky waved at Karen, but she was halfway over. 'Get a check on a Noel Liam Russell, please.'

'Oasis fan or what?' Karen turned away, phone to her ear.

Just as Vicky's rang.

Big Shug bellowed out a laugh. 'She calling you to get rid of me, eh?'

'Hardly.' Vicky checked the display. 'No, this is a complete idiot, unfortunately.' Vicky put her phone to her ear. 'Stephen.'

'Hey yo, Sarge.' Considine yawned down the line. 'Sorry about that. Listen, I've another five eyewitnesses to interview.'

'No need for that anymore.'

'Sure?'

'Sure I'm sure. Just get names and addresses, then you can follow up later.'

'Right. You know traffic's flowing again, aye?'

Vicky looked back over to the bridge and caught the acid yellow flash of a series of uniformed officers getting the cars moving. 'Not my decision or Forrester's. Have forensics finished up there?'

'Aye, wee Zoey's cleared off.'

'Okay. Can you get that ANPR check underway, okay? Find that van.'

'Sarge.' And he was gone.

But Vicky expected the van to be way past Cupar now, maybe down towards Kirkcaldy. They'd never see it again or it'll be a forensically neutral hunk of charred metal by the time they found it.

Big Shug was laughing. 'Clowns in all walks of life, eh?'

'Tell me about it.'

The laughing and joking from the pathology team stopped. Vicky looked over.

A blue people carrier pulled up. Shirley Arbuthnott got out of the driver side and smoothed down her salon perfect hair. She'd lost a ton of weight since Vicky last saw her, but not much of it from her behind, though it was more of a bum than a shelf like it had been. 'Sergeant.' She walked up to the boat and shivered against the air. 'Well, this doesn't really need a pathologist of my stature, does it?'

Vicky gave her a smile. 'But seeing as how you're here?'

'Well.' Arbuthnott crouched low and inspected the body. 'Okay, so this is the lad who fell from the road bridge?'

'Correct.'

Arbuthnott looked away from Vicky and focused on the victim. 'So what happened to him?'

'From what we've seen on the CCTV, he escaped a moving van, ran across a road and climbed a rail to evade the passing cars. Then he slipped back and... this. Could he have survived?'

'No chance. An impact like that would likely mean a broken neck and instantaneous death. Very clearly broke his on the way in. A human head really can't move like that. And if he'd gone in feet-first from that height, didn't hit any debris, didn't get the wind knocked out of him and could swim... it's a maybe, but with his hands tied, no chance.' She was pointing a finger at the bridge, but it was like she was assessing heights rather than indicating anything. 'Given the bridge height, the acceleration and speed at impact... I'd expect him to break his back.'

Vicky stared at the kid again. 'He looks like he's sleeping.'

'Indeed. A lot of the cases you and I have done over the years, vicious stabbings or what have you, and it's clear to see what's going on. Sometimes too much blood, if anything. But in a case like this, most of the damage is internal. Hitting the water like that causes a massive impact to the lungs, kidneys, liver and heart, and it creates internal haemorrhage. So even if he'd survived the initial fall, he would be bleeding inside. Meaning the post-mortem will be somewhat worse than it would initially appear to be.' Arbuthnott inspected his hands. 'I see.'

'See what?'

'This looks like some form of fossil fuel. I'm guessing petrol?'

'That's what our CSI believes.'

'Well, I shall confirm that finding. But I'd say this chap lost his grip due to the presence of petrol or diesel on his hands and arms.' She looked over at the bridge. 'Chances are you're falling... Yes. Instant death. I'll validate that with the internal organ shock trauma.' She pressed a device against his flesh and held it there for a few seconds, then checked her watch. 'I'd say that death occurred at roughly ten ten, plus or minus ten minutes.'

Vicky nodded. 'That's consistent with when he—'

'—took a header.' Big Shug grinned wide. 'Or a bummer.'

'Well, quite.' Arbuthnott gave a flash of her eyebrows. 'I take it you—'

'Aye, we fished him out.' He gave a big satisfied sigh. 'Boy drifted out to the buoy.'

Arbuthnott looked out to sea, twisting her lips back and forth. 'Okay, so there's no crime scene to preserve here, I'll get Archie to take— What's his name?'

'Noel. Noel Liam Russell.'

'I see, well I'll get young Noel's body taken for post-mortem.' She was frowning. 'But the petrol in his hair. Hmmm. I'd say there's a fair chance of finding diesel in the water, given boat engines, but not petrol. Strange.' Her frown deepened as she scanned across his body. 'Oh, and it appears your victim was a self-harmer.'

Vicky inched over to join her. 'How can you tell?'

'Well, these look like scratch marks, don't you think? From a knife too. And barely healed, so I'd suggest the wounds are fresh, maybe the last couple of days at most. I'll have to pay particular attention to it, of course.'

Vicky stared at the marks on the inside of his forearm. Not the usual marks you'd associate with a self-harmer, the grids and latticework on the skin.

Wait.

She got out her phone and snapped it, then zoomed in on the flesh. Noel was peely-wally, as Vicky's old man would say, and being in the cold water had made his wounds a deeper red than she'd expect.

Aye, the marks were definitely numbers.

1985110056

She put her phone away. 'Does that look like a number to you?'

Arbuthnott considered it for a few long seconds. 'I'd say so. Could it be a date?'

'What, November 1985?' Vicky pinched the image and zoomed in. 'But what would the 0056 mean?'

'Search me.' Arbuthnott eased herself up to her full height. 'I merely examine dead bodies.'

Vicky had no idea what the ten digits could represent.

'Sarge?' Karen jogged back over, waving. 'Just got a positive on the name, Sarge. Noel Russell is fifteen. Lives up by the Law on Killin Avenue.'

4

They were so close to the peak of the Law, but they couldn't see it.

Killin Avenue was another of those Dundee streets built in the sixties and named after rural countryside towns, filled with council houses that probably had a great community spirit for a few years until they were all sold off.

A slim avenue between surrounding houses showed the view over to the Perthshire hills in the distance, with the last few remaining Dundee multis in the foreground. Maybe it even pointed towards Killin.

Considine tried the doorbell again. Noel Russell's house was near the corner, a brown-harled two-storey affair.

Vicky checked her phone for notifications. Nothing, not even her mother complaining or Rob checking she was okay. She looked back at Considine. 'Keep trying.'

Across the road, a sharp-cheeked woman was hanging out her washing. Given the lack of railings or fencing, it was hard to tell if it was her garden or a public park.

'Yo?' A distorted voice burst out of the speaker.

Considine pressed the button again. 'Sir, it's the police. Need a word with a James Russell.'

'That's me, aye.'

Considine paused, but then, 'Sir, we should—'

'Fine. I know the drill.' His sigh was louder than the buzz.

The front door clicked open but Considine took three goes at opening it. 'Someone should tell the lad his door's buggered.' He stepped into the bright hallway, that two-tone communal stairwell thing you saw everywhere.

Vicky pocketed her phone and followed him inside. The place smelled like it had been freshly cleaned, and with industrial cleaner like you'd get in a hospital.

The flat door opened and a man popped his head out, yawning into his tight fist. His haircut was about twenty years too young for him, that style that Jamie wanted to get but Rob wouldn't allow. Shaved at the sides and long on top, with a long fringe dusting his tired eyes. He was just wearing tight boxer shorts, but his plunging gut hid most of his modesty. 'Aye?'

Considine clearly didn't know where to look, so held up his warrant card. 'Sir, may we come inside?'

'Sure, sure.' He craned his neck round to look out the front door, like someone was after him.

Vicky tilted her neck at him. 'You okay, sir?'

'Just... Aye. Aye. Come on.' He sloped inside and padded through to a kitchen that looked out onto a drying green.

Vicky led in, but didn't know where to stand. The place wasn't exactly a welcoming family home. In fact, it was an absolute tip, discarded clothes and pizza boxes everywhere. A half-drunk pint glass of beer sat on a side table. The TV was playing *Sky Sports News*, just like so many old men would have on now. The walls, though, were covered in framed Oasis posters, mainly of Liam Gallagher leaning into a microphone. One wall was taken up with a display case showing off their albums on vinyl, with a large collection of bootleg CDs from concerts. That explained his son's name. 'Mr Russell?'

'Call me Jim.' He slurped down a glass of orange in one go. 'And aye, it's me.' He flicked up his eyebrows.

But Vicky had absolutely no idea who he was.

Considine did, though. 'Thought it might be you. Big Jim, eh?'

Though he was hardly big, not even Considine's height, let alone Vicky's. Russell was sturdy, though. While he had that big gut, he still had a muscular frame, like he lifted weights three or four times a week. And heavy ones. 'You watch us play?'

'For United, aye.'

'You don't seem old enough, son. You must've been a wee laddie when I was in my pomp.'

'Aye, I was. My big brother and my old boy used to take us to the games, lift us over the turnstiles. Stood in the Shed, getting lifted from one end to the other whenever the Terriers scored.'

'Those were the days.' Russell looked off into the distance, a wash of sadness dulling his bright eyes. He smirked at Considine. 'Not that there's a lot of scoring at Tannadice these days, mind.'

'Getting there, though, eh?' Considine clocked Vicky's glare. 'Anyway, what happened to you?'

'Mind when I got sold to the Rangers, I was banging them in for big Walter down at Ibrox for a couple months, but I twanged my ACL in my second European match. Out for ten months.' Russell rubbed at his knee. 'I was never the same again. Kept playing afterwards, but never the same, son, never the same.' He picked up the half-drunk can of beer and sniffed it, but put it back where it came from. 'Lads these days get taken to America where they've got the best surgeons, but back then... we didn't earn that much. And I was on an incentive deal, you know? Play well, score and I'd get paid. Score enough and I'd get a new contract. Buggers, eh? Thing is, my basic was pish and I needed to be on the pitch, scoring. So I rushed it back. Ended up finishing my career early having earned bugger all from the game. Never stayed anywhere long enough for a testimonial. Some of my teammates live in mansions and have gigs on the radio, some just have pubs. Not me. I live in this shithole.'

Vicky knew she was in danger of heading down a winding rabbit hole of rehearsed after-dinner speeches. 'Sir, we need to speak to you about your son.'

Russell rolled his eyes and laughed. 'What's he done now?'

'You should probably sit down.'

'Right.' But Jim Russell stood there in his tight pants, shaking his head. 'Just a sec.' He went into the fridge for a carton of orange juice and refilled his glass. 'Right. I see.'

Considine was thrown by it, his forehead creasing and re-creasing. Fingers twitching. He'd been a cop a long time, so Vicky would've thought he'd given his fair share of death messages. Then again, he could be a work-shy sod. 'Is Noel's mother—'

'My wife died three years ago, son. What's happened?'

'Sorry to hear that.'

'Cancer, eh? Tragic.' Russell downed the glass in one then wiped his lips with the back of his hand. 'So, how'd Noel cark it?'

Considine cleared his throat. His cheeks were flushed. 'Eh, he fell from the Tay Bridge and was found—'

'Rail?'

Considine frowned. 'Road, sir.'

'Right, right.' Russell shrugged his big shoulders and gave a "What can you do?" look to Vicky.

Now she had his gaze, she held on to it. 'We'll need you to formally identify your son.'

'You're not sure it's him?'

'We found his wallet on him and the photo on his—'

'Aye, aye.' Russell sighed. 'Fine, I'll come with you.' He grabbed a T-shirt from a dining chair in the middle of the kitchen area and hauled it on, showing the faces of his son's namesakes, Noel Gallagher on the left, Liam on the right. A large curry stain ran down between them. Russell slumped back against the worktop, shaking his head. 'I want to help you find my boy's killer. Anything I can do.'

Now *that* was interesting. 'How do you know he was killed, sir?'

'Well, I heard on the news there was a fall off the Tay Bridge. And there's *no way* my boy's killing himself. Noel was a fighter, just like me.'

'Do you know anything about—'

'So someone has tried to kill him, right?'

'I see. Listen, he may or may not have been abducted, so we're trying to confirm his whereabouts this morning.'

'I see. Well, he was at the school.'

'Which one?'

'Rockwell High.' Russell thumbed out of the window behind him. 'So you're saying someone took him from the school, then what?'

'We don't know, sir. Right now, we need—'

'On the bridge, you think someone's chased him?'

'It's possible.' Vicky gave him a nod, but really, that was all he was getting. Despite his rough, hungover look, it was entirely possible Jim Russell was one of the men in the back of the van. 'Sir, we need to—'

'Aye, aye.' But he wasn't moving. Barely breathing.

'Did Noel have any enemies?'

Russell just stayed by his sink, staring at the floor tiles. 'Why would anyone *kill* my boy?'

'That's what we—'

'I want you to find his killer.'

'We will, but we need to absolutely confirm that it is your son lying in—'

'Look, no enemies that I know of.' Even Vicky was struggling to follow his roaming thoughts. 'I mean, you know what schools are like, right? Rockwell High is worse. You know what that place does to people. It's feral. And Noel's... Noel's a fighter, but he's wee like his mother, not a big strong lad like me.'

'Did he have a girlfriend?'

'Not that I know of. But laddies... I was a nightmare. I mean, when I was at school, I was playing for United's boys' teams, but I was shagging anything that moved. Stayed single for a long time after, likes. Until I met his mother, you know? Lot younger than us. Ended up falling for her big time. Big Jim finally settled down.'

Aye, Jim Russell was a man who lived his life rooted in the past.

'Thing is...' He scratched his neck. 'Noel's alone a lot, you know? I work nights as a concierge.'

'At a hotel?'

'Nah. It's apartments. Some boy Airbnb'd the hell out of it. All these wankers, eh? Coming in to stay and they check in with me, and half of them recognise Big Jim. I mean, there are five signed shirts of us hanging in the lobby, so it's hard to miss, eh?'

Considine had his doe eyes again. 'You own the shirts?'

'Nah, gave them to charity in my golden years, you know? Wish I'd kept them; I'm my own charity case now!' His laughter rattled around the room. 'Still, it's good, eh? These old boys come in with their wives for a weekend in Dundee, potter around the V&A. The town's changed a lot, hasn't it, at least that's what I say, but half of them at least recognise us. Not just my glory days, but their own. And they love speaking to us, getting stories of the old days. That goal against Motherwell. The header against the Hibs. Anderlecht. My one goal for Scotland. Or that free kick against the sheepshaggers. Tell you, that's where Ronaldo got that trick from! Hitting the valve, son, letting it rattle around and it dips down.'

Considine was just another of his Airbnb residents listening to Jim Russell's war stories.

Vicky cleared her throat. 'So you left Noel on his own at nights?'

'Didn't have a choice.'

Vicky had seen younger, any kid who could dial 999. 'So a fifteen year old was—'

'Woah, woah!' Russell held up his hands. He nodded to the front door. 'My sister lives just over the back. She looked in on him, put him to bed and that. And I've got security cameras here. Can keep an eye out, and she can come round if needs be. Thing is.' He burped into his fist. 'The boy liked having all that time on his own. I mean, I was always back to make sure he got up for school. Important to get a nice stretch of the legs, you know.'

'Okay, so we need to get you to—'

'Aye, aye.' Russell poured out another glass of orange, but didn't down it in one this time, just stayed there, letting the sour tang fill the room.

Vicky wasn't getting him anywhere near the mortuary anytime

soon. Happened like this fairly often, people avoiding making their loved one's death a reality. Understandable, and totally fine in most cases. But this was a murder and she needed clues. 'When did you last see him?'

'Well, last night before my shift. I watched the game with Noel. *Monday Night Football*. Southampton were on. Played for them on loan after my injury. They were pish at the time, but I was worse.' He laughed. 'Still, I've got a soft spot for the place, had a great six months there, even though I was away from home all the time. They were playing Man U.' He grimaced. 'Had a trial there in my United days. Dundee, that is. Ferguson didn't know if I was good enough, so got us to play in a match. Obviously thought I wasn't. Not that he told us. Just had to drive back up, eh?'

'So, last night?'

'Well, I had to go to work at halftime, so the wee fella went to his room. He's been playing this game with his mates online. I mean, back in my day, we'd be out all hours in the park kicking a ball around. But kids nowadays, they're just staring into computers, eh?'

That was maybe a lead, or just some more intel. A lead that might point to some friends. 'You any idea who he was playing with?'

'Hardly. I've no idea if he even was, to be honest. Could've been watching a film.'

'But you think he was?'

'Aye, aye. Come on through.' Russell led them back into the hallway, then opened a door. The curtains were shut but it was still pretty light in there. He flicked the switch.

The room was pretty spartan, just a bed and a big desk covered with a giant gaming rig like Vicky's brother had in his bedroom at their parents' house. The walls were covered with *Star Trek* posters, some of the classic sixties stuff and some from the modern one on Netflix that Vicky couldn't get into, but mostly the nineties shows. Another thing Noel shared with Vicky's brother. The times may change, but kids didn't that much.

'My boy was a geek. Got it from his mother. Met her in a club.

She was a student. Lot younger than me. I was working for the club in an ambassador role and had the patter. She fell for it. I fell for her. I mean, Noel would watch football with his old man, but...' Russell scratched his cheek. 'He's a fiend for the computers. Kept suggesting he think about doing all that laptop stuff in the game, you know. Stats and that. Like that *Moneyball* film with Brad Pitt and the wee fat fella who keeps losing weight.' He frowned, like remembering Jonah Hill's name was more important than processing his son's death. 'I mean, I'm all old school, did a bit of scouting for the Terriers when I was club ambassador, meant heading into deepest, darkest Fife to watch Raith Rovers games and it's a bugger of a journey in the middle of winter.'

Vicky waited until she was sure he'd finished. 'We're going to have to seize everything, I'm afraid.'

Russell shrugged, not even batting an eyelid. 'Take it all. It's useless to a guy like me, but if you need it, well, then whatever.'

Vicky walked over to the computer. A boy that age left alone and online all the time, they could find everything about him on that computer. Lots of stuff his father didn't know. She locked eyes with Considine. 'Constable, I need you to escort Mr Russell back to Bell Street. Can you arrange for someone to transport this computer back to the forensics lab?'

'I'll do it.'

'No, we need an expert. Call Jenny Morgan.'

'Aye, aye.' Considine left the room, scowling like he'd taken a drink from the wrong coffee cup again.

'Do you recognise this code?' Vicky got out her own phone and found the photo of Noel. She didn't show it to Russell, but she read out the numbers. '1985110056.'

Russell shook his head. 'No idea, sorry. Like I say, my boy was all about the numbers and the stats, but I can't do my two times table.' He laughed, but it came out hollow. '1985, though. Hmm.'

'That mean anything to you?'

'When my kid sister was born. But that was January, not November.' He shrugged. 'Look, it doesn't mean anything to me, but it might to his mate Hayden. Hayden Milne.'

5

While it was made of red bricks, there was something off about Rockwell High. Long banks of disconnected buildings, all separated out, presumably for age groups. Had a strange feeling about it, more like a borstal than a modern high school.

And where the hell was the entrance? Vicky had rounded three sides of the site now and—

There. On the left. She slowed and indicated.

The main building was like a mill, probably built at a time when the locals would be heading down to work in those dotted around Bell Street nick. But you could see the shape of the Law from over here. And another Perthshire name, Strathmore Avenue.

She pulled in, driving past the ugliest building she'd ever seen, a normal brick house with a two-floor bay window stapled on the side, and stopped at the gates guarded by an Eentrycom system. She got out and her phone rang.

Considine calling...

Vicky let out a sigh and got back in, keeping her eyes on the wing mirrors. 'What's up?'

'Well, he's identified the boy.'

'Already?'

'Drove like a demon. Hard to keep up with him, even in the Scorpion.'

The Scorpion...

Vicky wished she could be saved from Considine's constant obsession with cars. 'It's him?'

'Aye. Boy seemed a bit thrown, but he kept banging on about this boy he played with at Rangers who died during a training session.'

'Aye, I can imagine. Did he say anything that could give us a lead?'

'Not really. Just seems lost. What do you want me to do?'

'Can you chase up Jenny Morgan and get—'

'Aye, she's just left.'

'Can you sit with Mr Russell until—'

'He's already gone, Sarge. Said he's going to sit with his sister.'

'Well, follow him home and check he does.'

Considine barked out a laugh. 'Sarge, the lad's just lost his son!'

'Aye, and there are unknown men in balaclavas in a van who abducted him.'

'You don't think Big Jim Russell is one of them, do you?'

'We don't have any idea who they are. He might be one of them, he might know them. All of that. Getting anywhere with the van?'

'Still nothing on that either.'

'Well, can you follow him home and check he doesn't do anything daft?'

'You're the boss.'

And don't you forget it. 'Then come to Rockwell High, presuming Hayden's here.'

'Right. Just up the road from there, eh?'

'Not far. But I had a bit of a detour.'

'Greggs?'

'No, Stephen. Trying to track down Hayden. Your friend Big Jim could've told us Hayden was a school student.'

Something hard rapped on the door. A wiry man in tweeds was glowering at her.

'Just get here as soon as you can.'

'ASAP, Sarge. Sure.' And he was gone.

Vicky wound her window down and held out her warrant card. 'Police, sir.'

That seemed to throw him. 'Oh. What's happened?'

'Need to speak to the headmaster.'

'Well, that's me.' He thrust out his hand, but there was no angle that would allow her to shake it. 'Derek Archibald.' He frowned as he took his unshaken hand away. 'What's the nature of your visit, Sergeant?'

Vicky got out into the driving wind. 'I'm afraid one of your pupils has passed away. Noel Russell.'

Archibald exhaled slowly. 'I see.' He looked off into the distance, stroking his chin. 'First pupil I've lost in five years and young Keegan was to MND.' He stared hard back at her, those fierce teacher's eyes drilling into Vicky's skull. 'How rude of me. I should invite you in for a cup of tea.'

'I'm actually here to speak to a pupil who might be a friend of Noel's.'

THE OFFICE LOOKED like it hadn't been touched since Vicky's dad had attended the school way back when. Maybe not from either grandparent on that side.

She sat in front of the headmaster's desk;, not the first time in her life she'd done that, but the first in her professional one for a good few years. 'I thought this place had shut down twenty years ago.'

'Constant rumours and threats but I'm keeping it afloat, inch by inch. Meeting by meeting.'

Vicky nodded along, sharing his pain. 'My dad was a pupil here in the sixties.'

'Did he enjoy his time?'

'Hated it, sadly. And my late gran too.' A strange memory stabbed at Vicky's heart. 'She said they sang the school song every morning back in the thirties or forties. Something about Rockwell and Right?'

'Good heavens, aye. That's going back deep into the archives.' Archibald typed at his computer, but it looked like he was doing it for the first time. Each keystroke took a frown. 'Well, according to our morning registration, young Noel was here at school.'

'And Hayden?'

'Ah, yes.' At this rate, it was going to take a week to find anything.

Vicky couldn't sit waiting. 'Did you know Noel Russell?'

'Eight hundred and fifty-two pupils and students, Sergeant. Hard to get to know them all. But Noel, no. Sorry. Never on my radar.'

That was a reality Vicky had seen a few times. Only the exceptionally good or bad catch the attention of the headmaster, while the average remain anonymous and faceless. Noel may have been bright outside of school, but that didn't often translate to traditional school. And Rockwell seemed very traditional.

Archibald ran his finger across the screen. 'Well, well. Hayden Milne was indeed at registration today.' He stood up with a lot more speed and guile than he typed. 'I'll go and see if I can find him for you.' He walked over to the door. 'Ah, come in.'

A towering kid ducked under the door and crept in. Must be six foot seven, at least, and all skin and bone, like all his energy went on growing and growing. He wore as little of a uniform as he could get away with: black trainers, the stripes painted over; loose black trackie bottoms; white polo shirt with the school tie poked through so you couldn't see the yellow stripes, just the mid-blue bottom. He sat down, shoulders slumped, avoiding eye contact.

'Mr Milne, this is Detective Sergeant Dodds.'

Hayden looked over at her and tilted his head. 'Sup?'

She held his gaze as long as he'd let her. 'Hayden, do you know Noel Russell?'

'Dax.'

'Dax?'

'Noel's nickname.' He shrugged. 'Bout it?'

'Hayden, I'm afraid I have to deliver bad news. Someone has passed away unexpectedly...' She paused, watching his reaction. Eyes shooting around the room, frowning, then staring at the floor. Confusion. 'I'm afraid that Noel Russell passed away this morning.'

Hayden looked over at her, forehead twitching, tears in his eyes. 'Wuh?'

'We believe he fell off the road bridge this morning.'

'Crap.' Hayden gritted his teeth, then snorted like he was trying to control himself. But he just lost it. The cool fifteen-year-old trying to act like an adult now just looked like a child, crying over the death of his best friend.

Archibald got up from his desk and mouthed at Vicky, 'Can you give us a minute?'

Vicky got to her feet and gave Hayden a polite smile, but the kid was elsewhere. She eased the door open, slipped through and shut it carefully.

'Do you not remember Big Jim?' Considine was leaning over the secretary's desk, way too close to be anything other than pathetic flirting.

And she was buying it, leaning in just as close. Her pink lipstick matched her blouse. 'Sure he was at United?'

'Aye, left in '96, I think. Didn't make the squad for the Euros.'

'And that's— Bugger!'

Vicky glared at Considine. 'Don't mind me.'

The secretary smiled at Vicky. 'Do you need another cup of tea?'

Vicky smiled back. 'That would be nice.'

'I'll get you one too, Stevie.' She got up and sashayed away.

Vicky laughed. 'Stevie?'

'Kelly used to go out with one of my pals, eh?'

'Sure.' Vicky checked her watch. Time seemed to be running away from her. She was up here at the school, and had no idea what was going on back down at the bridge or at the station. 'Did you follow Big Jim?'

'Sure did. Boy drives a lot faster than he used to run on the pitch. But he just went to his sister's, aye. That battleaxe we saw outside, hanging out her washing, that's her.' He scowled out of the window. 'Bad day for it, surely?'

'You'd be the expert.'

'Wouldn't even bother, it'll just get wetter when it pisses down later.' Considine sat back and folded his arms. 'So, we're still waiting on young Hayden?'

'No, Stephen. He's in floods of tears at the loss of a friend.'

'Oh, right. So Noel and Hayden were bum chums?'

'Stephen, for Christ's sake. His best friend's just died. Have a bit of humanity.'

'Aye, but seriously. Boy's that upset, maybe it's more than just a friendship. Like his old boy said, all that time alone, maybe young Hayden was round there. Know what kids are like.'

'Maybe in Forfar.'

'Aye, very funny. But I'm serious.'

Vicky couldn't deny he had some semblance of a point, no matter how crassly he'd put it.

'Maybe there was something between them, and maybe Big Jim found them with their cocks in each other's hands and he wanted to teach his son a lesson. Him and a few mates, scare the living shite out of him. Pour petrol over him. But it went too far.'

'Maybe.'

The office door opened and Archibald appeared with a tight nod.

Vicky led Considine back into the office, but he seemed very reluctant. A hard look got him to shift.

Hayden was standing up by the whiteboard, hands in pockets. He had retied his school tie. 'Did he die?' His voice was a deep rumble, and he spoke like he was from Jamaica instead of Dundee.

'I'm afraid so.'

'Meant, was he killed?'

'Right. Well, we're investigating that.'

'Know who?'

'We don't. Yet. Wondering if you could help with anyone who might've wanted to harm him.'

'Nobody. Good kid. Bright, despite his old man.'

'Right. You know him?'

'Round there a bit.'

'Noel and his dad get on?'

A shrug.

'Did Noel have a girlfriend?'

Hayden looked away. 'Nope.'

And Vicky had seen that evasion before. Sometimes it was nothing, but sometimes it was a tell. 'Hayden, if he was seeing someone then—'

'No. He wasn't.'

'What about a boyfriend?'

Hayden laughed. 'Wasn't *gay*.'

Vicky still wasn't convinced that Considine's theory was without merit. 'When was the last time you heard from Noel?'

'Today. WhatsApped me this morning. Said he totally killed it on *Indignity* last night.'

'What is *Indignity*?' Of course Vicky knew, but she wanted to keep the kid talking.

Considine smiled. '*Indignity Online*, Sarge. It's a video game. Developers are based in Dundee, I think. Gangsters, gangs, guns. Great fun.'

Useless sod.

Still, Hayden looked over at Considine. 'You play, man?'

'I dabble. My brother's a bigger gamer than me. You?'

'Sure, man, sure.'

Considine kept hold of his gaze. 'You speak to Noel today? Or did you just message?'

'Saw him in reggie. Saw, man, that was it. Must've bunked off after.'

'What was his first class?'

'Maths.' Archibald flared his nostrils. 'That whole year all go to maths first thing on a Tuesday. Double period.'

'Okay.' Considine gave the kid a curt smile. 'Hayden, was Noel in your maths class?'

'Nah, man.'

'Okay, so we believe Noel died at around ten. So that's, what, an hour after he was last seen?'

'F'you say so, man.'

'You didn't walk with him?'

'He goes toilet.'

'He what?'

'After reggie, man, he goes toilet.'

'Every day?'

'Yeah, man.'

Considine frowned, like he found the idea of going every day a puzzling mystery. 'You didn't see anyone hanging around outside, maybe in a van?'

'No, man.'

'Anyone he was in trouble with at school? Teachers, bullies, anything?'

'Kids all liked him. Teachers? Maybe less, man. Maybe less. But Noel was well respected, man.'

'No enemies?'

'None.' Hayden slid forward to rest his elbows on his knees. 'Why ask, man?'

'Well, in my time at school there was always fights behind the bike sheds, that kind of thing. Soon as it got agreed it was all over the school.'

'Nah, man. Noel just lived for gaming.'

'Cool. You know anyone with a white van?'

Hayden looked away. 'No, man.'

'Hayden, is there anyone else we should be speaking to?'

'Like, people who own *vans*?'

Considine shrugged. 'You tell me.'

'Man, I can give you a list of names of his mates, if you want.

The kids he likes in class, kids he didn't, people we played with online. That's all I know.'

'That would be really useful.' Considine walked over to the whiteboard and smiled at the kid again. He uncapped a pen and started writing. '1985110056.' He tapped it. 'You recognise this?'

'No, man.'

'Sure about that?'

'Sure, man.' But Hayden was staring at them. 'Hmm.'

'You got something?'

'Maybe.' Hayden snatched the pen out of Considine's hand and added dots to the code. 'There you go, man.'

'198.51.100.56?' Considine tapped each set of numbers with his fingers. 'It's an IP address?'

'Don't know, man. Maybe. But it could also be a URL? Like for a website?'

Considine got out his phone and typed it in. Then he sighed. 'It's not that, Sarge.'

Vicky smiled at Hayden. 'Thanks for the idea, though.'

'Don't mention it. Might be dark web, man. Encrypted, man.'

6

Vicky pulled into the Bell Street car park and trundled across the tarmac towards her space.

A blue Skoda was parked in it. Souped up and tricked out.

She leaned on the horn and started winding down her window.

Considine's head popped up out of the driver's side. He gave Vicky the thumbs up and shut the door, then headed for the front desk.

Vicky hammered the horn again and shouted out of the window, 'Get out of my space!'

Considine stopped and scowled at her. 'But where will I park the Scorpion?'

Up your arse.

'I don't care, Constable, just not in my space.'

'*Sarge.*' The cheeky sod slouched back over to the car.

Vicky sat there checking her messages, engine purring. Nothing she needed to look at immediately.

Considine swerved back, casually slapping his hand on the wheel to guide it round. Almost hit her car. He shot off and bumped up onto the pavement.

Vicky slammed into the space and got out. 'You almost hit me!'

Considine was out of the car, sauntering away. 'You should try to calm down, Sarge. You're a bit tightly wound.'

Vicky blocked the doorway. 'I swear I will swing for you.'

'Would love that. Get you taken down a peg or two.'

Vicky could have it out with him, there and then. And maybe she should. 'Seriously, Stephen. I need you to just find that van. Okay?'

'But I can help with that code.'

'It wasn't a code.'

'Right, right. I mean, the IP address.'

'Just do what I say, Stephen. It'll make things a lot easier.'

'Fine.' He traipsed off past her like a sullen teenager. Or maybe a spoilt child.

Vicky watched him go. Aye, she needed to drag him into a room, lock the door and shout at him until he listened. Which might take an age of man. Maybe she needed to talk to him, then listen to everything he had to say. But whatever it was, she needed to do it soon enough, that was for sure.

The glass upstairs was distorting, flashing, and pretty fast. Like someone was waving at her. Someone in forensics.

Turned out the hand belonged to Jenny Morgan, who was now using it to beckon Vicky towards her across the lab. Not that there was any warmth in Jenny's smile. Her skin looked like vellum today, thin and very white, and her hair seemed that bit darker red, maybe a new bottle of dye or a new stylist. Not that she ever talked about that kind of thing.

Vicky cut through the busy lab, trying to take the shortest path, but the place was rammed full of CSIs all doing God knows what. Every time she visited, she swore there was a new set of machines lying against the walls, always humming away or beeping.

Vicky wasn't the only Dodds in there. Andrew was resting

against a workbench loaded up with laptops and tablets. Vicky hadn't seen her older brother in a few months and he was looking more and more like a mad scientist. His constant flirtation with stubble had blossomed into a full-blown marriage to a silvery-brown beard that reached down to his collar. And it looked like someone had replaced his eyes with balls of coal. 'Hey, sis.' He didn't move to meet her, just sat there, rubbing his temples.

'You okay, Andrew?'

'I'm fine.' Andrew shot one of his customary glares at Jenny. 'Supposed to be signed off. Yet another spell of stress, but she's begged me to come in again.'

Jenny raised her eyebrows, crumpling her smooth forehead. 'That's not true.'

Andrew chuckled at her. 'So, you telling me to work half hours on a secret project with people in Glasgow and London isn't begging me to come in?'

'Nobody's begging you, Andrew.'

'I mean, you didn't get down on your hands and knees, that's true, but—'

'Sorry to interrupt.' Vicky was smiling in a way that she really didn't mean. 'But I need help with some internet stuff.'

Jenny cupped her hands around her mouth. 'Zoey!'

A head peered around the edge of a machine, wearing goggles, but not crime scene ones, the sort you'd find in a school science class. 'What's up?'

'Can you help Ms Dodds here.'

'Aye, sure.'

'Jenny, you make me sound like an ancient divorcee. See you around.' Vicky tipped her imaginary cap and walked off to Zoey's bench.

She was working away at a whiteboard, but it was double Dutch to Vicky, a series of blobs all joined by arrows and illegible handwriting. It'd need a degree in something other than Vicky's to figure out what it was. Electronic engineering maybe? She finished writing in a box, her left-handed scribble smudging it before the ink had time to dry, then looked around at Vicky. 'What can I help with?'

'Well, first, did you get anywhere with that stuff on the railing?'

'Petrol.' Zoey opened a laptop, then swung the screen round like an owl's head so it was pointing towards Vicky with the keyboard still in front of Zoey. 'See?'

Vicky had absolutely no idea what it said, just another set of symbols. Chemistry, maybe? 'Take your word for it.' She pulled out her notebook and showed Zoey the numbers, without the dots. 'Need your expertise to look at this.'

She took one look at it and nodded. 'An IP address, right?'

'You're the expert.'

Zoey shrugged. 'I'd say it's 198.51.100.56.'

'That was quick.'

'You wouldn't believe how many times people in films make a mess of it. Four numbers, with each number a maximum of 255. Means it's easy to sort that chain out into something. There's only one possibility, really.' She swung the screen around and typed on the keyboard. 'Huh.'

'What's up?'

'Just...'

'We tried entering it on our phones. Got nothing.'

'No wonder.' Zoey scrubbed at her forehead. 'I mean, it's definitely a URL but the site you visit is a redirect.'

'A redirect?'

'Aye, it's just a dummy code to get you somewhere else. But where it redirects you to is blank.'

'Blank?'

'Aye. Well, that's the thing.' Zoey was focusing on something on her screen.

'So can you find out who owns the site where the redirection happens?'

'On it.' Zoey was working away like she was mentally connected to the machine and it could respond to her thoughts. 'It's owned by one Noel Liam Russell.'

'Great. That's our victim.' Vicky sighed. 'So it's a dead end? It just goes there?'

'Nope. Where it goes is probably somewhere on the dark web.' More typing.

Vicky shuffled round to look over her shoulder. 'I thought the dark web was... Look, I've been on a training course, but I was focusing on the criminal uses for it, not the tech itself.'

'Okay. How do I explain this?' Zoey stared up at the ceiling ductwork. 'Okay. The dark web is all encrypted. So you don't get URLs like www dot schoolbook dot com or bbc dot co dot uk. You get a string of text, then dot onion.'

'That's what I said. And what does onion mean?'

'It's a metaphor for layers of an onion.'

'I don't get it.'

Zoey made a ball with her fingers. 'Imagine an onion. Each layer is encrypted. You can only access it if you have the key.'

'Like a password?'

'Kind of. Basically, the encryption preserves anonymity. See how I found Noel's server in two ticks? Well, it'll take longer than the life of the universe to uncrack the locations of this site.' She tapped the screen.

A string of text then dot onion, just like she said.

'Right. So why do they do that?'

'Well, people can use it for criminal ends. Selling drugs or guns or gang hits with us not being able to trace them.'

A shiver ran up Vicky's spine. Why was Noel Russell into that kind of world? A fifteen-year-old boy?

Zoey sat back on her stool. 'There are no search engines, so you need to know the dot onion address of the place you're going. Like this code.'

'Which doesn't work.'

'In that browser.' Zoey nodded at Vicky's trouser pocket. 'Or whatever's on your phone. Chrome, Safari, Firefox.' She grinned. 'But I've got Tor on this baby.' She did more typing, precise keystrokes like everything was against a clock. 'Tor stands for "The Onion Router", so it's all circular really. But let's see where it takes us.' She hit another key and the browser slowly rendered a web page.

Really slowly, like Vicky was back at school and her brother was wowing her with this new thing called the internet. Before Amazon, Google, Schoolbook.

The page looked like a furniture store.

Vicky scowled at her. 'This doesn't make sense to me. Why scratch that code on your arm? Is it wrong?'

Zoey squinted at the screen. 'No, it's not wrong. Just...'

'It doesn't make any sense.' Vicky looked around the page. Very basic, a world away from the shiny modern sites she'd buy crap for Bella and Jamie. 'So, to me, it looks like a directory of furniture.'

'Filled with very expensive products.' Zoey tapped the screen. 'That shelving unit would be fifty quid in IKEA, but it's four grand here. Same with that sofa. Four hundred quid at Dunelm Mill, maybe, but it's twenty grand.'

'What the hell's going on?' Andrew was between them, panting hard. 'Oh, it had to be you, didn't it?'

Zoey arched her eyebrow. 'What is?'

'You. That site.' Andrew grabbed the laptop away from her. 'I've been looking at that site for weeks, and you've just set off a hundred alerts all across the UK.'

'How?'

'Because I'm doing my job.' He frowned. 'How did you find that? What are you doing on it?'

'Long story.' Vicky took the laptop from her brother's arms and passed it back to Zoey. 'But you've got more explaining to do, big brother.'

'Don't big brother me.'

'Come on, Andrew. What's going on? Why do you have alerts running?'

Andrew shut his eyes for a few seconds. 'You're not going to take a no, are you?'

'Andrew, I swear to God, I will tickle you until you tell me.'

He laughed. Then sighed. 'Look at the names.'

Vicky got close to the laptop again and scanned down the product page. Emmy-Kate, Norma, Jenna, Ashlynn. Douglas, Josh, Isaac, Noah. 'High-end products named after girls and boys. So what? Looks innocent to me.'

'That's the point.' Andrew shut his eyes again. 'Read the descriptions.'

Vicky checked the shelving unit, Emmy-Kate:

A chance to own a unique and special piece. Thirteen-year matured wood sculpted into a tight product to house your most special item.

Vicky felt her skin crawl, like ants were climbing her spine. 'What the hell?'

'That case I'm working, dear sister, is full of web pages like this. It's a Met case, really, and we're supporting. The gist is that paedophiles select the products on this—'

'Paedophiles?' The ants were marching around Vicky's brain now.

'Correct. The site looks innocent, like you say, but they're really getting an actual girl or boy.'

'So this is for someone called Emmy-Kate?'

'Maybe. It's still early days. We're cataloguing places. But you don't hide stuff like this on the dark web unless there's something bad behind it.'

Vicky scanned the list again. Something had jarred earlier and now it stuck out like a sore thumb. 'Ashlynn. A coffee table. Sold out. What does that mean?'

Andrew swallowed hard. 'I don't know.'

'Has someone bought her?'

'Vicks, what's going on? What are you hiding from me?'

'I'm not hiding anything.' Vicky tapped the screen and it opened to a pale wood coffee table, circular and resting on a Persian rug. 'Ashlynn is the name of the girl whose disappearance Forrester is investigating.' She fumbled her phone and dropped it to the floor. 'Christ.' She bent over to pick it up and called Forrester, then put it on speaker.

'Doddsy, I'm pretty busy here.' He sounded it. Out somewhere wild and breezy. 'What's up?'

'That case you're working, what's the name?'

'The lassie? It's Ashlynn Thomas. Why?'

'Thought so. Well, it's come up in my case.'

'Huh.'

'Look, it's a long story, but how old is she?'

'Nineteen.'

'She's not at school?'

'Studying criminal psychology at Abertay. Grew up in Fintry. Why?'

'Okay, it's just... Noel had a code on his arm that leads to a website and... Well, it might relate to sex trafficking, sir. Ashlynn is a name on the catalogue.'

'It's a pretty common name these days, though.'

Vicky felt herself nod. 'Well, yeah, I mean Bella has Ashlynn Carstairs and Ashlynn McFarlane in her class at school.'

'Could just be a coincidence, but... I bloody hate coincidences. Who's working on it? Glasgow?'

'Met.'

'Met. Shite.' Forrester sighed. 'Look, we need to get our arms around this. Two abductions at the same time, fair enough. Seen it happen. But if her name's coming up in his? Okay. Can you work closely with MacDonald on this?'

'Will do, sir.' Vicky caught Zoey shaking her head, nostrils splayed. 'I'll pick up with him. Cheers.' She ended the call and tilted her head at Zoey. 'What's up?'

'It's just, I'd rather not deal with DS MacDonald.'

'Isn't he your husband?'

'Was. Is. I don't know.' Zoey snorted. 'Euan left me.'

Andrew took a couple of steps away, his eyes bulging.

Vicky frowned at Zoey. 'But you've—'

'Aye. We've got an eighteen-month-old and Euan left me, didn't he? In Dundee. I'm really struggling, Vicky. Being a single mother is so hard.' She looked close to tears. 'And the standard forensics Jenny's asking me to do, like those railings and petrol and... It's beyond me. I can't dust crime scenes. I'm no good at it.'

Vicky recognised another mother in a similar shitty situation to the one she'd found herself. She patted her sleeve. 'Look, I won't patronise you. Raising a kid is hard work. I've done it myself. Every day is a struggle. But you're good at this stuff. You found this site for me.'

'Andrew could've done it.'

Vicky looked over at her brother. 'Andrew would still be mansplaining the internet to me. You've helped me connect two cases together. Possibly. That's way more important than proving he was dowsed with petrol.'

'Right.' Zoey traced the bags under her eyes with her fingers. 'Still, I should be able to do that.'

'Should is a bad word.' Vicky tried another encouraging smile. 'Have you got hold of Noel's gaming PC?'

'Aye.' Zoey shuffled through some paperwork on her desk. 'Turned up ten minutes ago.'

'How about you look into that computer and see if there's anything else on this website.'

'Sure.' But she stayed by her laptop. 'Andrew, have you finished with it?'

Andrew had slouched back to his desk. He turned around and groaned at Zoey. 'Not yet.'

'You able to do that soon? Then I can get on with it.'

'Aye, I'll try.' He grabbed a crate and huffed it up to his desk. 'Should see the spec of it.'

Vicky walked around. 'It's a good machine?'

'Good doesn't do this bad boy justice, sis. This is primo stuff, even better than my rig.'

'Your rig?'

'Hush. That graphics card alone is like sixteen hundred quid.'

Vicky didn't know when young men stopped messing about with cars and switched their attentions to computers, but it had happened. Seemed like only Considine was left worshipping petrol instead of silicon. 'Noel is fifteen. Where did he get the cash?'

'Now, that is your job, sis. I'm just cataloguing it for Zoey, that's mine.'

'How long's it going to take?'

'An hour.'

'To extract everything?'

'No, to catalogue the components.'

'Why is that important?'

'It takes its time, sis.'

'No, why do you need to identify how much his machine cost before you do the bit that's going to help me?'

Andrew sat back, his lips twitching. He didn't have an answer for that. 'Look, it's incredibly hard to pin it down. And the sooner I start, the sooner I'll finish.'

'Can you start with a ballpark figure?'

'No.'

'Come on... For me?'

'Fine.' Andrew unscrewed a plate on the side and pulled the hinge down. 'The prices fluctuate like Billy-o, but the rest of it... Well, it could've cost over two grand.'

'So a kid has a three and a half grand computer?'

'Aye, aye. Need to spend that much if you want to play in 4K and at sixty frames per second.'

'Right, thank you. Zoey?'

'I've not finished.'

'You have, for now.'

'Fine.' Andrew shut the flap and hefted the machine over to Zoey's desk. 'There you go.'

'Thank you.' She set about working at it, attaching it to her laptop and hammering her own keyboard.

Andrew was hovering around her like an uncomfortable teenager. 'Cloning the drive first, yes?'

'Aye, aye. I know how to do it. The SSD on this thing will make it super-quick, but it goes faster if you're not standing there.'

'Right.' Andrew nodded at her, then walked back, slowly like he wanted to make sure she did the task well. He sat down next to his sister, but kept his focus on Zoey.

'She'll be fine, Andrew.'

'Maybe.' Andrew leaned in close. 'How did you do that?'

'Do what?'

'Get her to talk. We've all been trying for months.'

'Maybe instead of a computer, you try treating her like a human being?'

Andrew smiled. 'Aye, what's one of them?'

'Sarge?' Zoey was looking up from her laptop. 'Got something.'

Vicky headed over. 'That was quick?'

'Oh, cloning his machine will be the best part of an hour.' Zoey tucked her hair behind her ear. 'No, I've managed to trace that furniture store to a physical address.'

Vicky winced. 'Let me guess. Russia? Iraq? China? Vietnam?'

'No, the Hilltown.'

7

Vicky pulled up at the lights. 'That it there?'

Considine was shuffling papers on his lap, frowning and squinting into the low sun. 'Think so, Sarge.'

'You *think* so?'

He shielded his eyes with his hand. 'Aye, I mean it is.'

Vicky flicked the indicator to the right and sat idling, waiting for the lights to change.

Small Paul's Home Bargains occupied an old tenement block, with a chunk of the ground floor spilling out to fill what would've been a garden on the side street. It had the look of a corner shop, but instead of the painted-over windows, they were open and filled with a furniture display.

Well, a single bed and a reclining armchair in front of some chests of drawers.

The lights changed and Vicky swerved right before the oncoming traffic could get to them.

'And you've got the cheek to criticise my driving!' Considine was grabbing the oh-shit handle above the door. 'Just pull in there, Sarge.'

Double yellows on both sides. No foot traffic except for a

woman walking towards them, phone in one hand, cigarette in the other, not paying any attention to anyone.

Vicky drove on along the road. 'No, Stephen. We're trying to be subtle here. Parking on double yellows and sticking out a "police business" sign might blow any subtlety.'

'Ah, right. With you now.'

Vicky spotted a car pulling off and shot into the space before a BT van could claim it. A bit on the nippit side, but she slid back in and killed the engine. 'There.'

'Right, so what's the plan?'

Vicky let her seatbelt zip up. 'Okay, so let's go in and pretend to be a married couple buying a new bed. We'll—'

Considine snorted. 'I mean, I'm into MILFs, but—'

Vicky shot him a glare. 'MILFs?'

'You know, Mothers I'd Like to—'

'I know what it means. But seriously?'

'Nothing wrong with being into mature women, Sarge. Stop being so judgemental.'

'Stephen, on what planet could I be your mother? You're thirty-two. Physically. Mentally, closer to twelve.'

'Not *my* mother.' He was blushing slightly. 'But you *are* a mother, right?'

'I'm doing the talking inside.'

⁓

THE SHOP SEEMED MORE like a workshop inside, and stank of sawdust and glue. Up close, the products looked handcrafted and well made at that. But a lot cheaper than online.

No sign of the owner, though.

Considine was running his hand along a bed frame. 'Nice shit, Sar—ally.'

Vicky scowled at him, then gave him a harsh whisper, 'Sally? Really?'

'Really suits you.' Considine nodded over into the shop. 'Morning.'

'How do?' A burly man was cleaning his oily hands on a rag. He was dressed like he was chopping down trees rather than turning the wood into furniture. Wild black beard and wilder hair, though it was thinning big time. 'Help you with anything?'

Vicky walked over with a smile on her face. 'You Small Paul?'

He laughed. 'Small Paul's just a joke for the locals.'

'Well, it made us laugh, didn't it?' Vicky elbowed Considine a bit harder than she should have. 'You're a big guy.'

'Right. Six three in my socks. Anyway. Enough about me, what are you looking for?'

Vicky elbowed Considine even harder. 'Me and this lump here are moving into our forever home next month and we're looking to furnish the bedroom.'

The owner looked between them with a crafty grin on his face. 'So, bed, units, chests at the side?'

'Sounds good.' Considine ran his hand over the finish on a dark-stained chest of drawers. 'And a chair for shoving all our half-worn clothes on, aye?'

'Know what you mean, son.' The owner chuckled. 'Size bed?'

'Six foot.'

'Aye?' He walked over to a display. 'Here's the beds. All one price.' He held out a shaking hand and pointed at a price list on the wall. 'Per size, mind.'

Three hundred quid for a super-king bed was really cheap. Vicky got that tingling in her neck. Money laundering as well as potential child trafficking. Buy the beds at six hundred, sell at three, bingo – all that dodgy money was now legal money. Get the word of mouth out enough and you could turn a *lot* of dodgy money into a *lot* of legal money.

She ran her hand along the smooth bed frame. 'That's very good value.'

'Aye, well that's what happens when you make it all yourself, eh?'

Vicky crouched to inspect the workmanship. No way was that done by a machine. It was done to an artisanal standard, with a perfect varnish job. The wood was the kind of knotty pine you'd get in a display in a high-end place. 'Looks like good stuff.'

'Thanks.' The owner sniffed. 'Got a little workshop out back where I make it all.'

Vicky looked over to the staircase. 'What's upstairs?'

'Oh, there's dining and living room on the top floor. More beds on first.' He looked around the sofas, which didn't seem to have the same hand-built care as the woodwork. 'Better to keep the heavy stuff on the ground floor, eh?'

'Makes total sense.' Vicky frowned at him, emphasising it for his benefit. 'The stuff is a lot cheaper than on your website.'

He bounced her frown back. 'Website?'

'Aye, one of Jim's mates sent us a link.' Vicky flicked a thumb in Considine's direction. 'Took him a while to get on it.' She looked around. 'There was a set of shelves I quite liked, but I don't see it here? Emmy-Kate was the name.'

'Okay. Well, we've sold out.' Aye, he'd spotted a rat. He turned and walked back to the door he'd entered through. 'Give me a shout if you need anything.'

'Police.'

He stopped dead and his head bowed.

'Wondering if you'd be able to attend an interview.'

VICKY CLUTCHED a cup of canteen tea. She still wasn't that hungry after that brunch, but it must've been super salty because she could drink for Scotland right now.

Considine was eating as they walked along the corridor, spilling crumbs from his BLT onto the carpet tiles. And a splodge of mayonnaise. Not that he even noticed, let alone worried about who was going to clean it up. 'So, you think he's smuggling kiddies?'

'Let's just see.' Vicky turned the corner and stopped dead.

DS Euan MacDonald stood outside the interview room, tapping at his phone with a seedy grin. Like Vicky but unlike the rest of the squad, he was dressed down, jeans and casual shirt a button too low, showing off his tanned bald chest. He looked up with a glint in his eyes, then put his phone away. That soul patch was a big mistake. 'Alrighty?'

That word. It made Vicky shudder. 'Euan.' She nudged Considine and pointed at the door. 'Finish your sandwich and get the interview started.'

'Sure thing, aye.' He shoved the second half of the sandwich in his mouth, then pushed into the interview room.

MacDonald watched the clown enter the room. 'Maybe you bully him a bit too much.'

'It's nowhere near enough, Euan.' Vicky leaned against the wall. 'So, I'm going to ask why you're guarding my room?'

'Your room now, huh?'

'You know what I mean.'

'Nope. Might need to spell it out for me.'

'You're trying to steal this case, aren't you?'

MacDonald raised his hands. 'Forrester said you're in charge of the investigation into the kid's death.' He splayed his fingers. 'That's cool, Vicky. Totally cool. Just got back to the station as the lad's lawyer turned up, that's all. Escorted him up here, making sure he didn't, you know, kill him or anything.'

'A likely tale.'

'Seriously.' MacDonald put one hand back in his pocket, with the other playing his soul patch like a fiddle. 'Getting nowhere with Ashlynn's disappearance. Forrester told me you've connected it to your laddie and this furniture shop?'

'Possibly.'

'Possibly?'

'The name could be a coincidence, Euan. It's fairly common.'

'Either way, Forrester wants me to ask this boy about her.'

'You're welcome to watch.'

MacDonald nodded his head over the room towards interview room C. 'Mum's in there.'

Vicky smiled. 'And you don't want me to speak to her, right?'

'Not that petty.'

'But you're sticking the mother of a missing girl in an interview room like she's a suspect.'

'Maybe she is.' MacDonald walked over and opened the door. 'Louise? One of my colleagues would like a word, if it's not too much trouble.' He stepped into the room.

Vicky joined him in the room.

Louise Thomas looked barely old enough to have a child, let alone a nineteen-year-old student. Thin to the point of skinny, mouth hanging open. 'You found her?'

Vicky sat opposite her and gave a curt smile. 'I'm investigating another matter, madam. But we think it's possibly connected.'

'Don't call me "madam", please.' She rolled her eyes, then rolled up her sleeves to show a bandage that ran up her arm. 'They took her from right in front of me. Meeting for a coffee, then I turned my back to take a phone call from my mum. Next thing I know, I'm sprawled over the Desperate Dan statue. My phone's smashed and my girl's taken.'

'Just outside Boots on Reform Street, right?'

'Right.'

'Did you see them?'

'No.' Louise shook her head. 'Well, no.'

'So you were meeting Ashlynn for a coffee?'

'Right, right. I've got work this morning. Cleaning some arse-hole's flat for him, but I wanted a coffee with my girl. She's at the university. So proud of her.' Her mouth opened in a thin rictus, revealing rotten teeth. 'My girl, a student. First in our family.' She took a sip of water, her hand shaking hard.

'That's great.' Vicky sipped tea through the lid, acting like they were two old friends having a cup together. 'Everything we've heard, Ashlynn sounds like a good kid.'

'The best.'

Vicky hadn't heard anything, but it was great when that kind of ploy worked. She finished her tea. 'Have to say, you don't look old enough to have a kid at uni.'

'Thanks, doll.' Louise sipped her water. 'I had Ash young. Like, real young.' She looked up, her furtive eyes shooting between

Vicky and MacDonald. 'I was fourteen. Didn't even think I could get pregnant at that age, despite all the shite they tell you at the school. Daft wee cow, I was. Mum was great about it, but it's been tough.'

'I can imagine.'

'Can you?'

'Aye. I might've been older than you, but I was a single mother.'

'Right.' Louise looked away from Vicky's acid stare. 'It's been tough for me and Ash. But it worked out well for her. Made sure she didn't make my mistake. Had her on the pill as soon as she started talking about boys.'

It stung Vicky's gut. Maybe it was the tea, but maybe it was something a lot worse. 'Did Ashlynn ever speak about her boyfriends?'

'Don't ask, don't tell.'

'She ever mention a Noel?'

'Nuh.'

'What about a Dax?'

'Is that a name?'

'A nickname.'

Louise looked over at MacDonald. 'Is this who's taken her?'

He shook his head. 'It's a separate case. A murder inquiry.'

Louise was glowering at Vicky. 'This lad's been killed and you think my Ashlynn did it?'

'There's a possible connection between both this murder and your daughter's abduction to a shop in the Hilltown. Small Paul's Home Bargains.'

'Never heard of it. Try to avoid the Hilltown.'

'Why's that?'

'It's personal, you bitch.'

Wow, she turned fast there.

MacDonald raised his hands. 'Hey, it's okay.'

'How is it okay? My Ash is missing and you're asking *me*? How is any of this okay? Eh?'

'Louise.' MacDonald steepled his fingers on the table. 'Think you should tell us what happened there.'

'No, you nosy prick, I won't—'

'Please. It could be important.'

'It's not!'

'Let us judge that.'

Louise seemed to slow down to a snail's pace, her hand sliding down her face. 'That's where Keith... Where. I was at a party there as a lassie. It's... It's where Ashlynn was... conceived.'

Nineteen years ago would mean 2000, taking into account her maternity. Vicky was a few years older, but had seen that kind of thing happen. And it was always the mother's lives that were ruined, saddled with children when they were children themselves. And maybe things were getting a bit better, but it was unlikely.

'Thanks for telling us. It must be really hard. Is her father—'

'Prick's dead.'

'I'm sorry to hear that.'

Louise shook her head. 'No loss to the human race. He died overseas.'

'Sorry to hear that. Was he in the army?'

'In the army? Hell no. Keith worked in bars in Turkey, you know? Antalya. Shithole of a place. Different girl every night.'

'Was he older than you?'

'Aye, aye. He was nineteen. My cousin too.'

Abusing a fourteen-year-old in his family.

Great. Just great.

'While that prick was over there having the time of my life, I had to give up school and my future to raise my girl. Someone stabbed him to death outside his pub when Ash was six weeks old. Hard to feel sympathy, eh?'

'How did he react to the news?'

'Ran off, didn't he? My mum told his mum, her sister, and they haven't spoken since.' Louise reached out and grabbed Vicky's wrist. 'Will you rescue my girl?'

'We're trying.' Vicky shook herself free of the iron grip. 'DS MacDonald will do all he can and we'll work together to try to find her.' She got up and used that as an excuse to get away from

MacDonald. 'I'll be in touch, Euan.' She left the room and tried to process everything.

Noel fell off the bridge.

The code on his arm led to a website, which led to a store.

Ashlynn's name appeared on the website, out of stock.

Ashlynn was missing, abducted from the middle of Dundee.

Too much there for it to be a coincidence.

Right?

Time to see what the owner had to say for himself.

Vicky crossed over to room B and opened the door.

Considine was yawning into his fist, his eyes all twisted up. 'Sarge.'

Small Paul's owner sat opposite, stroking his thick beard and looking like he wanted to be anywhere else but in that interview room.

Next to him, a much taller man shot to his feet with a skip and thrust out his hand, then took it away. 'Ah, it's you.' Beige suit, blue shirt, white tie. Tanned face way too big for his tiny features. 'Victoria Dodds.'

She took the chair next to Considine, opposite the lawyer. 'Bruce.'

A lawyer attending an informal interview indicated some level of guilt. But whether the crime was money laundering, sex trafficking or unpaid parking tickets was unclear. Maybe it was all three. Maybe it was none.

Considine tapped the microphone. 'Also present is Bruce Watson of Nelson-Caird & Watson, the interviewee's solicitor.' He nodded at the shop owner. 'Can you identify yourself, sir?'

The shop owner snorted, then rubbed at his nose. 'I know your game, son.'

Considine sat back and folded his arms. He almost looked like a hardcore police officer, but the mayonnaise and brown sauce stains gave the game away a bit. Like he'd been crapped on by an eagle. 'Oh? What game is that?'

'I'm saying nothing, son.'

'So why have you come here?'

'When the police come knocking, you don't refuse the call.'

Bruce leaned across the desk, pleading with Vicky. 'Sergeant, my client has complied with your request to attend the interview. Please, let's get on with this before my client gets bored and leaves.'

'But we haven't asked him anything.'

Bruce held up a hand to stop his client talking. 'Before we get down to brass tacks, let's discuss what this is about, shall we?'

'Your client's business has come up in an investigation.'

'I don't own it.'

Vicky sat back, keeping her smile in place. 'Okay, the business your client is a front for.'

'A front.' Watson shot his tongue from one side of his tiny mouth to the other. 'That sounds like you're assuming his guilt.'

'Like I say, the business premises are associated with a criminal enterprise.'

'I trust you've got a valid evidence trail?'

'We do. Mr Whatever-his-name-is here hasn't been arrested, so I can't share it with you. Just like he can't share his name with us.'

'He doesn't have to.'

Vicky leaned across the desk. 'But you do work at Small Paul's Home Bargains?'

'Aye.' He sighed. 'I make all the stuff in there. Apart from the sofas. Working with wood's been my passion since I was wee.'

'It's good stuff. Very well made. And cheap.'

'Thanks.'

'But I can't connect the lovely stuff you've made with the stuff on your website.'

'Told you back at my workshop, there's *no* website.'

Vicky reached into her pocket for a printout and took her time unfolding it. She held it up beside her head. 'This is a website, but it's no ordinary website. It lives on the dark web. It's encrypted so police officers can't easily find it. Trouble is, the police found it and the hosting traces to your shop.'

'Well, someone's playing us both then.'

'Playing us how?'

'Whatever they're up to, it has sweet Fanny Adams to do with me. I just make furniture. You're investigating God knows what and it sounds vile. But whoever's doing whatever you're investigating, they're trying to point that to me.'

As excuses went, it was maybe at the more plausible end of the spectrum. Wouldn't be the first time some criminals pointed to an entirely innocent business as a deflection tactic.

Then again, it wouldn't be the first time criminals were taking cash from a shonky business.

'You've never heard of an Emmy-Kate or an Ashlynn?'

'What? No.'

'What about Noel?'

The owner smirked. 'Gallagher or Edmonds?'

'Russell.'

'Sorry. No.'

'What about a Dax?'

'Dax?' He frowned. 'Like in that *Star Trek* show? Deep something something?'

'Right. *Deep Space Nine*, I believe.'

'Still no.'

'Victoria.' Watson's grin wounded as much as his choice of name to address her with. 'My client is merely a simple craftsman trying to eke out a living. That's it.'

'I'm not sure I believe that.'

'You'd better because it's the—'

The door clattered open. DCI John Raven popped his head into the room. 'Sergeant. A word.'

Vicky scraped her chair back and got up, then whispered into Considine's ear. 'Pause it and keep them talking.' She straightened up. 'Just be a second.' She followed Raven out into the corridor, heart thudding. What did he want?

In the harsh light, Raven's combover looked even worse, just a few strands of hair hauled over pink skin. He folded his brawny arms, his shirtsleeves rolled up to his elbows. 'What's going on in there?'

'I'm interviewing a suspect, sir.'

'I can see that, Sergeant.' His creepy eyes shot all over her. 'I just...' He smiled. 'Cut him loose.'

Vicky folded her own arms. 'No.'

'I'm sorry?'

'No, *sir*.'

'Sergeant, that's an order. Get him out of here.'

'Sir, he's running a website connected to a paedophile network.'

Raven smoothed down a strand of his combover. 'Sergeant, all you've got is a gossamer thin audit trail connecting this shop to a dark web storefront. Correct?'

'It's a bit more concrete than—'

'What did Bell say?'

Vicky glanced at Forrester, who seemed as mystified as her. 'Bell?'

'Sergeant, tell me you've spoken to DCI Jason Bell?'

'No, sir, I...' The acidic tang was bubbling up into her chest.

'Who is he?'

'DCI Bell works in the Met. That's Greater London's police force to you.' Patronising sod. 'He's leading a strategic investigation on behalf of our prime minister into this so-called paedophile ring.'

'So-called.'

'I understand the victims are older than—'

'Right.'

'Sergeant, we're beholden to DCI Bell on such matters. And yet, you're running in like a bull in a china shop. Interviewing anyone you can find.'

'Sir, with all due respect, your forensics officers are working with the Met and didn't mention this connection when they unearthed it.'

'Right, well.' Raven looked her up and down. 'Do the work before you visit. Get evidence that Mr Johnston is connected.'

Vicky had to look away. 'I didn't have his name.'

'I know you didn't. It underlines my point. Get the evidence against him first, then you can go hard on him. We don't need lawyers making problems because we're running off half-cocked. Okay?'

'So you want me to pick up with DCI Bell?'

'That's not your job, Sergeant.' Raven sneered at her. 'I'll get back on the blower to him now I know what's going on here. You find that boy's killer. Am I clear?'

'Crystal, sir.'

'Right, good work.' Raven turned on his heel and stormed off down the corridor.

Arsehole.

Vicky blew out air, hoping she hadn't said that out loud.

Maybe he was right. Maybe she had been a bull in a china shop. But Met DCIs and strategic investigations were way above her pay grade.

She got out her phone and called Forrester.

8

Vicky tried to stand upwind of Forrester, but the smoking shelter's layout meant there was no such thing. The blue mist just surrounded her, like it wanted to choke her.

'Well?'

Forrester exhaled another lungful out of the side of his mouth, but it still snaked its way towards her. 'Standard practice, I suppose.'

'What, the Met being involved?'

'You hear about this case a few years back, where some bastards had been... Bloody hell, I can't bring myself to talk about it.' Forrester took another drag and held it in. 'Long and short of it, no matter what the Police Scotland brass think, the Met still have a national remit for some crimes. And this Jason Bell boy is the real deal. Know someone who can't stand him, mind.' He exhaled through his nostrils. 'But we've got to bow to their whims in cases like this.'

'I don't like it, sir.'

'Nor do I, but what can we do? Sex trafficking on this scale trumps a murder case.'

'What if our murder is connected to it, though?'

'Then we'll have to do the work, like that arsehole says.'

Forrester took a long drag, taking his cigarette almost down to the filter, and coughed it immediately into Vicky's face. 'You did jump the gun in bringing in the shop owner.'

'But if the Met are all over this, why doesn't Jenny Morgan know? Why doesn't anyone else know?'

'Good point.' Forrester stared into space like he was thinking it all through. Thinking the same thoughts as Vicky.

'Sir, the way I see it, these senior officers are playing games against each other. Jason Bell, whoever he might be, is trying to grab hold of our investigation, while Raven's playing a game back at him.'

'What, though?'

'Not sure.'

Forrester flicked his cigarette butt into the bin and waved over to the road. 'Aye, he's up to something that's for sure.'

At the far end of the car park, Raven stood by his Audi sports car, shaking his head, but it was like he was listening to someone.

Vicky's acid gut started bubbling again.

Turned out Raven was talking to someone.

Alan stepped forward, scowling at Raven. He was saying something, but Vicky couldn't tell what.

'Why the hell is your ex speaking to him?' Forrester stormed across the car park, hands in pockets, but going at a fair old lick. 'Sir, need a word.'

Raven and Alan either didn't notice or didn't care.

Alan jabbed a finger in Raven's face. 'You've got two cases now, John. You sure you don't want to go on the record?'

'No, son.' Raven gave a wide, beaming smile, hands on hips. 'I'm quite comfortable with our position on this matter.'

'You've got a Mancunian gang abducting kids off the streets of Dundee. First Ashlynn Thomas, then Noel Russell. That's a pattern. Who's next, eh?'

Raven laughed. 'Son, I'd love a bowl of whatever you're smoking. Just don't get caught with it in your possession, as it's probably a Class A.'

'I'm being serious, John. This is going national.'

'I'll pass that on to my superiors then. I'm sure they'll love being threatened by a daft wee nyaff just as much as I do.'

'A nyaff? Can I quote you on that?'

'No, son. You can piss off back to Edinburgh. Sure they've got proper stories for you to look into.'

'You're saying people trafficking isn't a proper story?'

'Son, I'm late for a meeting in Glasgow and you're in my way, so can you kindly bugger off?'

Alan stared at him for a few seconds, then stepped aside. 'By all means.' He looked over at Forrester, then at Vicky. 'Oh, didn't notice you there.' He nodded over the dual carriageway. 'When we were an item, do you remember how we used to meet in the cafe when you were on duty?'

Vicky felt her cheeks start to burn. 'Alan, you should probably listen to him.'

'Aye, aye. I'm not that daft.' Alan walked off in the opposite direction, heading for the city centre.

Raven opened his car door, but didn't get in, instead watching Alan leave. 'Boy is a twat.' Then he turned to face Vicky with the full force of his fury. 'You and him? Wait a second.' His face twisted, then untwisted, but still looked like a skelped arse. 'Did you leak stuff to him?'

'No, sir.' Vicky walked closer to him and rested on the car door. 'And I don't appreciate the insinuation.'

'Well, someone's been leaking again. If it's not her, David, how the hell does he know about both your cases?'

'Sir, it's nothing.' Forrester was grinning. 'Lad's just winding you up. Don't succumb to it.'

'Right. Well.' Raven stared at his door until Vicky let go. 'Need you lot to see if there's something in what he says. If there might be a connection between these cases and these Mancunian gangsters.'

'You believe that, sir?' Forrester narrowed his eyes like he didn't.

Raven waved back along Bell Street. 'Way the lad tells it, we should be chalking young Noel's death up to a drug deal gone bad.'

'A drug deal?' Vicky frowned. 'What evidence have you got?'

Raven wagged his finger at her. 'Naughty, naughty, very naughty.'

'Eh?'

'Using my own words against me.' Raven smoothed his hair over his head. 'No, Sergeant, we don't have any evidence, but I've been through both of David's cases and it certainly fits. Or it looks like it. According to your own brother, the kid's gaming computer cost a pretty penny, right? I've seen the estimate. Five grand. Where does a fifteen-year-old get that kind of cash, eh?' He left them hanging.

Forrester was first to bite. 'You think from dealing drugs?'

'Stands to reason. Rockie's a rough school. Attended there myself, for my sins. Place should've been closed twenty years ago, I tell you. Stands to reason the best way to get drugs to the kids is by getting some of the kids to do it. Give them a cut, keep them quiet, let them spend their pennies on daft stuff like computers. See who they can trust and move on up the ranks. Maybe that daft sod got greedy and it backfired, big time. Didn't expect it to be some gangsters from out of town.' He nodded at Vicky. 'Sergeant, I need you to prove it for me, then close the case. Okay?'

'Sir, I'm not sure—'

'This is open and shut. Easy. You've got gangsters abducting him, pouring petrol on him, then chucking him out of a moving van. Speak to the laddie's pals and see what shite they can put him in. And David.' Raven was looking down his nose at Forrester. 'Get Mac to focus on tying them to Ashlynn. I like these lads for that too.'

'Why, though?'

'She was a student. Students like drugs. Same MO.'

'If you insist.'

'Aye, I do.'

Vicky didn't like any of it. 'What about the website?'

'Look, we are aware of it and we're progressing it, but it's not our case.' Raven slapped the roof of his car. 'And that's why I'm heading down to sodding Glasgow. The powers that be are convening a conference call with the Met and some clowns in Manchester and Birmingham. Obviously Carolyn doesn't like me dialling in remotely and insists I drive halfway across the country, but hey ho. This baby can shift, so I'll only be a few hours. Look after the fort for me, David.'

Forrester stopped him shutting his door. 'Why would Noel scratch a code on his arm if he was just a low-level dealer?'

Raven sucked in a deep breath. 'I'd say that drug dealers and people traffickers are usually the same kettle of bastard, so it stands to reason if he was in one, he'd know about the other.'

Vicky had to laugh. 'I don't see how that all follows, sir.'

'It just does!' Raven licked his dinger and plastered his rogue strand of hair down again. 'Kid is a dealer, probably full of remorse and guilt when he took a swan dive off the Tay Bridge. Open and shut case, like I say. And when you get some experience you'll know better.'

Not for the first time, Vicky could've swung for him. But she shoved her hands behind her back.

Raven shifted his glare from Vicky to Forrester. 'I've asked Jenny Morgan to lead on that front, so leave it with her, okay? And David, can you go to the lad's PM? If he was high as a kite when he took that header, that'll slam the case shut.' He got in the car and slammed his car door with a bang like gunfire. He shot off out of the parking space at a fast clip.

Forrester stood there, flicking his lighter open and shut.

'Penny for them, sir.'

Forrester looked over at her. 'Bloody bullshit, Doddsy. Manc gangsters? Drug deals gone wrong? Load of shite. Load. Of. Shite.' He swaggered off, lighting another cigarette in the howling wind.

Vicky got out her phone, mainly to distract herself by seeing what Rob and the kids were up to. Whether Mum had tagged her on Schoolbook *again*. Anything but thinking about John Raven for a few minutes.

A text from her dad:

Nope! Never head of Big Shug the coastie! How's it going? X

And there was another text. Unknown number.

She hated having to, but she opened it regardless of who it might be. Or what it might contain.

Bit slow on the uptake, Vicks. I'm in the cafe, waiting to meet you. Alan x

9

Vicky hadn't been back to the Auld Cludgie Café since they refitted the canteen and it started selling edible lunches and tea that tasted like tea rather than a sewer. The place was pretty busy, even though it was now definitely post-lunch. Not that Vicky was hungry. The opposite after spending that much time with Raven.

The waitress looked pretty frazzled as she retied her apron. 'You here for some food?'

'Just meeting someone.'

'Oh, okay.'

Vicky spotted Alan in a table by the window, next to a couple getting up from one.

The filthy bastard waited a few seconds, then leaned over to the now-vacant table and swiped two slices of leftover pizza from a plate.

Vicky sat opposite him. 'Still a dirty sod, then.'

'Waste not, want not.' He took another bite.

'It's not like you're taking untouched slices. Someone's been eating that.'

'Not the crusts.'

'True. They only touch those with their mucky fingers.'

Alan shook his head. 'You're still a bit slow on the uptake, eh?'

'Not about germs.'

'I mean about me suggesting you meet over here after speaking to that daft wanker.' Alan took another bite of somebody else's pizza. 'I was trying to be subtle, but I forgot you need a brick in the face sometimes.'

'Look, if this is about Bella, we should have lawyers present.'

'Come on, Vicks, you wouldn't be here if you thought this was about her.'

'So what is it, then? Gangsters from Manchester and failed drug deals?'

'Got it in one. Maybe not so slow, after all.'

'Okay, so spill.'

'Well.' Alan tossed the crust back onto the plate at the next table. 'I've been doing a story. Found a couple of waifs and strays in seedier parts of Edinburgh and its environs. Wee lassies, just skin and bone really, and young. Working in a brothel in Broxburn, as it happens. Some drug dealer's mum's old house, turned into a knocking shop.'

'This better be going somewhere.'

'Aye, aye. These lassies started talking to me, okay? And like I say, I thought it was just drugs and prostitution, so I was going to pass it over to some cop contacts through there. Big Malky. But then I found another lassie, right. Turns out she's from Findhorn in the Highlands.'

'Wow, you must be waiting on the Pulitzer committee to call you up.'

'Sarcasm never suited you, Vicks. The lassie was reported missing seven years ago. She's twenty now.'

'And?'

'She went missing at the age of thirteen. Next thing we know, she's working as a prostitute in Broxburn.'

'So?'

'Well, it turns out that drug dealer is into human trafficking as the mainstay, with drugs just the sideline.'

Vicky's mouth went all dry. She needed to watch her mouth

here. Keep her powder dry. Hold everything back. Or Raven would be on her like a ton of bricks. Or feathers. Or anything, but enough to squash her. 'What, so they're trafficking young girls into the sex trade?'

'Maybe. I don't have the full picture. Way I see it, the drugs are the lure, right?' Alan waved a purloined pizza crust at her. 'You know how it works. Wee dealers in towns, offering free gear around. Get a kickback for getting any pretty young lassies hooked. Have some of this, then a bit of that, until they *really* have a taste for it. Then it's a case of, you know that cost me a packet, right? Put big guilt on them. Then say if you want to pay me back, Greedy Gus says he would pay to spend time with you.'

'Speaking from experience?'

Alan reached over and grabbed a few chips off the other plate. 'Aye, but not my experience.'

The waitress walked over and snatched the plates away before he could take any more.

'These lassies in Edinburgh, Vicks. It's *horrible*. There's a pipeline from north to south, and Dundee is just the tip. Inverness, Aberdeen, Fort William, Stonehaven, loads of places. Wee lassies getting taken to Glasgow, Edinburgh, then further south into England. Newcastle, Leeds, Manchester, Liverpool, Birmingham, London. Working sex clubs. And I don't mean lap dancing bars, but brothels. Horrible, *horrible* places where consent isn't even asked. Or the girls' mouths are taped shut. Or they're on so much smack they don't even know their own age, let alone what's going on.'

Vicky sat back and blew air up her face. Shit. Alan might be an arsehole, but he was good at his job. It all made sense, and it made her sick. 'How does this fit in with me?'

'Come on, don't be coy with me.'

'What do you mean?'

'Raven was denying it before you got there, but young Noel is on my radar.'

'What do you know about him?'

'Nothing. Just a name. Noel Liam Russell. And I know it's him.'

A cold shiver ran up her spine. 'What do you want?'

'Let's you and me work together. I'll share what I've got, you give me some info back.'

'Alan, I can't.'

'I know. But *some* info. Pertaining to a news story, not a criminal investigation. Any famous faces. VIPs, politicians. Any of it. That's all I ask.'

That was in the realm of the slightly possible, maybe. But if she got caught, she was already on Raven's radar. So it had to be worth it.

The waitress walked over and slid a pizza in front of Alan. 'Here you go, sir.' She laid out some cutlery. 'Can I get anything for you, madam?'

'I'm fine, thanks.' Vicky sat back and smiled, waiting for the waitress to leave. Mulling it all over. Aye, for it to be worth it, it had to be something really big. 'Okay.'

'Okay?'

'I'll do it.'

'Excellent.' Alan picked up a slice of pizza with stringy cheese and charred mushroom hanging off.

'But on the condition that you keep out of our lives.'

Alan dropped the pizza slice. 'So, I'm giving you all this golden info, and you're asking me to give up on my daughter's life?'

'Pretty much.'

'Okay.'

Vicky frowned. 'That's it? I expected more of a fight from you.'

Alan picked up his pizza again and took a bite. 'Thing is, as a father... I'm a good journalist.' He finished chewing and took a drink of water. 'And you're a lot better at sacrificing your career for your family. So, if you pony up some juicy worms from your end, I'll walk away totally. Bella will never see me again.'

'Fine, but this has to work financially too. The last two years, you've haggled over the fact you didn't know you were a dad and refused to pay anything towards Bella's upbringing. It's expensive. I need some of that back.'

'What, so you and Rob can blow it on a holiday?'

'Well, it's better than you blowing it on coke and hookers.'

Alan laughed. 'Fine. I'll tell my lawyer to speak to yours and we'll stop this petty nonsense.'

It wasn't petty, it was him being malicious, but Vicky nodded graciously. 'Thank you.'

'Cool beans.' Alan picked up the next slice of his pizza. 'So what is it you've got to share?'

'Me first, is it?'

He bit into the slice and blowing hot air out of his mouth. 'Aye.'

Vicky tossed around a few ideas in her head. 'Have a look into Small Paul's Home Bargains.'

'What the hell is that?'

'You'll see if you're good enough.'

'Good. Thanks.' Alan finished chewing and tossed the crust onto the plate. 'Well, my turn to show you mine, eh?'

'I've seen yours and look where it got me.'

'A lovely daughter?'

'*Alan.*'

'Fine. I've been digging into Noel as part of the story. Your boy Raven's right. The kid was dealing drugs at Rockie, as they call it.'

'How do you know that?'

'Kids at that school might not talk to cops, but they talk to me. Noel was into dope, weed, hash, grass.'

'So that whole thing about a drug deal gone wrong could be true?'

Alan laughed. 'Could be.'

'Come on, you're confronting Raven about it. You must have something?'

'Well.'

'If he was dealing drugs, how much would he be making?'

'Pocket money. Why?'

'Just that he had certain lines of extravagance in his life, which Raven is using to explain his drug dealing.'

'Which is?'

'Well, his old man was pretty broke, but his computer cost over five grand.'

'What, a computer costing that much? My laptop cost three hundred quid!'

'It's a gaming thing. Very high-end stuff. My brother's into it.'

'Your brother...' Alan wagged another floppy slice in front of her. 'Look, I don't know if Noel was dealing, but I did hear that he is a big gamer. Been playing that...' He frowned. 'That game I can't remember the name of. Anything newer than chess, I've no idea.'

'*Indignity*?'

'Right, right. This one kid, the way he explained it, he said there's a ton of money in it. Buying and selling like virtual clothes.'

Vicky got a flash of Jamie, accidentally spending over a grand on such shit. 'I've heard about that.'

'Right. Right. But the way I hear it, Noel and a few others had been chatting on there.'

'Isn't that kind of the point? They're hanging out on there, playing a game with their headsets on.'

'It's not the what, Vicks, so much as the who.'

Back in the forensics lab, Jenny and Zoey were huddled by a workbench, scowling at a laptop screen. They stopped talking when they spotted Vicky's approach.

Jenny tilted her head forward. 'Back so soon?'

Vicky took a seat at the bench opposite them. 'Just wondering how it's going with Noel's computer.'

'Which bit of it?'

'I need to see what games he was playing online, and who with.'

Zoey took the hint and left Jenny's desk. 'I'll see how he's getting on.'

Vicky watched her go, then looked at Jenny. 'Andrew?'

'Right. Disappeared about half an hour ago. Zoey's looking at that Ashlynn's laptop, so I got Andrew to take lead on Noel's machine.'

'That what you two were discussing?'

'Can't tell you of all people, Vicks. Come on.'

'Right.' Vicky leaned in close, though the place was so empty that she didn't really need to bother. 'Have you been dealing with DCI Raven on anything?'

Jenny gave a distant-eyed nod. 'This Met shit. For Ding Dong.'

'Jason Bell?'

'Right.' Jenny focused on Vicky. 'Mate of mine down in the Met hates the guy. But aye, Raven's been pushing me to get Met to lead it.'

'And you don't necessarily agree with that?'

'Correct. He's a lazy sod, looking to balance his budget by getting people to do his job for him. But I think a case like this will definitely benefit from local expertise.'

'Even with Mancunian gangsters?'

'Well, that's up to them, isn't it? Greater Manchester Police are like a wee dog, rolling over and expecting its tummy to be tickled. By the Met. Same as Police Scotland. There's definitely a Dundee angle to this.'

'Just Dundee?'

'Well, what have you heard?'

'Nothing much.'

'Look, I don't think we're doing enough here.' Jenny shook her head in disgust. 'Typical Police Scotland, it's all gone to shite since we merged. It's all about budgets and cost centres, not about catching the bad guys any more.'

'Jen!' Zoey called over from the far end of the empty lab. 'Got something.'

'Well, let's see what's behind the mystery door.' Jenny vaulted up and charged across her domain.

Vicky followed at a slower pace.

Zoey was working at Noel's gaming PC, but with electricity flowing through it was like seeing a corpse coming back to life. Not a black box any more, but glowing with neon green and acid yellow lights, with vivid blue veins. 'Well, I've no idea where Handy Andy has gone to, but we couldn't get it to clone earlier, so we have to access it directly. I'm into Noel's online accounts. Steam, Epic Store, GOG.'

Vicky stood there, hands on hips. 'You just got in like that?'

'Happens a lot, Vicks.' Jenny was nodding along to the beat of Zoey's mouse clicks. 'I haven't met him, but Zoey said Noel's dad seems computer illiterate, so Noel saw no need to protect everything with a password. His phone might be different, but we haven't recovered that.'

Zoey tapped the screen. 'His username is DaxTheDestroyer. I've got a list of friends on Steam.'

Vicky scanned the names, but they all looked like codes to her. ZippyBongo1000. BvggerLvgsKid. AchyBreakyF4rt. And all childish gibberish. 'What about any others?'

'Well.' Zoey clicked into another window. 'Thing is, I could look through Epic and GOG too, but you said he's spent most of his time playing *Indignity Online*, right?'

'Why didn't you start there?'

Zoey shrugged. 'It's the one I know least. Handy Andy is the pro there.' She frowned. 'Does Hayden69er mean anything?'

'Noel's best friend is Hayden Milne.'

'He's got a lot of *Indignity* DMs from him.'

'DMs?'

'Direct messages between users.' Zoey switched to her laptop and started typing. 'As far as I can tell, Noel's contacts are most likely other kids from school, judging by IP addresses.'

'You can see that?'

'Well, not publicly. I've just got a backdoor into the game.'

'That was quick.'

'Another case, Sarge.'

Vicky rolled her eyes. 'I've been bitten by fake IP addresses before. People can mask their locations, like if they want to watch American Netflix. That kind of thing.'

'Not this time. PC gamers all plug into their router to get the fastest time. It's incredible tech, really, but to make it seem like they're all playing the same game, they need to trim the latency close to nothing.' She stopped, clocking Vicky's confusion. 'Latency is the delay between the computer and the server and back. They need to trim that to single-digit milliseconds, if possible. And to do that, they make sure everyone is locally paired. So the servers are in Dundee, nearer the players. It means people in Dundee can't play someone in Australia or Russia or America without it getting all janky. So, to stop that and preserve the experience, they pair up locally.'

Vicky could see a week of just chasing down school kids, interviewing them with concerned parents causing mayhem with the press and senior officers. 'Okay, can you extract the chat records? I'll get my team to go through them.'

'Trouble is, Sarge, well.' Zoey sighed. 'Two things. First, Noel's wiped his chat records.'

'But you said you had his chats with Hayden?'

'I did, but that's just an outlier. And Hayden sent a ton of messages last night. They were unread, so this was presumably after Noel went to bed. So he didn't get time to even read them before...' Zoey swallowed hard. She was still young, almost a kid herself, despite having a child, and sometimes murder could hit at the weirdest times.

'Zoey, what's the other thing?'

She snapped back to the present. 'The person who logged the most hours playing with Noel stopped doing so two weeks ago.'

'Any idea why?'

'Well, the game is about a gang like in that old film about robbers. You gang up and go around doing stuff. People talk to each other online and that. But it's a fixed gang, like in real life.'

'Okay. So what do we know about this person?'

Zoey tapped into her laptop. 'Well, the username is 5318008 but that's all—'

'Oh, shit.' Vicky felt her stomach churning again, tightening around her brunch.

Jenny waved a hand over her face. 'Earth to Dodds. Earth to Dodds. What's up?'

Vicky slapped her hand away. 'I think it could be someone I know.'

'How?'

'Well, they use that everywhere as their username. Twitter, Netflix, whatever.'

'It means something to you?'

Vicky rolled her fingertips along her palms. 'It's that calculator thing. Type it in, turn it upside down and it reads BOOBIES.'

Jenny laughed. 'So it's Alan?'

Vicky shook her head. 'Worse.'

10

Onscreen, Karen and MacDonald took the lead in the interview, while Vicky was in the obs suite. Stuck, hemmed in, trapped. 'I should be in there.'

Jenny was between her and the door. 'So should I, really. But we're not. Vicks, you need to let this play out.'

Vicky gripped her thighs tight. Anything to avoid punching the screen.

'Alrighty, then.' Onscreen, MacDonald was giving it his all, sitting on his chair back-to-front, drumming his thumbs on the back. 'Easier if you just admit it now.'

Andrew just sat there, arms wrapped around his chest, eyes clamped shut. Vicky's brother, so deep in the shit. He opened them again and glowered at MacDonald. 'You need to tell me what I'm supposed to have done.'

'Come on, Andrew. You know it's easier if you tell us. *Much* easier that way.'

'Okay, so I picked my nose and ate it when I was twelve. Is that it?'

'Certainly take that into account. But no.'

'I'm not under arrest here, so I don't need to say anything, right? And I can go at any time.'

'Just have to arrest you, then.'

'Do it. Then I'll find out what the hell I'm supposed to have done.'

'Andrew, Andrew, Andrew. Better for you to be as open with us as you can. Look better for you in court.'

'In *court*?' Andrew laughed. 'Don't kid yourself. This is going nowhere near court.'

'Because your old man's an ex-cop? Because your sister's a serving officer?'

'No, because I haven't done anything, you chopper.'

MacDonald did a little fill with his thumbs on the chair back. 'Alrighty.' He smiled at Karen, but she was ignoring him, so he looked back at Andrew. 'Don't worry. Can totally understand how it is. Play a lot of *Indignity*, am I right?'

'*Indignity*?' Andrew was frowning so much his forehead looked like a stack of unopened post. 'What are you talking about?'

'More of a *Red Dead Redemption* man myself. Sink *hours* into that. Given your condition, I—'

'My condition?'

'Sickness record shows a lot of absences. Presume you've got an underlying condition? Or a drugs problem?'

'You really want to bring that up on a recorded interview?'

MacDonald focused on the recorder, then started drumming with his thumbs again. 'Mean it in the nicest possible way, Andrew. You're not a well man. Anyone can see. Everyone appreciates you coming into work, as you've got very special skills.'

Andrew nibbled at his thumbnail. 'And this is the thanks I get.'

'Spent a *lot* of time playing that game, haven't you? Logged a minimum of sixty hours a week for the last six months.'

'It's not a crime, you know?'

'No. It's not.'

'But snooping on me without a warrant might be.'

'No warrant needed for publicly available information.' MacDonald held up a sheet of paper that made Andrew look away.

If Vicky was in that room, she'd have a word with MacDonald. At least. Drag him out into the corridor. But she'd done the same thing to suspects. Probably done worse, if she was being truly honest. But that was her *older brother*. And he was *abusing* him. It was like MacDonald was trying to get at Vicky. Snide bastard.

'Lot of time spent in a virtual world, Andrew. Maybe you confuse reality with—'

'Don't. Seriously.'

'Spend all that time shooting and maiming and—'

'It's a *game*, you dick. It's not real. We go in and we muck about.'

'Muck about, huh? Like, how?'

'We troll people. You know, messing them about. Bullying them.'

'Sounds childish.'

'Sure you get up to all sorts on *Red Dead Redemption*, right?'

'Maybe.' MacDonald smirked, but it settled into a scowl. 'Who's we, Andrew?'

'Just some guys on there.'

'Anyone I might know?'

'Depends.'

'Come on, Andrew. Best if you're honest with me. Who are you talking about?'

'I don't know their names.'

'You mean in real life?'

'Right. I know just the handles on *Indignity*. It's just some people I've met on raids and stuff. Hit it off and we hang out, form gangs and...'

'Troll people. I get it.' MacDonald gave another display of chair drumming. 'Doesn't look very good, though, does it?'

'How?'

'Well.'

'You're the one playing games here.' Andrew pushed his chair back and stood up over MacDonald. 'Look, you wee shite, all I've done is play a video game online with some people. That's it!'

'Sure. Be okay if it was just anyone you were playing with.'

Andrew frowned at him. 'Who are you talking about? What am I supposed to have done?'

MacDonald sat back and it looked to Vicky like he almost fell off his reversed chair. He caught himself before he did. 'Did you murder the boy?'

'Eh?' Andrew's eyes bulged. 'What boy?'

'Come on, Andrew... Open up. Confession is good for the soul.'

'Seriously, you need to quit this. Who are you talking about?' Andrew was tugging at his beard, like he was going to tear big clumps of it out. 'Is this someone I've been playing online with?'

'Would expect someone who worked in IT forensics to check who they were playing with.'

Andrew swallowed again. 'You need to tell me who you're talking about.' His voice was thin and shrill. 'Or I'm out of here.'

MacDonald reached over for a sheet of paper. 'Noob241, Rock-wellHard, KellasBwoi.'

'That's some of them, aye. I've no idea who they were in real life.'

MacDonald put the sheet back on the table, just out of Andrew's reach. 'What about DaxTheDestroyer?'

'What about him?'

'Spent a lot of time with him. Raids, sure. But chats too. Trouble is, you've wiped your chat records, haven't you?'

'I haven't.'

'Really?'

'Why would I do that?'

'Hide them from us?'

'They're still there, you arse.' Andrew wiped his hair across his face. Both were slicked with sweat and that room was notoriously cold. 'Look, if I delete my messages, they stay on the other user's account.'

'So you're saying you've got a chain of messages between you and DaxTheDestroyer?'

'Right.'

'Share them, then.'

'I would, if I liked you. And you were being honest with me.'
Andrew collapsed into his chair like a sulking kid.

'Still got your copies of these messages, that's good. Just share them, then you can maybe get out of here.'

Andrew sat back, kneading his beard with his fingers. 'Okay. But I don't think it's what you're looking for.'

'What *am* I looking for?'

'I honestly have no idea, you clown. But these messages are just about us arranging bank robberies, train robberies, home invasions, carjacking. Or rearranging them.'

'Lot of virtual robbing going on.'

'That's the game. Don't blame me. I just play it.'

'Of these kids, who do—?'

'*Kids*?'

'Play the daft laddie all you like, Andrew. Must've *known* they were all fifteen.'

Andrew slumped back in his chair. 'Shite.'

'Honestly didn't know?'

'No.' Andrew looked broken and defeated. He surely knew where this was headed — Noel, the kid whose computer he'd catalogued, that price he'd pulled together that seemingly gave proof to Noel's drug dealing. Surely.

MacDonald pulled himself forward, leaning over the chair back. 'When you're playing, though, surely you use headsets to talk, right?'

Andrew nodded. 'Thought they were older.' He tugged at the beard stubble on his neck. 'Like eighteen, twenty. Thought they were students.' He shot a look at MacDonald. 'Do you think I'm abusing them?'

'Are you?'

'Fuck off!'

'Older guy like you hitting on young boys. Happens a lot.'

'FUCK OFF!'

'Okay to be gay, Andrew. Just that, well, if they're underage... Tut tut.'

Vicky was on her feet now, ready to smash the monitor into a thousand pieces. Or take it through to the interview room and batter it over MacDonald's head.

Jenny rested her hand on Vicky's arm. 'Calm down, Vicks. I've seen you go apeshit in an interview. Like I said, let this play out.'

'But he's my brother.'

'And if he's a paedophile, it'll be really tough on you and your folks. I totally get that. Completely. But you should want him to get done for it. Aye?'

Vicky knew she was right. But Jesus, her older brother. Could he really—?

Could he?

She sat down and put her head in her hands.

'You need to tell me who these kids are.' Her brother's voice, but was that the voice of a paedophile? A *killer*? Christ. 'You need to tell me who's dead.'

MacDonald leaned back again. 'Noel Russell.'

'The kid who died?'

'Right. Know anything about that?'

'I mean, aye. I catalogued his computer.'

'Delete anything on there?'

'What? Of course not! It wasn't plugged in to—'

'Heard you couldn't get the cloning to work. You do that?'

'Shut up!'

'Why did you get banned?'

Andrew slumped back in his chair, tears streaming down his cheeks.

Vicky was on her feet again. She couldn't just sit there and let that arsehole do this to her brother. Could she?

'Vicks, I know this is tough, but you need to let him finish.'

Vicky looked round at Jenny, frowning at her. She was right, but she couldn't just... sit there, watching that prick tearing her brother apart. Maybe she should go to the canteen, get a cup of tea, wait it out.

But that was even more passive than sitting here and watching. She'd have no idea what was going on. No way of knowing if

MacDonald was playing fair. No way of reassuring her parents she did all she could.

MacDonald rubbed at his eyes, looking bored more than anything. 'Here's how I see it. That kid, Noel, you did something to him. Said something that got you banned. Maybe he threatened you back. So you needed to send him a message. So you—'

'Shut up.' Andrew's voice was a low hiss.

'Was it one of the other kids you played with? Hayden Milne, say? Andrew, if you were flirting with them, it's best to—'

'FUCK OFF, YOU PRICK! I didn't do anything! Nothing!'

'See, we found a code on Noel's arm. You know that, right? The furniture catalogue. You know what it represents. Selling children. You involved in that?'

'No!'

'Sure? Because it'd need a lot of technical know-how to pull off. Dark web is your speciality, right?'

Andrew shot to his feet and stabbed a finger in the air. 'If you accuse me one more time of anything disgusting like that, I swear to God I will come over the desk and belt your jaw.'

MacDonald leaned forward and drummed with the heels of his palms. 'Bring it on.'

Vicky had no choice here. Her brother. She needed to know if he was innocent. Her parents deserved the truth, no matter how heartbreaking it would be. But she was the only one who could get it out of him.

'Sod this.' Vicky stormed out into the corridor, then stepped into the interview room. It felt like a freezer in there, but it smelled of rancid meat.

Andrew was sweating so much his shirt was soaked through, showing coils of hair in the damp patches.

MacDonald pushed up to standing. 'Erm, Sergeant, you shouldn't be in here.'

Vicky walked over to the recorder and ended the session without speaking. She leaned in close to MacDonald. 'Euan, I'm stopping this.'

'Idiot just threatened me. Keep it going!'

'Euan, how would you react if someone accused you of... Of being involved with that site?'

'Not doing himself any favours here.'

'Doesn't matter. Our priority is finding Ashlynn and catching Noel's killers. Tormenting my brother isn't getting you what you need.'

'What if he's connected to those people?'

'Then I'll get it out of him. All you're going to achieve is needing surgery after he batters you.'

MacDonald laughed. 'Really think he could?'

'He can and will. Give me a minute with him and I'll get him talking.'

MacDonald snorted. 'Could do with a coffee.' He got to his feet. 'Come on, Constable.'

Karen joined him standing, but her gaze was locked onto Vicky. She mouthed, 'You okay?'

Vicky nodded back. But she wasn't okay, even worse than after an hour with Raven belittling her. She waited for them to leave, her neck throbbing, then righted MacDonald's chair and sat on it. She stared deep into her brother's eyes, searching for the truth. 'Andrew, whatever's going on, I just want the truth. You owe me that. You owe Mum and Dad.'

He looked away.

'Andrew, I don't care about anything other than the truth. Okay?'

He couldn't look at her. What did that say? Shame? Disgust? Or feeling betrayed?

Vicky reached over for his hand but he snatched it away. 'Andrew, the microphones are off, okay? Nothing's being recorded, nobody's listening in. That's it. Just you and me. Just tell me what happened.'

He looked at her now with wounded eyes, blinking way too fast. '*Nothing* happened.'

'Okay. But you know these kids, right?'

'Vicks, all I've done is shoot and rob virtual people in a gang with these kids. That's it. It's fun, pretty much the only enjoyment

I've got in my life. It's like a Tarantino film or *The Sopranos* or something. Pure escapism. And you know what I need escape from. I'm really, really ill. I can't sleep half the time. I keep waking up, or just not getting to sleep. And it doesn't matter how little caffeine I have. I can't switch my brain off. All I can do is play these games.'

'Why didn't you say any of that to DS MacDonald?'

'Because he's a wanker. And he's not interested in the truth. Just wants to make me suffer.'

'Andrew, he's just doing his job. I've done the same to suspects. So many times. Just so I can get a confession or just gain some intel. Dad would've been the same.' Vicky grinned at her brother. 'Actually, Dad was a lot worse.'

Andrew laughed through a snotty nose.

'So, why don't you tell me the truth?'

Andrew sat back, caressing his temples for a few seconds. 'The truth of it is I didn't know it was Noel. I swear.' It was like he was trying to drive his thumbs into his brain. 'I feel bad because I collected his PC from his house and catalogued the equipment. You won't be able to use it as evidence.'

'Not necessarily. Andrew, if you're not involved in his death—'

'Of course I'm not!'

'Even so. You're connected to his account. We need to speak to you.'

'You can't think I—'

'Andrew, just stop it. Okay? Keep telling me the truth. That's it.'

'Right. Which one is Noel?'

'DaxTheDestroyer.' Vicky watched his shoulders slump. 'And we know you're 5318008, Andrew. Which is stupidly immature, but you haven't changed.'

'Okay. I didn't know who DaxTheDestroyer is. Honestly. But I spent a lot of time on there, playing with him and the others. The names that twat read out.' He flicked his hand towards the sheet of paper. 'But I've no idea about anything other than chatting to him on *Indignity*. He was a good laugh. Similar sense of humour to me.'

'What sort of thing?'

'Well, we had nicknames for other players. It was fun. Just daft fun.' Andrew looked right at her, deep into her eyes. 'The thing is, I can't do it anymore.'

'Because you've been banned.'

'You know?'

'Right. For the last fortnight. Why?'

But Andrew stared at the desktop, shaking his head.

Vicky felt the floor swallowing her whole. Her worst fear was coming true. She rested her elbows on the table and cradled her head in her hands. 'Andrew, what did you *do*?'

'Nothing!'

'You don't get banned for doing *nothing*.'

Andrew leaned forward, resting on his elbows, mirroring her body language. 'I killed too many people.'

'In the game?'

'Right.'

'Isn't that the point?'

'It was kind of over the top. It was just a laugh.'

'Was Noel banned?'

'Not that I know of.'

'It was just you?'

'Right.'

'And you don't think that looks bad?'

'I was just mucking about.'

'By killing innocent people?'

'They're not innocent.'

'Come on, Andrew. It's all virtual nonsense. You got banned for killing too many people. Why weren't they innocent?'

'Look, I'll try and explain. Every so often on *Indignity*, you have to go on these big skirmishes. It's part of the game world. The rules. Usually it's a squad of four. But this one, we were in teams of twenty, cops and robbers. We were robbers. A few of them were really annoying, but this one time...' Andrew ran a hand through his hair, slicked with sweat. 'A group of four of us got to the map early, got into place and waited. The rest turned up and we killed them all.'

'Twenty people?'

'No, thirty-six. Sixteen of our team and twenty on the cops side.'

'You and DaxTheDestroyer?'

'Noel, if that's him. It was great fun. We robbed their corpses, got some good gear, then ran off.'

'And you got banned for that?'

'I think so. The next time we logged in, we were doing a bank job. I was the getaway driver, it was going really well. They came out with millions in cash, and I hit the gas but someone shot a rocket launcher at our car. We somehow survived but this guy... He had all the best gear, I swear. He could mow us down from miles away. It was like a sniper rifle but *fast*. And we took all of our stuff, the shit we'd glommed on that raid. Then every time we logged in, he kept hunting us down and killing us.'

'This all sounds really childish, Andrew. And complete nonsense.'

'I'm serious. It's what happened. The last time, this guy starts speaking to us. And he clearly wasn't a kid, judging by his voice.'

'You thought fifteen-year-olds were older.'

'Aye, but this guy, he was thirties. And he's got all the best gear, must've spent tens of thousands. Like fifty grand's worth. A hundred grand maybe.'

'He could actually be a kid with very angry parents, maybe.'

'Nah.'

Vicky winced. 'Rob found that Jamie's spent a grand on clothes on there.'

'Ouch.' For a fleeting moment, Vicky's brother was back. Andrew, not a sexual predator grooming kids online. Potentially. 'But this guy told us to stop.'

'And did you?'

'No. Next day, we shot these guys and stole their gear.'

'Who was it?'

'Well, I have access to some hacker tools, don't I, so dug into his profile, even used some of my work skills. His handle is King-VietCong, but he... The KingVietCong thing panned out. It said he lives in Vietnam. So it's obvious he's used a VPN. I couldn't track him down after that.'

'Zoey said you can't use them on *Indignity*? Something to do with only local players?'

'And she's completely right. It's a bugger, but they're creating this amazing virtual world that's light years ahead of everyone else's and they do that by making it weirdly local.'

'This better be going somewhere.'

'It is. I think. Look, when I got banned I kept messaging the guys I was with. Sounds like he kept on killing them. Every time they logged in, bang, a sniper rifle.'

Vicky grabbed the sheet of paper and showed it to Andrew. 'Any of this lot?'

'Hayden69er, Noob241, RockwellHard. All of them were getting targeted. As soon as they logged in, they were wiped out. Every time.'

'But not Noel?'

'Nope. Look, the last time I messaged with DaxTheDestroyer, if that's Noel, he told me that KingVietCong had been. He threatened him.'

'How?'

'He didn't say.'

'In the game?'

'No, in real life. He knew his name. He called him up on his phone.'

'Andrew, we haven't got Noel's phone.'

'But you can check his call records.'

'We can see he's been called, but it won't back up the message.'

'I know. But after Dax didn't stop, every time he logged, King-VietKong would kidnap him, pour petrol over him and set him on fire. He kept doing it.'

Vicky's blood ran cold. 'Andrew, that's pretty much what happened to him.'

'What?'

'Come on. Of course you know. You've been working this case, and you've been privy to lots of confidential information.'

'I swear I don't. He fell off the bridge, didn't he?'

'He got away.'

'Christ.' Vicky looked at a grieving man, not a guilty one. A shocked, stunned one. 'Okay, so assuming I believe you, how can I prove any of this?'

'I don't know.'

'So this is just he said, she said?'

'No. But Dax told me that he kept doing it. Every time he logged in. Into a car, petrol, fire. Every time.'

'So who could it be?'

'Well, KingVietCong was warning him. He might work for the company.'

Vicky got out into the blustering wind. Cars and lorries hurtled along the Kingsway, barely metres from her face, just the black-painted mesh fence between them. The putrid stink of spent diesel and burnt tyres.

'Worked here when I was at school.' Considine slammed the passenger door and shot off towards the entrance. 'Brilliant fun, have to say.'

Vicky set off across the car park after him. Fair to say their pool Focus was the worst car in the place. At least half of them were electric models plugged in to fast chargers, though Vicky was pretty sure you didn't have to do that every day. Then again, this exact spot would let staff drive in from miles away and the commute wouldn't be anywhere near as bad as the average internal Glasgow or Edinburgh one. Probably a fair few estates in Perthshire, Aberdeenshire, maybe even up in the Highlands. Let that sports car hammer down the A9 every morning, then across country roads.

A few months ago, the office frontage had been done up to look like a giant rocket ship. The local papers were up in arms about it. As much as it was a rich man's folly, it added a bit of colour to an industrial estate in the armpit of Dundee. Still, you could probably see it lit up from Fife if it weren't for the Law being in the way.

The front door opened with a swoosh like in *Star Trek* and a big man stormed out into the fresh air. 'Come on!' He was followed by two kids, a boy and a girl. They looked a lot like Rob, Bella and Jamie.

Vicky approached and saw it was them. She stopped dead and locked eyes with Rob. 'What are you doing here?'

Considine shifted his focus between them. 'This is your dad?'

'My *dad*?' Vicky shot him her police officer's glare. 'Go inside and ask to speak to the CEO, please.'

'Aye, aye.' Considine trudged off with a smirk on his face.

Vicky let Bella bury her head in her jacket. 'Didn't expect to see you lot here.'

'Aye.' Rob huffed out a sigh. 'Wouldn't have come, but I was on the phone complaining to them for over an hour, and they just wouldn't listen.'

Vicky hugged Bella tight and let Jamie join in on the cuddle. 'Rob, it's okay, we'll manage.'

'Aye, but it's the principle of the thing.' He was speaking in a low voice. 'How can they let someone spend a grand on *virtual clothes*.'

Vicky held his gaze as Jamie hugged closer, but it was like he was trying to barge Bella out of the way. 'Like I said, it's okay—'

'No, it's not.'

'You did put our credit card info on the Xbox.'

'Aye, Vicks, but I put it behind a password. I want to know how they can let my son *actually* play the game despite me setting the parental lock and him, for once, not circumventing it. Makes me wonder how many other kids are on it. And...' Another sigh. 'And he's *nine*. It just shouldn't be allowed.'

Jamie was hiding from Bella now and reaching out to poke her arm.

'I took him into PC World and showed him the size of telly we could've bought with that money.'

Vicky ruffled Jamie's hair. 'I'm sure he understands.'

'Not convinced.'

Vicky hugged both children tight. 'Anyway, I've got a contact at the *Sunday Argus* who does consumer rights stuff. Worth a chat with her?'

Rob clenched his jaw. 'This contact is through Alan?'

'Rob, it's someone I've known for a long time and independent of that ar— him. Sally Wilson, she's good. I'll text you her number. And, to be honest, just mentioning her name will probably frighten them into giving us the refund.'

Rob looked at her for a few seconds, then swallowed. 'Thanks, Vicks. Look, I'm sorry about this. I'm just frantic with worry. I *hate* being in debt. I felt so *embarrassed* back there. Your mother had to pay. You know?'

Vicky nodded. 'I know. She loves to pay, though.'

Rob frowned at her. 'Why are you here?'

'It's about the case, sadly. I've got to go.' She leaned in and kissed him. 'Give them a call back, mention Sally Wilson and you'll get the refund.'

SOMETIMES CONSIDINE COULD SURPRISE VICKY, and right now was one of them. While she'd been talking to Rob outside, he had secured a meeting with the CEO. No fuss, no messing.

And his office was right up in the tip of the rocket ship, at the top of the tower, though it wasn't outfitted like a command module, just a generic office with windows giving a three-sixty of northern Dundee, where the city's housing estates blended into the Angus countryside, then as much of the city centre as he could see from up there.

Trouble was, there was no sign of him.

Vicky sucked through the straw of her fruit smoothie, hand blended and tasting like about eighty quid's worth of fruit, and not the bruised reduced stuff Rob would buy when the price reductions were done in the Arbroath Ashworth's. 'Is he burning files or something?'

Considine slurped at his own smoothie, finishing the dark blue drink, but he kept sucking through the straw until it hissed and rattled. And just kept on doing it. 'Boy's probably gone for a jobbie.'

Or a line of coke.

Vicky rested her drink on the desk. Most of the time, guilty people wouldn't leave two cops alone in an office, but there was nothing to rummage through here. Just a brushed steel desk with a fancy laptop plugged into three screens. And the laptop was password protected – Vicky had tried.

The *Star Trek* office door swooshed open and a rock star walked into the room. Tight jeans, tight grandad collar shirt rolled up to show athletic arms, and hungry eyes that scanned the room. 'Sorry about that, we're on a tight schedule just now.' He swanned over to them and thrust out a hand. 'Heard it said they'll stop us shaking hands, so let's do it while it's still allowed.' He tightened his grip around Vicky's hand. 'Jason Kellas, pleased to meet you.'

'DS Victoria Dodds.' She didn't know why she'd used her full name. She *hated* it. Christ, this guy already had her on the ropes. And Vicky didn't know why. 'This is DC Stephen Considine.'

Kellas grabbed Considine's hand. 'Know your face from somewhere, don't I?'

'Worked here about ten years ago.'

'Jeez, that was a long-ass time ago.' Kellas shoved himself down in his chair. He clicked his fingers and the door opened. His assistant raced in with another pint-sized smoothie, though this was bright green. 'Thanks, Dennis.' He sat back, silently sipping through his straw, but with much more elegance than Considine who was *still doing it*. 'So. How can I help, guys?' Not a Dundee accent, but lost somewhere over the Atlantic.

Vicky got up and walked around the room. Her hands were shaking, so she stuffed them in her pockets. Christ, what was up with her? She looked out of the window. Across the Kingsway, a man was hanging out bedsheets on the line and making a right mess of it, getting them all caught up by the wind. 'Impressive place you've got here.'

'It's taken a while, but I'm proud of what we've achieved here.'

'Must be worth a packet.'

'I've done okay.'

'Hundreds of millions is better than okay.'

Kellas raised his eyebrows. 'That's a bit forward, Sergeant.'

Vicky turned around and appraised him from a distance. His rockabilly haircut looked dyed, the shaved sides a bit greyer than the black fringe hanging loose. Not an ounce of fat on him, though. And he was wearing more make-up than she was, and it was her *birthday* too. 'I mean, you're a global power in the video game industry.'

Kellas raised up his pale palms, a defensive gesture but it showed his tan wasn't out of a bottle. 'Hey, I wouldn't go that far.'

'You make hundreds of millions each year, don't you?'

'Maybe.'

'And you haven't sold up and you've kept the business in Dundee. That takes a lot of courage.'

Kellas slicked his long fringe out of his eyes. 'Look, it's not as magnanimous a gesture as you think. Okay, so we can boost the local economy and pay our taxes, but we can harvest talent from Abertay's video game degree. Get the cream of the crop each summer. And because it's here rather than in America or London or wherever, we can also pay a lot less than the standard rate. That's how you keep the best talent locked in.'

Considine finished blowing air out of his straw and set the cup down. 'When's the next season of *Indignity Online* out?'

'You game?'

'Massive fan of it, aye.'

'Here.' Kellas tossed him a silver pen. 'That's a limited edition. Have it.'

'Is this what Jack Snyder uses to stab—'

'In the prologue, yeah.' Kellas grinned. 'And to answer your question, we're in the middle of a crunch, which is when I ask my guys to work twenty-hour days for a few months back-to-back. Nature of the beast, but they're on bonuses like you wouldn't believe.' He waved out of the window. 'Every time we ship an update, I can look out and see the new cars rolling in from the bonuses.'

'This the new revision?'

'Yeah. It's going to be huge. Going to change things in a big way. And it's risky changing stuff like that.' Kellas laughed hard. 'When we work all the hours, it makes me appreciate what it must be like being a cop.'

'Don't know the half of it, mate.' Considine was looking around, though Vicky couldn't tell if it was for somewhere to stick his empty, or where to get a refill.

And she was losing control of the situation. The more nonsense Considine threw at him, the harder it was going to be to get what they needed. It was her own fault for goading him about his wealth. She waited for Kellas to look over at her. 'My son plays your game.'

Kellas nodded slowly. 'The *Charlie the Seahorse Adventures*, right?'

She frowned. 'You make those too?'

'Our mobile division does. Easy money.'

'Right, no. My daughter plays that. My son is into *Indignity Online*.'

'But you don't look old enough to—' Kellas shut his eyes. 'Wait a second.' He reopened them and waved a finger at her. 'We had some guy just in here, saying his partner's a cop, threatening us unless I unwound a grand's worth of transactions.'

Vicky fought against the physical urge to wince. 'Sorry about that.'

'That's your husband?'

'We're not married, but aye. Problem was, we blocked Jamie from spending but he hacked in.'

'Seriously? That's what this is about?' Kellas smiled, but there was more than a hint of malice in there as he slurped smoothie. 'Isn't this an abuse of police power.'

'That's not why I'm here.'

'Sure? Because I can't just—'

'He's *nine*.'

That hit Kellas in the face. 'Shit. Okay.' He put his smoothie down, then hit the laptop keys like he was drumming, hard and precise to a silent beat. 'Okay, I've unwound those transactions. And I've thrown in a free year of *Charlie the Seahorse* for young Jamie.'

Vicky smiled. 'You don't have to do that.'

'No, but I want him to keep playing our games, ideally an age-appropriate one until he's old enough.'

'That's an eighteen-rated game, right?'

'Yeah, sure, but it's next to impossible to sift through our user-base and find out who's underage.'

'That mean you get a lot of kids on your servers?'

'I've no idea of exact numbers. The game engine handles it all anonymously, so it's really tough to pinpoint exact users. It's a bit of a thorny issue with our investors, as they want us to maximise our monetisation of every user, but I've got to have some principles in this racket.'

'Sure you do.' Vicky walked back to her chair and sat down. She took her time sipping the smoothie. 'The reason we're here is to get your help in tracking an IP address.'

'Of a player?'

'Aye. Connected to a case.'

'Like I said, we can struggle to pinpoint users, but I'll do all I can to help.'

'Thanks.' Vicky put her smoothie down and got out her notebook. 'I need you to look into a user for me.'

'I can ask if you've got a warrant, Sergeant.'

'So go on, then. Ask.' Vicky gave him space, but he didn't fill it, just sucked on his straw. 'A warrant makes me think you've got something to hide.'

'Okay, look. What do you need?'

Vicky glanced over at Considine. 'I need you to look into the username DaxTheDestroyer.'

Kellas reached back for his laptop, then typed. He sat back, cradling his hands behind his head. 'Ah.'

'What's that mean?'

'That user has been problematic.'

'In what way?'

'Well, we've had complaints from users about this gang of wee pricks.' His accent slipped back to a local Dundee one. 'Wee shites who had been robbing other players of stuff. Cars and guns. All items they've spent a fortune on buying or a ton of time earning.'

'I really don't understand why people spend money on clothes for a *game*.'

'Look, these kids spend *hours* on these games every day. They want to look as good as you did at your school disco. You spent twenty quid on a T-shirt that cost two quid to make, just to be seen by friends with the right logo. It's exactly the same for them.'

And maybe it was, but it melted Vicky's brain.

'But the clothes and guns are different. The cosmetics are always owned by the user, so they look as cool or as daft as they want. But each weapon in the game is a unique object and you own it. You and only you. You can't copy it, but you can sell it to someone else. And, yes, I'm that kind of CEO – I take it personally when people try to screw with my game. So I'm trying to fix it. I'm trying to stop them doing that kind of thing.'

Considine was nodding along. 'Happens a lot, eh?'

'Heck of a lot.' The mid-Atlantic accent was back. 'I mean, *Indignity* is supposed to be rough and tumble, don't get me wrong. Losing all of your guns is part of the fun, right? The excitement. But some gangs in the game have been killing players maliciously. Stealing their equipment over and over. So I've personally found them all, and I've gone into the game and taken them down, grabbed all their stuff back, then I've banned them.'

'You can't just do it remotely?'

'We used to be able to, but then we caught some of our staff taking bribes to gift upgrades, so we stopped it. Makes our platform very unique.' Kellas sighed. 'This user, DaxTheDestroyer, I remember the name, because we had an incident blow up overnight, so I banned him this morning, along with a couple of other players.'

'So you're KingVietCong?'

'What?' Kellas scowled. 'No.'

'Come on, you've been very honest with us so far.' Vicky leaned forward on her chair. 'Why start lying now?'

'How about a bit of quid pro quo here? Who is DaxTheDestroyer?'

Vicky didn't even have to think about it. 'Okay. We fished his body out of the Tay this morning.'

'Shit.'

'He was fifteen. His name is Noel Russell.'

'Never heard of him. Was it suicide?'

'Looks like murder.'

'Looks like?' Kellas shot a steely look at her. 'Is it standard practice to interview every video game company CEO when a player dies?'

'Thing is, Noel was abducted in broad daylight. The kidnappers poured petrol over him. He managed to escape before he was torched.'

'Shit.'

'That user, KingVietCong, he did the exact same to him in the game. Over and over.'

'You've got proof of this?'

'No. That's why we need your help.'

'You really should have a warrant, you know?'

'My boss is speaking to a judge about this. It's an unusual one, but we're confident we'll get it.'

'Okay. Look, I don't respond well to threats. Unless we're in a bedroom situation.' Kellas wasn't looking at her, but his words were coiling around her like a snake. 'Good news is I'm going to help you, okay? My privileges let me see behind the scenes here. I'm the only one I can trust.'

Vicky wondered if he was deleting information, evidence, whatever, so she got up and joined him on his side of the desk.

The middle monitor was filled with rows of spreadsheet data, indecipherable to anyone but Kellas.

Vicky rested her knuckles on the cold desk. 'What's this?'

'Chat logs from that user to anyone.' He tapped the middle screen. 'You recognise that name?'

Username 5318008. Andrew.

'Aye, that's a person of interest in the case.' Vicky scanned down the message chain.

Torching you?

Then Noel:

> *Every time I log in.*
> *Kidnaps me.*
> *Shoves me in a van.*
> *Kicks me out.*
> *And sets me on fire!*

Dude.

> *I know, right?*
> *Said if we don't stop, it'll be in real life.*
> *Not the game.*
> *But it's not like I've *done* anything since!*
> *He just keeps killing me!*

But that was the end of the chain. 'Any idea why it stopped?'

'Because I banned user 5318008.' Kellas tapped on a profile page with a photo of a big hulking brute. And it wasn't a photo, it came from the game. Looked so realistic. 'But there's something here.' He tapped on the right screen.

Noel was chatting to Hayden69er. Didn't take a genius to figure out who that was.

Hayden:

You believe him?

Noel:

Sent me my address, dude.
My *home address*.
Like IRL.
So yeah, I'm shit scared, dude.

It'll be okay.
Surely?

Don't think so.

Kellas sat back, arms folded. 'Shit.'

'Someone is threatening players of your game, then doing it in real life.'

'You don't have to tell me how serious this is.' Kellas leaned forward and typed, revealing another page of data on the left screen. He tapped the display, but Vicky couldn't make head nor tail of it. 'There you are.'

She squinted and read the words:

I will keep finding you. And if you don't quit, I will kidnap you.
Douse you in petrol. Set fire to you. Nobody will find the body.

'This is from KingVietCong?'

'Right.' Kellas brought up another user's avatar. This one was athletic, but wearing camouflage gear. Shaved head, tattoos up his neck. South-east Asian features, but that could be a ruse. It was all virtual. And whatever, Vicky didn't recognise him.

Vicky leaned back against the window behind the desk. 'Could it be someone who works here?'

'It could be. Well, I'd very worried if it wasn't as it'd mean someone's infiltrated our security system.'

'This is all because DaxTheDestroyer has been killing people in the game?'

'Aye, but...' Kellas swung around to look at her. 'When these players steal guns off corpses, they can sell the gear to other players. Making a few quid in real money.'

'Real money?'

'Right. You buy our in-game currency. Ten "Digs" for a dollar or a quid.'

'So it's like real life theft?'

'Just like it. In fact, it legally is in a few American states. Probably be over here soon.'

'Okay, do you have any idea who KingVietCong is?'

'I do.'

'Do they work here?'

Kellas nodded. 'Mark Agnew.'

'And who is he?'

'He's currently heading up QA here for the upcoming release.'

'QA?'

'Quality assurance. Testing. Making sure the game does what it says on the tin with minimal glitching.'

'Okay, so you're going to show us where he is.'

12

Vicky stood in the doorway to an empty room, some kind of circular office with glass on all sides except a red brick wall, filled with framed stills from violent films, mainly ones that starred Robert De Niro. In the middle, a glass desk at standing height was perched over a treadmill. Chrome bar stools were dotted around, with a couple of damp-looking towels on them. The room had the reek of salty sweat, but no trace of who had left the towels.

'So, where is he?'

Kellas had his mobile out. A man of his wealth might have some pre-market prototype of a next-generation smartphone, but he was using a vintage Nokia. He tapped at the keys, getting that click that gave Vicky a wave of nostalgia for not very long ago. 'Sorry, he usually replies to my texts immediately.'

Vicky didn't want to perch on any of the stools, in case she sat on something she didn't want to.

It didn't stop Considine. The lazy sod thumped down onto one. 'Nice crib.'

Vicky had to fight to not roll her eyes at him, instead focusing on Kellas. 'Any idea where Mr Agnew might be?'

Kellas was typing away on his Nokia. 'Sorry, no idea.'

Considine was staring at the desk. 'He can work walking on that treadmill?'

'It's deceptively easy. And I actually encourage everyone in the business to— Gary!' Kellas dashed back out into the hall.

Vicky followed him out.

Kellas was blocking a young man from passing. 'You seen Marco?'

A hipster type, with a thick beard that made him look ten years older than his fresh eyes indicated. 'Not since the stand-up, no.' He looked round at Vicky, then back at Kellas. Then did a double take. 'You.'

Vicky frowned at him. 'Do I know you?'

'Eh, you should.' He shook his head at her, then focused on Kellas. 'Marco said he was heading out for a couple of hours. Want me to give him a bell?'

'There's a good lad, aye.' Kellas watched him go, then smirked at Vicky. 'You got previous with Gaz?'

It hit Vicky — that case a few years ago. 'Gary Wilkie, right?'

'Right. One of our lead testers here. Currently heading up *Indignity Online*.' Kellas sniffed, then rubbed at his nose like he had a six-gram-a-day coke habit. Maybe he did. 'Kid's going places. He'll be after my job soon enough.' He shook his head. 'My own fault, really.'

'Why's that?'

'Well, we have a no-policy culture here.'

'What's one of them?'

Kellas looked at her like she'd just crawled out of the Dark Ages. 'It means that people can turn up whenever they want, leave as often as they need to, so long as they achieve everything set by their line manager, so long as the work gets done.'

Considine was grinning. 'So, smoking crack would be okay?'

Kellas shrugged as he put his phone to his ear. 'So long as we get shit done, I don't see a prob— Bugger me!' He charged into the office. 'Marco's left his phone here.'

Vicky shared a worried look with Considine. 'This isn't good.'

'Aye, I know.' Kellas was scowling at the high-end mobile

dancing across the treadmill desk. 'Despite us being bollock deep in the final phase of testing, my QA lead has decided to bugger off home for the day. That's *fucked*.'

Vicky fixed him with a hard look. 'So, one of my colleagues will be out to get hold of those messages.'

'Right. Sure.' But Kellas was staring at the phone like it was going to come to life and attack him.

'You will play ball, won't you?'

'Of course. Sure.'

'Do you have an address for Mr Agnew?'

DUCHESS HILL WAS the highest point in Dalhousie, a crap town somewhere between Montrose and Arbroath, which were both competing to be the crappest of crap towns and whose only function seemed to be to make Dalhousie seem nicer by comparison.

Mark Agnew's home was at the top of the hill and gated off from most of the crap, with a nice view of the old town, the harbour lights glowing in the February gloaming.

'Some place, eh?' Considine was peering through the windows, his thumb pressing the doorbell down. 'Must be making a mint there.'

'I don't like this, Stephen. He should've been at work.'

'Know what you mean, Sarge, but—'

'Hello?' A woman's voice, coming from behind them.

Considine swung around first.

A massive BMW sat on the drive. The sort that could fit two football teams in there, and substitutes and referees. A woman was leaning out of the driver's window. Soft face, maybe a bit puffy, but had clearly been beautiful at some point, though age and the three children fighting in the back of the car had taken its toll on her. 'Can I help you?'

Considine was charging across the pebbled drive. 'Mrs Agnew?'

'Ms Healey.' She stepped out onto the drive, engine running, and looked Considine up and down. 'Deanna Healey. To whom am I speaking?'

'Police, ma'am. Looking for Mark Agnew.'

The back door opened and a small version of Deanna clambered out, hugging into her mother's legs just like Bella would've done to Vicky at that age. Maybe four or five, but small and delicate. Something in the physical contact made Deanna's expression harden. 'Well, I'm afraid my husband isn't here.'

Considine held out his warrant card. 'Is it possible for us to come inside and see for ourselves?'

'No. It's not. I've just collected our children from school and have to ferry them to a number of after-school clubs, so if we can do this another time?'

'Sure, I get that.' Considine nodded slowly. 'When did you last hear from him?'

'Last night.' Deanna lifted her daughter into the back seat. 'My husband's an early riser, so I usually don't see him when he shoots off in the morning. Now, I really must get on.'

'Okay. Thanks.' Considine stepped aside to let the car pull into the drive. 'Well, Sarge, what shall we do? Batter inside, see if he's hiding?'

Vicky looked back towards the town. 'Know any good local cops?'

'Well, aye, there's Goth.'

'Goth?'

'Richard Guthrie. Bit of a fanny, but he's okay. Want me to get him to pop in once she's away?'

'No, when she's back.' Vicky checked her watch. Just turned five. Just too early to bugger off home, even though it was much closer than going to Dundee and back to Carnoustie. 'Let's head back to the station. I'll see what Forrester wants us to do with a dead end.'

～

THE INCIDENT ROOM was a hive of activity. This early in a case, that was a good sign. Then again, free pizza was a much greater lure than solving someone's death. Or rescuing an abducted teenager.

Forrester dipped his crust into a tub and scraped it around until he'd got the last atom of dip onto it. 'Well, that sounds like we need to speak to the lad.'

Vicky stopped chewing her slice of pepperoni long enough to shake her head. 'That's what I've been saying for the last ten minutes.'

'Aye, well. You know what's it like.'

'Do I?'

'I hope so.'

Vicky had no idea what Forrester was on about. He looked beaten down, like he'd taken so much bullshit over the years that he just had nothing left to give. Or just that managing two cases simultaneously, that might or might not be connected, was too much for him. 'So why scratch that IP address into his arm? It's got to all connect, sir. Hasn't it?'

'Maybe.' Forrester finished eating his crust, then looked over at the open box on the desk. He took a slice that seemed to be more onion than cheese. 'Well, the PM gave us absolutely hee haw.' He snapped the crust in half, folding it so it straightened out his pizza wedge lengthways. 'Maybe Raven's right, Doddsy. Maybe it's just a drug deal gone wrong.'

'You don't really believe that, do you?'

'I don't know. Seems a bit funny to me, and nothing makes any sense to me.'

'So, you don't think there's anything in Mark Agnew constantly logging in and torturing Noel in the exact way he was—'

'You got proof of that?'

Vicky checked her phone. No new texts, no missed calls. If Jenny had bothered to head up there, she was keeping quiet about it. 'I don't know.'

'Well, why don't you find out?'

Vicky knew then that Forrester was more interested in stuffing his face than in solving the case. 'I will.' She left him to his slice and found a computer far enough away from Considine and the Three Amigos, deep in a discussion of Dundee United's prospects for the rest of the season. Maybe. It seemed to involve a lot more uses of 'United' than was warranted in a police incident room.

Her phone chimed. Text from Jenny:

Just got the messages extracted. Can't prove the threats were Agnew.

Superb. Just superb.

The case was slipping away from her.

She replied:

But? Can you check he was doing it?

Vicky finished her pizza. She just knew that Forrester was going to take the easy way out, wasn't he? Listen to Raven, put it down to some drug deal gone wrong, let it go cold. Sorted.

All the while, Jim Russell was struggling to come to terms with what happened to his son.

All the while, Louise Thomas had no idea where her daughter was.

All the while, Mark Agnew was at large.

'Sarge?' Considine was standing too close to her, his lips slapping together. 'Just got a call from Goth.'

'Richard Gordon?'

'Guthrie.'

'Right, sorry. What was that about again?'

'Paid the Agnew-Healey home another visit again. No sign of the lad.'

'Okay, thanks.'

'You need anything?'

'No, I'm just assessing what to do next.'

'Right. Sure.' Considine walked off, shoving a whole slice into his mouth.

Sod it.

Vicky opened the PNC and entered the name Mark Agnew. Eleventy-billion results, or what felt like it. There he was, address in Dalhousie, with a few hits relating to him. He was mugged a couple of times in Dundee, his wallet the first time, his phone the second. House burgled when on holiday. Drink driving a couple of times.

And what was that?

She clicked the link and the screen filled with an old murder case file dating back to 2013. A cold case murder in Edinburgh linked to a live murder in Glasgow.

Curious.

Mark Agnew had a few actions attached to him, all assigned to the Edinburgh MIT.

And one Scott Cullen.

Christ.

Vicky got that old, familiar sick feeling. Just had to be him, didn't it? She blew air up her face and got out her phone, tapping in the number on file and hitting dial.

'Hello?'

'Scott, you of all people shouldn't answer strange numbers.'

'Oh Vicky, but yours is saved on my phone.' She could hear him grinning down the line. 'How's it going, trouble?'

She rubbed her forehead. 'Okay, I suppose.'

'That suppose is doing an awful lot of work there, isn't it? Listen, I'm— Elvis, I told you! No sugar.' Vicky heard a mumbled apology in the background. 'Sorry, the boy's a clown.'

'You were saying?'

'Aye, sorry. I'm busy with a case. A dead body in a supermarket and it wasn't a fight over toilet roll. This Covid shit, it's going to get bad, I'm telling you.'

'Believe that when I see it.'

'You Dundee cops are alright, stuck away in the arse of Scotland. Different world down here in Edinburgh, Vicky. But I'm assuming this isn't to rekindle our great lost love?'

'I'm spoken for, Scott.' She was blushing, though. 'Not that it usually stops you.'

He laughed. 'So what's up?'

'Got a hit in a search for a Mark Agnew?'

'Remind me?'

'He's a person of interest in a case.' Vicky squinted at the summary notes. 'Body found under the—'

'Oh God, that one. Aye, Mark Agnew. Think the victim was from my hometown. Dalhousie. Absolute nightmare.'

'I forgot you were from there. Just visited.'

'Place doesn't change much.'

'What did you need from Agnew, Scott?'

'He was a mate of the victim. That's it.'

'That's it?'

'You need him to be a gun-toting mass murderer?'

'Something like that.'

Sounded like Cullen was clicking something in the background. 'Turns out someone made me admin on the file, so I've given you access.'

'Cheers, Scott.' Vicky managed to click through this time. A quick scan showed it was exactly as he said. Just seeing a man about a dog. 'Well, thanks, Scott.'

'Nothing on it, see?'

'Right. I see.'

'So, what do you need from him?'

Vicky was inspecting the action assigned to Cullen. 'It's got two mobile phone numbers there.'

'Work and play, Vicky. Sign of a true shagger.'

'And you'd know, Scott. Thanks.'

'We should catch up sometime, Vicky.'

'Sure. But not for anything other than a coffee.'

'No, totally. Don't be a stranger.' Click and he was gone.

Vicky tapped the numbers into the location tracker.

THE LAST-KNOWN location for Mark Agnew's other mobile number turned out to be a brand-new block of flats at the riverside, wedged between the V&A and Road Bridge Noel Russell had tumbled off. White and shining in the dark evening, the place was the embodiment of new Dundee, clean and corporate. Maybe twenty in there, with everything above the first floor having a wide balcony to look across the mucky Tay to Fife.

Good news is it pinged a couple of nearby cell sites, long enough to triangulate down to the room, at least using Jenny's newest gizmo.

Vicky nudged Considine's side and pointed at the blue-and-yellow signage of the two squad cars Control had sent over. 'Right, Stephen, look lively.'

Considine blinked awake and looked over at her. 'Huh?'

'Backup.'

'Right.' A big yawn and he opened the door to let the frigid air in. 'Let's get going.'

Vicky got out too and waved at the pair of lumps getting out of the first squad car. 'I'll take lead.' She marched inside, then up to the concierge desk, warrant card out, a no-nonsense look on her face. 'Is there a Mark Agnew in here?'

The concierge tilted his head. He was absolutely stacked, like he spent four hours a day in the gym lifting massive weights. 'I'm not at liberty to—'

'I'm working a murder case, sir.' Vicky leaned against the counter. 'We also need to speak to Mr Agnew in relation to an abduction. Now, if you want to stand in my way, that's fine. But I wouldn't—'

'Aye, aye.' The big lump stepped back and folded his arms. 'Marky Mark's in flat seven.'

'Need access to—'

'You don't have a warrant and I don't have the key.'

'No, you do.'

'What makes you think that?'

'A block of flats in Dundee having a concierge is a strange one. I imagine part of your job here involves letting tradesmen in?'

He looked behind Vicky at the squad of goons, some almost as big as him. 'Listen, this place is mostly Airbnbs for punters visiting the new V&A museum just over the way.'

Vicky took another look at her team, assessing her options. MacDonald walked through the door with a uniform carrying the battering ram. Vicky turned back and held out her hand to the concierge. 'Key, please.'

'I can't.'

'I gave you a chance.' Vicky turned around. 'Stephen, let's get upstairs with the battering ram.'

MacDonald joined them, lugging a big metal tube. He handed it to Considine.

'Come on, you can't just do that.' The concierge just stayed behind his desk, arms folded. 'Fascists.'

MacDonald squared up to him. 'What did you say?'

'Fascist bastard.'

'Euan, leave it.'

'Not taking this shite from him.'

The concierge stuck the head on MacDonald, or at least tried to. MacDonald sidestepped him and the concierge stuck the head on a pillar instead. He went down like a sack of potatoes, moaning and groaning. MacDonald grabbed him in an arm bar and pushed it up his back. 'What's your name, sir?'

'Fascist!'

MacDonald was proving his point.

Vicky sighed. 'Stephen, follow me. The rest of you stay here and make sure he doesn't go anywhere.' She led them up the stairs, then followed the signs for flat seven to the end of the corridor. "Smith" was stencilled on a brass plate below a looking glass. She put a hand to the door, ready to knock, but stopped.

'No! Stop! You're hurting me! I want to go home!'

'You heard that, right?' Vicky stepped back. 'As good a reason as any to force the door.'

Considine placed the battering ram against the door. On his fingers, he counted down three, two, one, then hit the ram off the door. It collapsed in and he pressed himself against the door.

Vicky led them inside, snapping out her baton and inching forward.

A long corridor, with two doors halfway along. At the end was a large open space. Loud dance music played, almost drowning out the voices.

But not fully.

'I told you, no!' And a scream was dampened, like a hand was placed over a mouth.

Vicky stopped in the doorway, baton poised, ready to strike.

A wide open living space overlooking the harbour. Both bridges were lit up in the night on either side. Kitchen area to the right, grey units with black marble worktops.

In the living area, a young woman was sitting on a grey sofa, swaddled up in a loose dressing gown, hugging her knees to her chest. She was heavily made up, her hair done like she was at a wedding.

Two men stood to the side, watching a phone screen with eager eyes.

The larger one was wearing a tracksuit. 'See what I mean?' Northern English accent, hard to place. 'With you all the way, man!'

His friend wore a dressing gown, tucked tight around him. 'You caught it all, Phil. Excellent work.' Local accent. 'You want a go now?'

'Damn right, mate.' Phil swung around and his eyes bulged. 'Shite!'

'Police!' Considine was brandishing his baton.

Phil's mate cowered behind him.

The woman was squealing and trying to hide under cushions.

Phil dropped his phone and drew a gun. 'How do you like them apples?'

Vicky stopped dead.

Shit.

Shit, shit, shit.

She was staring down the barrel of a gun.

In Dundee.

'No need to do anything rash, mate.' Considine walked up to the man with the gun and smacked it out of his hand.

Phil watched the pistol spin away from him across the kitchen floor and get stuck under the steel fridge. 'What the fu—'

Considine grabbed his wrist and bent it back, then pushed him onto the floor. 'Now, are you going to behave?'

Two of the uniforms stomped into the room. Considine hauled Phil up to standing and handed him over. 'Take him to Bell Street, aye? And send your mates up for the other one.'

They led Phil out of the room. All of the fight had left him.

Vicky stayed guarding the door. 'Stephen, you could've got us killed.'

Considine slapped his cuffs on the man in the dressing gown. 'Relax, Sarge. It was a fake.'

'How did you know?'

Considine looked over at the fridge, frowning. 'I didn't, I suppose, but that twat needed to learn never bring a gun to a fist fight in Scotland.'

Lucky, lucky bastard.

Vicky walked over to the woman on the sofa. 'Ashlynn?'

Up close she looked young, but made up like she was much older. Far too much around her eyes, hair dyed a bright yellow rather than a natural-looking blonde. 'Who are you?'

'I'm Vicky. I'm a police officer, you're safe now. Can I take your name?'

'No.' She was still trying to hide behind the cushions.

Great. She motioned the uniform over to take care of her.

At least they had Agnew, though.

Vicky grabbed the phone from where it had been dropped. Bastard thing had locked, but they didn't know that.

Considine was cuffing the other man. 'Mark Agnew?'

His head dipped low. 'Don't suppose there's any chance I can pay you off?'

Vicky stuffed the phone in a bag. 'Not a hope.'

Agnew didn't say anything.

13

Vicky opened the interview room door and stopped dead. The only thing worse than indigestion from too much stale pizza and having *a gun aimed at your head* was Fergus Duncan.

The lawyer was dressed for shooting: Barbour jacket, plus fours and tweeds. He didn't have one of those hats on, so his lank black hair was slicked back like a mobster. He nodded at Vicky, then ran his hands down his clothes. 'Been shooting pheasants, in case you're wondering. Our firm's senior partner owns an estate near Dunkeld. And I'll miss the supper tonight, so be thankful I'm here.'

Vicky sat opposite, next to Considine. The recorder was already blinking red. 'Thank you for getting here so quickly.' She got her first look at Mark Agnew, now he wasn't having sex with an underage girl and she didn't have a gun pointed at her.

Agnew was clearly very tall, hunched up at the desk like when Vicky was at primary school for Bella's parents' evenings. He was dressed like he was underage too, skinny jeans and Supreme-branded trainers, and a too-small cyan T-shirt with no logo, so it probably cost a bomb to buy. His NHS glasses were genuine — thick and distorting his features. His hairstyle matched Fergus

Duncan's, like they'd been to the same barber who specialised in haircuts from Scorsese films.

Vicky eased off her jacket and let it hang over her chair back.

'We saw your office at *Indignity*, Mr Agnew. Pretty cool place.'

'Not the first cop to be in there.'

'No. And I know the last one pretty well. I gather you knew a murder victim.'

'Something like that, aye.' Agnew looked down his nose at her. 'You going to get on with this, or do you want more of my CV? How I used to head up design, but moved sideways as I was creatively burning out?'

'No.' Vicky took her seat next to Considine. 'How about we settle for discussing why you were having sex with a fourteen-year-old girl.'

Agnew's eyes bulged. 'Fourteen?'

'Well, I assume she's fourteen.' Vicky gave him a shrug. 'Could be thirteen, or maybe even twelve. Thing is, she seems pretty traumatised by her ordeal. Understandable. But she won't give me her name.'

Agnew blew air out and seemed to deflate like a football with a knife in it. 'I can't believe you're accusing me of... of... of *that*.'

'Sorry. But I am accusing you of having sex with a minor.'

'Do I look like the kind of person who would do something so horrible?'

'Like there's a look shared by all sexual predators. It was recorded on video.' Vicky patted her thick file of blank paper. 'We've got some stills here.'

Agnew looked at his lawyer, then back at the pile of paper. 'Are you trying to ruin my life?'

'No, I'm trying to prosecute a hebephile.'

'A what?'

'A paedophile, but targeting older victims. Hebephiles are attracted to young adolescents and pubescents between ten and fourteen.' Vicky felt herself hiding behind the formal language, the only thing she could do to keep her voice from wavering. 'Children who have at least started puberty and have signs of adult sexual maturation, but are still young and developing both mentally and physically. Still children.'

'This is such bullshit.'

'Given we caught you having sex with someone under the age of consent, Mr Agnew, I'd say you fit that profile.'

'Bullshit.'

'I mean, you seemed to be enjoying yourself, so I'd say you were attracted to her.' She left a long pause for him, dangling it like a worm. 'Unless your friend there was coercing you?'

Agnew looked over at Vicky, but he didn't seem to be ready to take the bait. 'Why don't you go after real criminals?'

'Like your friend? I mean, you were merely sexually abusing a minor. He's guilty of manufacturing child pornography. He is also guilty of the sexual abuse. Abetting the offence carries the same charge. And I don't think he's got a permit for that gun.'

Agnew leaned over and whispered in Duncan's ear. He got a reply, but Vicky couldn't hear any of it. As much as she hoped Agnew would give up his accomplice, she doubted it. He sat back and smoothed down his hair again. 'She told me she was seventeen.'

'Sure that's the avenue you're going down?'

'Well, it's the truth.'

'Because it doesn't really matter, Mr Agnew. You had sex with her.'

'She *definitely* told me.'

'Did you check?'

'Do you check every man who pumps you?'

Vicky stared at her feet for a few seconds, trying to hide the smile forming. She had him. And he knew it. 'But you didn't check.'

'Right.'

So Vicky didn't have to tell him he needed to show he took all reasonable steps to prove her age. Given she barely looked fourteen, that was a ridiculously high obstacle to overcome in a court. She looked back up. 'Mr Agnew, I have sex with people roughly the same age as me. And either way, I'm in a relationship.' She left a pause. 'As are you, Mr Agnew. In fact, we met your wife. Seems like the same age as you.'

'Been going out since we were young.'

'How young?'

'I don't need to answer that.'

'I see. Makes sense then, doesn't it? You hanker for her when she was that age. So you abuse young girls. Like your daughter.'

Agnew thumped the desk and shot to his feet. 'I don't have to listen to this bullshit!'

'You have to listen to everything I say, Mr Agnew. You're under arrest.' Vicky switched her gaze between Agnew and his lawyer. 'How about we talk about DaxTheDestroyer.'

Agnew frowned. 'I don't know who that is.'

'No spaces. All one word.'

'Sounds like a username?'

'Right. You should know it.'

'No idea.'

'So you deny threatening him?'

'What? Of course I do.'

'What about targeting him every time he logged into *Indignity*?'

'Shut up.'

'Weird thing is, every single time he logged into the game, you kidnapped him, poured petrol over him, and burned him with it. Game over for him, sure. But it's strange how he was then abducted and had petrol poured on him in real life. No game over for him, no second lives. Because he's *dead*.'

Agnew swallowed hard, his Adam's apple bobbing up and down.

'Do you want to say anything to that?'

'No.' Agnew massaged his temple. 'I don't know what you want me to say.'

'Did you have Noel Russell killed?'

'Noel?'

'You know him?'

'Aye, I was coaching Noel on how to code and develop 3D video games.' Agnew sat back, arms folded. 'He's dead?'

Vicky focused on Agnew. She could confront him with all sorts of evidence, but she'd keep her powder dry. They had an accomplice to interview and a victim to help. Who knew what else might shake free? Either way, she was looking at a guilty man.

VICKY FINISHED her tea and tossed the cup in the recycling. She'd lost count of how many she'd had that day, but her head was throbbing from it, and her tongue was tingling with the metallic taste she couldn't get rid of. She pushed open the door to check if Considine had things rolling again.

And Fergus Duncan was gawping at her, again.

Vicky beckoned him out into the corridor and held the door until he joined her. 'You don't think defending a sex offender *and* the man who videoed him abusing a child looks bad for you?'

Duncan adjusted his sleeves. 'Sergeant, Sergeant, Sergeant. That's just coincidental, Sergeant, and you should stop seeing conspiracies everywhere. My client in there made his phone call to a firm aligned with mine. I happened to be here, defending an innocent man.'

'But you've got to—'

'We're done.' Duncan pushed back into the interview room.

Cheeky, cheeky bastard.

Vicky followed Duncan in and sat opposite him. She kicked his shin, then raised her hands. 'Sorry. You're manspreading a bit there, Fergus.'

He shot her a glare. 'Just get on with this, Sergeant.'

Vicky stared at the Mancunian gangster. 'Sorry, I didn't catch your name.'

He was as big as the concierge at the apartments, stacked with heavy muscles that cost a lot of protein and did absolutely nothing for most women. His face looked like he'd dropped some weights on his own skull and the scars hadn't healed. 'That's cos I haven't given you it, sweetheart.' He spoke like all those thugs who wore baggy jeans in the nineties. Bands her brother had been into, but who all sounded the same. Jangly guitars and funky drums and Mancunian accents.

'So what is your name?'

'Ain't saying nothing, sweetheart.'

'You're saying *some*thing.'

He just laughed at that.

'I admire the misogyny, though.'

He frowned like the word was Swahili.

'It means sexism, really. Hatred of women.'

'Call everyone sweetheart, don't I? Term of endearment, yeah?'

'Take your word for it.' Vicky sighed, trying to feign boredom, when really her heart was racing. Sitting opposite a violent man like that, one who'd pointed a gun at her... Christ. 'You got a permit for that weapon?'

'What, my cock?'

'No, the handgun.'

'What handgun?'

'The one you pointed at me.'

'Did I?'

'Come on, don't give me that.'

'Don't know what you're talking about, sweetheart.'

'You might remember it being in your pocket at the same time as your friend was having sexual intercourse with a child.'

It didn't knock him off his stride. He blinked, slowly like he was stoned beyond this realm. Maybe he was. 'That right, yeah?'

'It is. But my colleagues downstairs will need your name for charging you.'

'Like what, sweetheart? What do you think I've done?'

'For starters, you're a party to the offence of sexual abuse of a minor, when you aided or abetted Mr Agnew.'

'Did nothing.'

Vicky nudged Considine with her elbow. 'Can you read out what the victim said?'

Considine flicked through his notebook. 'When we were

outside, we heard the victim shout "No! Stop! You're hurting me! I want to go home!"' She paused, but the gangster didn't react. 'Then, when we broke into the property, she shouted "I told you, no!" to which our friend here said, "See what I mean? With you all the way, man!" While he recorded it. Then Mr Agnew said, "You caught it all, Phil. Excellent work. You want a go now?"'

Vicky waited for Manc Phil to look over at her. 'Is it Philip with two Ls?'

'Ain't nothing to you, sweetheart.'

'This is poppycock.' Duncan was shaking his head. 'I should get your chief constable on the phone here. Get her to put a stop to this.'

'Heard that threat from you before. She won't take the call.'

'You really want to test me?'

Vicky ignored the slimy prick and focused on his client. 'I need your full name, sir.'

'And I need my dinner, sweetheart. You going to cook it for me?'

'Okay, it makes no difference. We're going to charge you as a John Doe. Then we can take your fingerprints too, and your DNA.'

IT HAD ONLY BEEN a few minutes since her last cup of tea, but Vicky was yawning into her fist. She needed another or maybe something a lot stronger.

She stood in the hallway in Ninewells hospital. The inner courtyard was lit up, but only one man in there, sitting on a bench and sucking on a cigarette, leaning against his drip.

The door opened and Alison Carmichael shuffled out. Her hair was cut way shorter than the last time Vicky had seen her, an elfin cut and dyed black, but way too thin to pass for her natural colour. She wore staff nurse blue scrubs a size too tight for her squat frame. 'Evening. You here to see this one?'

'I am. How is she?'

'She's really, really bad.' Alison shook her head. 'Took me ages to perform the rape kit, but we can prove they had sex. The issue we've got is the girl saying she consented to everything. We've had a couple of cases like this where the child can't legally consent to the sex but they withhold consent for the rape kit. I mean, in this particular case you have video evidence to the sexual acts so the kit is less crucial but it is still an oddity...'

'But she let you perform it?'

'Right. Eventually. Just as well you interviewed those two raping bastards before her, as it would've taken even longer with cops present, I think.'

'You got a name for her?'

'Nope. And the age of fourteen is only a guess.'

'So she could be older?'

'God no. She could be thirteen. Maybe twelve.'

What a world when the age of a sexual assault victim going down was a relief. Vicky knew how hard rape was to prosecute, but very few juries wouldn't convict a child abuser.

'Can I speak to her?'

'I mean, you can try. She won't let me call her parents, or give me her name and, like I say, she's in complete denial about this.'

'Well, I'll give it my best shot.'

'Godspeed.'

Vicky flashed a thankful smile at Alison, then stepped into the room.

The girl was sitting hunched up on the bed. Not the body language of a girl who'd just had consensual sex. But it wasn't a child who'd been abused while some animal recorded it either. She looked up at Vicky. No make-up on, so she really did look like a child.

If she was thirteen, then she was *four* years older than Bella and Jamie.

Christ.

Vicky was almost sick. Her child getting old enough to overlap with a victim's age. All the theory, the textbook stuff she'd thrown at Agnew and Phil the Mancunian mystery man, it was all real. In this room. In her head. 'How are you doing?'

She looked away.

That was how she was going to play it, then.

Vicky leaned back against the door. 'Do you remember me?'

The girl looked back at her. 'You...'

Vicky held her gaze until she looked away again. 'What's your name?'

'Fuck off, you old witch.'

Charming.

'You know, I've encountered a lot of girls like you.'

'That your thing, eh? You a dyke?'

'No. But I like consensual sex with other adults. Not children who can't legally consent being forced into having sex with a grown man.'

'I consented. He consented. No problem.'

'Whatever your name is, you're too young to be able to consent to what he was doing to you.'

'Fuck off.' But there was a fragility to her voice.

'It's true. But whatever, you can believe you consented. I get that. And I could talk about how you've lived a life of neglect, starved for affection by your parents. Maybe a single parent, a mum or a dad struggling to raise you and maybe some brothers and sisters. Or it's just that they didn't care enough. Maybe they think they loved you, but you think it's all empty. I don't know. But I know that you strive for the affections of older men, which gives you the semblance of feeling important to someone.'

'Fuck off.' She was sitting head in hands. Sometimes Vicky would just leave, but she was getting somewhere now. 'Fuck off!'

'I could say all of that, but the bottom line is that while you were having intercourse with that man, another man was videoing the whole thing.'

'So?' But see could see she was sickened by it. Her lips were turning up, nostrils flaring.

'Because you don't have any control over that video. They do. And it'd be all over the internet by the time they've finished recording. Other men with fetishes like theirs will be masturbating over your torment.'

She looked at Vicky through tearful eyes.

'And it didn't sound consensual to me. It sounded like they were forcing you to do it. Is that true?'

She huffed out a sigh. 'Maybe.'

'Look, I get it. If you don't want your parents to know, I completely understand. If they're bad parents, then there's child welfare legislation. If you are underage and don't want to live with your parents any longer, I can notify the authorities. A social worker will be appointed and they'll deem you "in need of protection". They'll do everything they can to put you in a loving home with foster parents to help you and where these men can't exploit you anymore.'

She nodded. 'Okay.'

'Okay?'

'I'll tell you what you want to know.'

'How old are you?'

'I'm fourteen next month. The fifteenth.'

She was thirteen, then. Vicky had to grit her teeth and take a deep breath. Acid burnt in her throat. 'What's your name?'

She stared up at the ceiling. 'Emmy-Kate. Emmy-Kate Mitchell.'

Vicky didn't even have to ask if it was Emma. Didn't have to question the hyphenation.

Because it was one of the names on the furniture website.

14

Vicky drove along the Marketgait, the old mill buildings all hidden in the night-time gloom, away from the road's bright glow. Her phone was ringing through the car speakers. 'Come on, come on, come on.'

Why did nobody ever answer when you wanted them?

Her birthday evening. Interviewing a victim of abuse and two child molesters.

She killed the call to Forrester and hit the dial button for Rob. Somebody who would always answer her. 'Hey you.'

'Hey.' Vicky turned along West Bell Street, then kept it slow as she passed the station. 'How are you doing?'

'This is you calling to say it's going to be a late one, right?'

'We've already had the pizza, so that should indicate how late it's going to be. Like I've been to a nightclub and I've got chips, cheese and coleslaw after.'

'That's *barbaric*.'

Vicky laughed as she pulled around the bend into the station car park, feeling that gnawing at her heart. 'How are they?'

'Ach, fine. Keeping them from murdering each other. Bella's reading, Jamie's playing that game. Not *Indignity*.'

'Good! But it sounds like bliss.'

'It is. Just missing you, that's all. How was it up at that game company?'

Vicky wanted to say disgusting, sickening, vile, anything, but some stories had to stay in her head. 'It was useful. Oh, and you might get a refund for Jamie's little splurge.'

'Really? I'll have a look when I get a minute.'

'Anyway, just checking in.' She shot into her space and killed the engine. 'Got to go. Love you, bye.'

'Love you too.'

Vicky ended the call and opened the door. But she had to just sit there, the cabin light on, feeling empty. Drained. Chasing down as many leads as she could find in a horrific case, all while her family was growing up apart from her. Aye, it was tough. And it *was* going to be a late one.

At least forensics had got the memo — their lights were still on full blast.

Vicky got out into the cold and slammed the door.

'Careful, or you'll break it.'

She swung around and felt her mouth hang open.

Ryan Ennis was standing by his beaten-up BMW, which looked old enough to vote. He'd lost a ton of weight since Vicky had last seen him, and a few inches of height. He seemed to stoop over. His thick beard had spread up the sides of his head, previously shaved, but still couldn't conquer the top. 'Strange night, eh?'

'Is it?' Vicky reached around for her baton. Just to check it was there, as much as anything. 'You okay, Ryan?'

'Well, okay's a relative term.'

'How long have you been off the force now?'

Ennis frowned. 'I'm not, Vicks.'

'You can't still be signed off, surely?'

Ennis wore every scar of that stress on his face, dark bags under his eyes and pale, grey skin. 'No, I'm back. On a special assignment through the superintendent's office, special projects and all, very hush-hush.'

Then again, even Police Scotland with its low resourcing had places to bury the useless and lazy, counting paperclips and using rounded scissors. 'I hadn't heard.'

'Two years now.' He yawned into his fist. 'How's my replacement doing?'

'DS MacDonald?' Vicky felt that sting of disgust, but gave a polite shrug. 'He's doing okay.'

'Just okay?'

She waited for eye contact. 'Ryan, it's quarter past nine. Why are you here?'

Ennis blew out air, misting in the night. 'Never you mind.'

VICKY WALKED through the forensics lab, yawning into her fist. The lights were on, but there was nobody home. It stank of a stale Chinese takeaway, but it had been forensically cleaned afterwards, except for the garlicky tang. 'Hello?' Her voice echoed around the room.

Zoey shot up from behind a workbench, her mouth filled with prawn crackers. 'Sarge?'

'Hi there.' Vicky stopped by the desk, but didn't ask her what she was up to, just waited for her to stop crunching her snack. 'Is Jenny around?'

'She muttered something about Raven half an hour ago and hasn't been back since.'

Raven. Just great.

Vicky took a stool and sat next to her. 'How's your investigation into that website going?'

'Nowhere. She's had me processing the crime scene all night.'

'Seriously?'

'Why, should I have been doing something else?'

'That website, can you find the product called Emmy-Kate again?'

'Aye, sure.' Zoey wiped her hand across her mouth, then logged into a computer.

Onscreen, the Emmy-Kate shelving unit sat there.

A chance to own a unique and special piece. Thirteen-year matured wood sculpted into a tight product to house your most special item.

Christ.

Vicky almost fell on the floor.

Her worst fears laid bare.

It all tallied. The name, the age, the predilection.

Zoey tapped the screen. 'That's just changed.' She was pointing at the price. 'Currently out of stock, please select from our other items.'

Someone knew.

Vicky opened the door and peered into Raven's office, but it was empty. Where the hell was he? And where was Jenny?

She set off down the corridor, trying her phone again but it was like a zombie film where all the mobile networks were down. Nobody was answering.

She stopped outside the incident room and looked inside. Jenny was in the corner, stuck between Forrester and Raven.

Bingo.

Vicky walked over to them, but Jenny caught her approach and shook her head.

Vicky raised her eyebrows, checking.

Another shake.

Great.

But Vicky headed over anyway. 'Sir, I need a—'

'Not now.' Forrester wouldn't even look at her.

'Sir, it's impo—'

'I said, not now.' Forrester looked at her with wide eyes and tight lips. 'Wait in my office, this'll just be a minute.'

'Okay, but it's—'

'Sergeant.' Raven laughed. 'There's a hierarchy in the police service for a reason. When he speaks, you listen. Okay?'

'Fine.' Vicky stepped away from them, fists clenched, finger-nails biting into her palms, and set off towards the door, the corridor, Forrester's office.

But Considine was waving at her, his phone stuck to his ear.

Vicky walked over and sat next to Considine, but angled so she could keep an eye on proceedings with Jenny, Raven and Forrester.

'Got your text, Sarge.' Considine shoved a sheet of paper over. 'Take a look at that.'

Vicky dragged her gaze away from the argument to read the name.

Emmy-Kate Mitchell.

Date of birth: 13th March 2006

'And she's lived a life already, Sarge.' Considine turned the page over. 'Turns out young Emmy-Kate was done for street prostitution last month.'

'How isn't she—'

Considine tapped his phone. 'On with her social worker just now. She's just checking some stuff for me. Bottom line, mum died ten years ago, and her old man doesn't care. Heroin addict or boozer, not sure which. Social worker tried to get them separated, but it's taking too long. And her grandparents won't have anything to do with it. And if they manage to get her to a foster home, she'll probably run away to head back there. Dad with a substance problem and a daughter like that, is he passing her around friends in exchange for cash or drugs?'

Vicky slumped back in the chair. Such a sad life. It didn't always have to end in street prostitution, but undetected parental neglect on that scale left a child wide open to men like Mark Agnew. And whoever else.

Considine tapped the middle of the sheet. 'Home address is old. Sent a uniform around, but they moved last month. Hello?' He sat forward. 'Aye, still here.'

Vicky logged into a machine. Something didn't feel right about it. Neglectful fathers were one thing, but to release her back into his care after an arrest? That felt all kinds of wrong.

She pulled up the investigation file.

And frowned.

The case was closed, released without charge.

Vicky nudged Considine, then pointed at the screen.

He squinted at it, then stood up tall. 'Just looking at the case file now, aye. Seems to have been closed at our end?'

Vicky scanned the record for the commentary:

"The investigation was closed due to unreliable accounts from the witnesses."

She scanned back up. The case was closed down by Superintendent Brian Masson, head of Dundee Local Policing.

Why would a super get involved in stopping a street prostitution investigation?

Then he'd been at the Tay Bridge, trying to get them to open up way too quickly.

Vicky looked across the room, but they'd taken their argument elsewhere.

Something stank about this. Something rotten.

Vicky sat back, itching like she was covered in an army of ants, and checked the name.

Colin Woods.

Karen's husband.

～

PC COLIN WOODS was standing in the custody suite, sipping a coffee, his other thumb tucked into his stab-proof. Sixteen stone of monster, bulging out of his uniform, so big that nobody would mention the crescent-shaped birthmark on his left cheek. 'Aye, well, we shall see if we get promoted this century.'

'That'll be lucky.' Martin Saunders chuckled, then looked back along the corridor. 'Shite, here comes trouble.'

Vicky stopped by the desk and smiled, but her guts were churning.

Karen's husband. Rob's friend. Someone Vicky knew well and had known for a good few years, someone beyond reproach.

Wasn't he?

Of course he was. Colin was a good guy. One of the best.

'Colin, you got a minute?'

'Always for you, Vicks.'

'It's a private one.'

'Oh. Right.' He looked over at Martin. 'Any rooms free?'

'Eh, try six.'

'Cheers, Maz.' Colin left his coffee cup and set off at a pace much faster than his huge frame should allow. 'Nights are a bugger, Vicks. Weren't you supposed to be off today?'

'It's my birthday, aye.'

'Happy birthday, then. Sure Rob will save up his special treat for you later.' Colin opened the door to room six. 'This about Karen?'

Vicky let him go first. 'Not really.' She paused in the doorway. 'Why, is there something going on?'

'Not that I know of. Just wondering if there's something I should.' He sat down and eased off his stab-proof. 'Won't need this, will I?'

'Depends.'

Colin laughed. 'Okay, so you're here as a sergeant, right?'

'Correct. This evening, we picked up a—'

Colin shot forward, cracking his elbows off the wood. 'Wait, is Karen okay?'

Vicky raised her hands to placate him. 'Aye, she's at home with your kids.'

'Thank God.'

'As I was saying… This evening, we picked up a young girl from inside a flat. She was having sex with an adult.'

'And she was underage?'

'Correct. Name is Emmy-Kate Mitchell.'

Colin blew air up his face. 'Right.'

'That's it?'

'Don't know what you want me to say, Vicks.'

'Something other than "right". You picked her up for soliciting.'

'Her? Right, aye. Me and Dougie spotted her up in the Hilltown, back in December. Wouldn't speak, but we found out she was thirteen. The girl's a mess.'

'Why did you let her go?'

'The girl's father came in. Had a nightmare with him. Tried to get her social worker to... I don't know, do her job? She tried but couldn't. Court case is due for April.'

'Colin, we found her in a man's flat, having sex with him.'

'Oh no.'

'Why did you let her go?'

He made bunny fingers in the air. 'No reasonable prospect of conviction.'

'Says who?'

'Masson.'

15

Vicky was by the window, looking back to the queue of cars on the Marketgait. She turned to face them, and just didn't know who the hell she could trust.

Forrester's hand was shaking as he sipped coffee.

Jenny was inspecting her shoes.

Neither was looking at her, or each other.

'Doddsy, I can't tell you. Seriously.'

'No, I'm not giving you a choice. You two need to tell me what the hell you were talking to Raven about.'

Jenny looked at her for a fleeting moment, then went back to her shoes.

'Right, so that's how you're playing it?'

'Vicky.' Forrester shook his head. 'You don't want to know.'

'Don't I? Because it's looking very, very strange to me.'

'Vicky. Shut up.' Jenny turned and walked over to the other window in the corner office.

'Are you helping him?'

Jenny glowered at her. 'Helping who?'

'Masson.'

Jenny glowered at Forrester then at Vicky. 'What are you talking about?'

Vicky handed over the wad of evidence to Forrester. 'Have a look through that. This is a list of sexual cases over the last year. Seventeen went to trial of over three hundred. Five years ago, the rate was closer to half of two hundred and eighty.'

Forrester scanned the list, his frown deepening as he went down. 'What's this supposed to show me?

'Brian Masson has been closing down cases, all sex crimes.' Vicky handed him another sheet. 'I checked through a few of the abandoned ones and the same thread of language kept cropping up. "Intellectual frailties of the victim." "Unreliable." "Known liar." "Mental health issues." "Prone to exaggeration." "Prone to flights of fantasy." Sir, this doesn't look good, does it? These are vulnerable women, who are brave enough to come forward about their ordeals and this is how they're treated?'

'Bloody hell.'

Vicky felt her blood boiling. 'Not only have they been messing about with investigations into sexual crimes, but these women won't get justice for what happened to them. And they'll lose trust in the system after what's happened to them.'

'I know that.' Forrester grabbed the top sheet and scanned through it a few times. 'These are underage street walkers, right?' He sifted through the pages. 'This goes back years. How didn't we notice?' He shuffled through more pages then looked at Jenny. 'Can you dig into this for me?'

'Even after—'

'Aye. You don't report to Raven. He's just a wee nyaff; I'll cover your arse. Get deep into the system files, see who's been in there, okay?'

'Right, will do. And thanks.' Jenny nodded at Vicky as she passed.

Forrester waited on the door to shut before looking at Vicky.

'What happened with Raven?'

'Jenny slapped him. All that crap with your brother. Raven wants her to turf him out, but he's central to some investigation. He got angry, called her a "goth cow", she slapped him. I was trying to stop them killing each other.'

Which was maybe too cute to explain things.

Christ. Vicky was doubting her friends now. She'd worked for Forrester for a few years now, first as a DC to his DS, now as DS to his DI. Her old man worked with him back in the nineties.

But people changed. And people got into bad situations, situations that needed help from people. Happened to the victims of these crimes as much as the people covering it up.

'Sir, did you know anything about this?'

'Of course I didn't! Who do you think I am?'

'I don't know anything, sir. All I'm seeing is some really dodgy shit going on.'

'But you can't—'

'I can. Listen to me. We recovered Emmy-Kate just after she'd been sexually abused. She's thirteen. She's in Ninewells right now.' Vicky handed him the top page. 'The code on Noel Russell's arm led us to that shop, sir. One of the names on that site is Emmy-Kate. Try telling me that isn't linked.'

Forrester let the page fall to his desk. 'This is... This is...'

The door opened and Jenny came back in, cradling a laptop. 'It all checks out. Colin Woods closed those files.'

'Aye. I just spoke with him. Emmy-Kate Mitchell was picked up by Colin Woods and his partner.' Vicky stared hard into Forrester's eyes. 'They let her go on Masson's orders.'

Jenny tapped at her laptop. 'There's only one other officer who's been in the files. Sergeant Ryan Ennis.'

Christ.

He was all over this case, turning it inside out.

'Ennis?' Forrester collapsed back into his seat. 'Ryan Ennis?'

'You might remember him, sir.' Vicky was scowling at him. 'He used to work for you.'

'Why are you looking at me like that? Vicky, if you think—'

'You see how this looks, right? Ennis and Masson are covering up sex crimes. And when Ennis got bucketed, it was you who kept him on. Remember? Doesn't take—'

'Come on, Doddsy, you—'

'Stop calling me that! Doddsy was my dad's nickname. And I'm not him. Vicky or Sergeant. You choose, but not Doddsy any more.'

Forrester folded his arms. 'Vicky, I haven't seen Ry for years. And he was off sick for two years before that. Masson took his file over from me. Look, me and your old man worked with Ennis. The Rube, they called him. He's just a daft sod.'

'So it's just a coincidence that Ennis showed up the same night I recovered Emmy-Kate?'

Forrester stood up tall. 'This doesn't... No.' He collapsed back into his chair and tugged at his hair. 'Bloody hell.'

'Sir, the question right now is what we do with it.'

'Only one thing for it.'

VICKY WALKED past the glass-windowed meeting room, trying to act all calm and casual.

Ennis was sitting there, scowling as he jabbed his meaty thumbs off his phone's screen. Definitely playing a game on there. And definitely not paying attention to anyone else. Some cop.

Vicky continued past and stopped at the end, then turned to give Forrester the thumbs-up.

He opened the door. 'Ry?'

Ennis looked up from his phone, his big eyebrows meeting in the middle of his thick skull. 'Alright?' He went back to his phone like he hadn't just bumped into his old boss he hadn't seen for over two years.

Forrester took the seat opposite. 'Been a while.'

'Aye. So it has.'

'What are you up to?'

'I don't work for you.'

'Come on, Rube.' Forrester flashed a wide grin. 'That's what we used to call you, eh? Vicky here's old man too.'

Vicky took the chair between Ennis and the door.

Ennis glanced at her, then went back to his phone. 'I *hated* that name.'

'You played along with it, though. Smart man. Earn your stripes by sucking up to the bosses, eh?' Forrester nodded at the phone. 'What are you playing?'

'That *Charlie the Seahorse* game.'

'Right.' Forrester chuckled. 'Got a bit of a problem with that myself. Absolute nightmare.'

'It's so addictive.' Ennis sat back and stretched out. 'Fills the time, eh?'

'Right. Right. Not seen you in a while, Ry. What brings you here?'

'Meeting Masson.' Ennis let out a sigh. 'Boy's a bit of a fiend for late-night catch-ups. Nature of the job, you know? I mean, I work from home normally. Reading reports, tabulating stats, you know the deal. Usually I put him off, but I need to do it today to get my pension letter.'

'You're retiring?'

'Finally decided to, aye. Need to move on with my life. After all that's happened, eh?'

Vicky waited for him to look her way. 'Retiring when you should've been kicked off the force.'

Ennis scowled at her. 'Excuse me?'

'Four years ago, Ryan.' Vicky circled her fingers around the three of them. 'We were all there. We know what you did. That you should be in prison, let alone still being a cop.'

'This is a load of shite, Davie. You shouldn't let *her* speak to me like this.'

'What, about you shutting down sex crimes?'

'Wait a minute here. Sex crimes?'

'Come on, Ry.' Forrester repeated Vicky's circular motion. 'Just open up to us. We're your friends.'

'Aye, bollocks you are.' Ennis pushed his seat back. 'I'll see where—'

Forrester grabbed his hand. 'Stay right where you are, Sergeant.' He pressed his thumb into the bone, making Ennis wince. 'You could start by talking about Emmy-Kate Mitchell.'

'Never heard of her.' But he wasn't looking at them.

'Sure?'

'Aye. Now, can you let me go?'

'See, Ryan, we know that you arrested her last month. And you got one of your guys to close off her file.'

'Not me.'

'No, it's you. You're all over the records, Ry. There is an audit trail. Who read that file, who edited it, when, where. And all former versions are still there, just suppressed from view. You're a guilty man. Aiding and abetting child abusers.'

Ennis kept looking at the door, like someone was going to save him. 'This is bullshit!'

'Right now, we've got a warrant for your phone records. From that, we'll get your movements over the last few years. Piece all that together, see who you've been talking to and meeting. I understand it's difficult to process. You're in too deep, I get that. But believe me, talking to me and Vicky will take a load off. How about starting with your family.'

Ennis snatched his hand away from Forrester, then sat back and ran it down his face. 'Wife left me. Daughter won't speak to me.'

'Why?'

'Because of what happened, eh? I was off sick, aye, but I went to pieces. Fell apart. It was horrible. Couldn't save my marriage, no matter how hard I tried.'

'But you came back, right?'

'Aye, working for Masson.'

'Masson. Right. Helping him cover up a sex ring.'

'A sex ring? What are you smoking, Davie?'

'What's going on, Ry?'

'Nothing!'

'Look, if you spill on Masson, we can get a deal going here.'

'Shut up. You and your deals.'

'I'm serious. I'll call the PF, get her to sign off on what you've done. Get off without doing any jail time. But you need to open up. Unless you're abusing girls yourself?'

'What?' Ennis looked ready to go apeshit. Start breaking heads.

'I get it, Ry. Really, I do. Starts when you were kept on after that incident a few years back. I put you on long-term sick as a favour, but Masson took over. But he got you to fudge some records, right?'

Ennis shook his head. 'Look, I just want off the force. I don't know anything about whatever you two think you've cooked up. I'm here to get my papers and retire.'

'Come on, Ry. We're going to take you downstairs and charge you with criminal conspiracy. This is your chance to get away. Maybe see your kid again this side of a prison cell.'

Ennis sat back, rubbing his tongue over his teeth. 'Okay, when I was at my lowest point, you wanted me to pay for it, right? You were going to do me for... For what I did. That slippery shite, Fergus Duncan, said he was going to struggle to get me off. But Masson... He came round one night, and he set me up with a bent doctor. He got me signed off sick, full pay, all while accruing pension. Even covered the period in question where I'd... The doctor said I was on a prescription that I wasn't, which explained why I went a wee bit overboard. That's why all that nonsense went away.'

'Masson?'

'Masson.'

'And in return, you just had to close down some cases?'

'That's all he asked of me, aye.'

16

F orrester stormed through the top-floor office space, buzzing with late-night operational activity and stinking of rancid curry. Phones buzzing and computers beeping. Vicky jogged so she could stop outside Masson's office and block Forrester from going in. 'I'm not sure we should do it this way.'

'Vicky, if we go through formal channels, he will get wind of it and run. He can bugger off to Vietnam or Russia or wherever. But if we arrest him now, he's going to be downstairs. We can trust Martin to look after him. Right?'

'You're friends with him, aren't you?'

'Thought I was, aye. Golfed with him a few times. Went to a few golfing trips with him to the Algarve. Great craic.' He shook his head. 'Hard to believe he's involved with this shite.'

'Sir, if you—'

'Vicky, believe me. You're going to have to stop me from killing him, not from letting him go.' The fire in his eyes showed he meant it.

'Fine.' She stepped back, hands up.

Forrester knocked on the door and popped his head in the door. 'Need a word, sir.' He turned to beckon Vicky in.

Masson sat at the coffee table, playing with a tablet computer. He looked up at them, narrowing his eyes. 'I'm just heading out of the door.'

Vicky followed Forrester in, but stayed next to the door, leaning back against the glass. 'It's very important we have that word now, sir.'

Masson hauled his massive frame up to full height. 'Right, David, you bloody arsehole, you want to tell me what's going on?'

Forrester smiled. 'I think you know.'

'What are you talking about, Inspector?'

'Don't pull rank on me, sir. Right now, you need to tell what you're up to.'

'Heading to the pub to meet an old pal. Now, if you—'

'That's not what I'm talking about.'

'No?'

'No, we're interested in how you've been covering up sexual abuse.'

Masson stared hard at him for a few seconds, then switched his focus to Vicky. 'Seriously?'

'Seriously.' Forrester tossed the prints on his desk. 'It's all there, you daft bastard.'

Masson sat back in his chair, arms folded. 'You're making a big mistake here. Who have you told?'

'I'm not the one making—'

'David, this isn't what you think.'

'Because that's what innocent people say, right?' Forrester snapped out a set of handcuffs. 'Brian Masson, I'm arresting you for—'

'David, don't do this. This goes way above your pay grade.'

'Brian, you're under arrest, you bloody arsehole. Stop playing games, thinking you can get off.'

'David. This isn't what you think.'

'No? How about you tell what I think, then? You've been covering up sexual abuse. Closing cases left, right and centre.'

'Your name is all over this case.' Vicky pulled out the wad of papers and held out the top record. 'Emmy-Kate Mitchell. She'd been picked up for prostitution last year. By an unimpeachable officer.'

'No officer is unimpeachable.'

'This one is. Then you ordered her to be let go. She lives with a neglectful father, who doesn't care what she's doing.' Vicky paused. 'She's *thirteen*.'

'I know.' Masson's jawline was throbbing. 'It's a real tragedy.'

'What are you talking about?'

'Emmy-Kate Mitchell, right?' Masson snatched the sheet off her. 'Right. Aye. We had her in for prostitution. Not even fourteen and she's selling herself on the street. What kind of life is that?'

'Still, you ordered her to be released without charge.'

'I sat in an interview with her and offered her *everything* in exchange for testifying against the people who forced her onto the street, but she's too far gone, too deep into it. And her father... He just didn't care, like you say. When he came in, he was shouting at her, but nothing too severe, nothing we could do him for, nothing we could do to get them separated. I tried to get the local authorities to do something about it, but the gears move too slowly these days. It broke my heart. It really did.'

'You expect us to believe this? You expect us to—'

'David, I'm not perpetrating these crimes.' Masson let out a deep breath. 'I'm investigating them.'

'But you've been shutting down cases.'

'Deliberately, David. But it's to gain an in.' Masson looked at Forrester then at Vicky. 'I'm working for Chief Superintendent Marcus Ogilvie, of Professional Standards and Ethics, and DCS Carolyn Soutar, your boss. We're bringing down a sex ring that has infiltrated Police Scotland.'

Vicky didn't believe a word of it. A guilty man, caught red-handed. Of course he was going to spin a line like this. 'So if I phone her, she'll back this up?'

'No, of course not.' Masson sucked in a deep breath. 'Unless you use the codename "Kestrel Super".'

'This sounds like nonsense to me.'

'It's on the level.' Masson held her gaze, then switched to Forrester. 'Call her.'

Forrester took a long look at Masson, then got out his phone. He tapped the screen and put it to his ear, then stood there listening. 'Ma'am, it's DI David Forrester.' He set off. 'Aye, from Dundee. Aye, one of Raven's lads.' He motioned for Vicky to let him past, then whispered, 'Stay with him,' then left them to it.

Masson stood up, hands in pockets. He didn't look like a man in deep shit. Maybe Soutar was going to dig him out. Maybe they were all complicit. 'Well, while he's getting told what for, Sergeant, I'll start with you.'

Vicky didn't move from her perch. Only one way for him to go and that was through her. She stood there like a statue, arms folded. Her baton was tucked inside her jacket, one movement to grab it, another to be able to hit him with it. Besides, she'd been here before, so knew how to play it. Just keep quiet, let him exhaust himself. Men like Masson never resorted to violence.

He didn't seem perturbed by someone entrapping him in his own office. 'You know how the PNC generates silent hits on certain searches?'

'I do.'

'If someone searches for "chocolate biscuits", someone else gets notified without the first person knowing.' Masson reached for his tablet again. 'This bad boy is super locked down. And I have a lot of silent searches running. Anyone searching for sexual crimes in Dundee over any period, I get notified. So when I received the latest notice this evening, I wondered who else was involved in this conspiracy. But it came up with Jennifer Morgan and Vicky Dodds and, well. I knew you were coming at it from the good side.'

'If you're trying to—'

'Sergeant. Vicky.' Masson grinned at her. 'I know your dad. Worked with him a lot over the years.'

'That won't wash either. If you're trying to pin any of this on me, forget it.'

'Look, there's something big going on. I've had a lot of notifications like that one and the rate is increasing. A big conspiracy, shutting down sexual crimes over the last few years.'

A knock at the door, behind her.

Vicky swung around to see Forrester standing there, still talking, but pointing to be let in. She opened the door.

'Cheers, Carolyn. No, but I'll pop in next time I'm down that way. Cheers, bye.' Forrester killed the call and slumped into the meeting chair. 'Well, she backed up your tale.'

Masson smiled. 'So you believe me?'

'Let's just say I'm going to verify it.' Forrester looked over at Vicky. 'Operation Kestrel Super is real, though. According to her, this big lump from Edinburgh was investigating a gang of bent cops in the Highlands and Grampian.' He looked over at Masson. 'You want to continue it, or shall I?'

'Sure. Like he said, Big Luke was up there, working as a DS while he investigated a couple of bent officers. All of them remained tight-lipped, until Luke got one of them smashed last summer. Bottle of whisky on a fishing trip. The guy started speaking, inviting Luke into their gang. And when one starts talking, they don't stop. Like one arsehole revealing to him what was going on in Dundee.' Masson was looking at Vicky. 'You've got someone, aye?'

'Ryan Ennis. He's been all over these records.'

'When do you plan to speak to him?'

'Half an hour ago. He's in the cells now.'

'You spoke to him?' Masson darted over to his desk and hit the buttons on the phone. 'Martin? It's Brian Masson. Aye, have you got Ryan Ennis still there? Sure. Keep an eye on him, okay? Aye. Cheers, Martin.' He looked over at them. 'You daft sods.'

'You didn't think to come to me when you got your silent hit?'

'It was on the cards for tomorrow, aye. I had my work cut out for me with Ryan.'

'He's the friend you were going drinking with?'

'Aye. Need to see what the latest is.' Masson was staring hard at her now. 'Why are you so interested in Emmy-Kate?'

She looked over at Forrester, and got a nod in return. 'Because we found her having sex with a man.'

Masson's eyes lit up like a child on Christmas morning. 'You caught him red-handed?'

'Not quite red-handed, but there were two of them.'

'Two?'

'A local man and a gangster from Manchester. It was filmed.'

'Man alive.' Masson stared at Forrester. 'David, this is the motherlode. Having independent eye witnesses and a *video*? That's... This is child-abuse gold. All we need to do is to produce a birth certificate and push play, bang. Automatic conviction. We can take that into the room with this bloke.' He frowned at Vicky. 'What's his name?'

'Mark Agnew. He's downstairs, just waiting for you to let him go.'

'Right, well, this is one that won't get away.' Masson sighed. 'I've been working as head of Local Policing, trying to get close to the local officers here, putting my details all over the records and seeing what shakes loose, but nothing has really. Just caused a lot of pain and distress. Until tonight. So I owe you both a huge thank you.'

'It's Vicky's work, really, sir.'

'Aye, aye.' Masson smiled at her. 'Now, it's late, so how about you clear off for the night? David and I will interview Ennis.'

THEIR HOME WAS DEATHLY SILENT. Not even Rob's snoring rattling from their room.

Vicky eased her coat off and hung it up, then kicked off her shoes. Her feet were all swollen and aching. She'd dressed for a birthday, and ended up... Working.

Rescuing a child from being raped.

Christ.

Vicky padded through to the kitchen, cold and dark.

The dogs lay in their big puffy beds by the French doors. Holt looked up, farted, then put his head back down again. Peralta was out for the count.

Vicky spotted a Post-It on her place setting – "Lasagne in the fridge".

Fantastic.

She got the tub out and grabbed a fork out of the dishwasher, still warm, then attacked it cold. Absolutely fantastic. She could say a lot of things about Rob, but he certainly knew the way to her heart and it was most definitely through her tastebuds.

Holt stood up and groaned as he stretched, then padded over to Vicky, his feet a lot louder than hers.

'Are you here just to be lovely, boy?' Vicky rubbed his head. 'Or are you ratting at my birthday tea?'

Tinkle hopped up from Rob's chair onto the table and waddled over. She let Vicky rub her head, then smacked Holt on the head. The poor dog scuttled off back to his friend and hunkered down in his bed.

Vicky's phone rang on silent, the screen the brightest thing in the room.

Forrester calling...

She put it to her ear and spoke in a whisper. 'Hey. How'd it go with Ennis?'

'Hey, Dod— Vicky. Just finished up. Ennis isn't really talking. We'll go at him again tomorrow.'

'Sounds disappointing. Suppose we were lucky to get what we did out of him.'

'Right.'

'Think Masson's on the level?'

'Done some digging, Do— Vicky. Aye, he's on the level. Soutar's got a couple of lads working with him. The Sexual Offences Unit in Bathgate are working the Glasgow and Edinburgh end of the operation too.'

'I take it Ennis knows nothing about what happened to Noel Russell?'

'Correct. And that Ashlynn lassie's still out there.' Forrester's yawn hissed into the microphone. 'Never rains, but it pours.' Another yawn. 'Listen, can you get into the station early tomorrow?'

'How early?'

'Before six would be good. Need to hit Ennis while he's shattered.'

'Right, I'll try.'

'No trying about it, Vicky. Catch you later.' Click and he was gone.

Vicky finished her lasagne with a wobbly lump of pasta and tossed the dish into the sink. It didn't set well in her stomach.

She set her watch alarm for half five. Enough time to get up, get a bit damp in the shower, then hoof it up to Dundee for six. Barely any sleep, mind.

She walked into the hall and caught a blast of Rob's snoring from their room. Great. Just fantastic.

She opened Bella's door. She was lying on her back, making the quietest sound.

Vicky eased the door shut again and checked Jamie's room.

The lights were on and he was looking right at her. 'What?'

'Hey.' Vicky walked over to the bed. 'You okay?'

His eyes were all red. He'd been crying. 'Bit stressed.'

'What about?'

'The money. Dad was *raging*.'

Vicky tucked the duvet around his shoulders. 'Don't worry about the money, okay?'

'I swear I didn't know what I was doing.'

'I know that. Your dad does too. The important thing is not to do it again. If you're worried you might be spending money, ask me or your father, okay?'

'So I did do something wrong?'

'Jamie, lots of people will try to exploit children, okay?' Vicky got a visceral flash of Emmy-Kate's angry face and shook it away.

'It's not your fault. We'll all make sure you don't get caught out, okay? Just talk to us. And I'm always here for you.'

Jamie nodded, his eyes getting heavy. 'Thanks, Mum.'

Vicky felt her heart flutter. She leaned over and kissed his forehead. 'Sleep tight, Jamie.'

DAY 2

Wednesday
26th February 2020

17

S omething throbbed at Vicky's wrist. A sound blared out, digital and harsh. She opened her eyes. Pitch black, just a flash of green light to her right.

What the hell was that?

Her watch.

Her alarm, buzzing away.

She pressed the button and snoozed it. Half five. She lay back. Just another couple of minutes, then she'd get up.

No.

Adrenaline jerked her up to sitting. She needed to get in the shower, get into work. Solve the case.

Not that she'd managed much sleep. Her head pounded like she'd drunk half a bottle of wine when she'd got in. Her mouth was dry. Her heart was thumping in her chest.

Get up!

She patted the other side of the bed. Rob wasn't there.

What the hell?

No sounds of flushing toilets, no radio blaring from the kitchen.

Her heartbeat sped up.

She sat up, woozy as hell, and flicked on her light. Her dressing gown was under her work clothes on the chair. She walked over and grabbed it, then tied it around her waist. Should be more used to this over fifteen years' service, God knows how much of that on shifts. Still, shifts gave you enough time to sleep – David Forrester didn't.

In the hall, a thin channel of light cut through from the kitchen. Rob was standing in his gown, sipping tea with one hand, stroking Peralta's head with the other. He turned around and smiled. 'Morning.'

'Gogga hechen.' It sounded like gibberish even to Vicky. 'Got to get in.'

Rob smiled at her. 'Here.' He handed her a cup of tea. 'I was asleep when you got in last night, presumably.'

'Well, it was more like someone was attacking you with a chainsaw.' She took a glug of boiling hot tea. 'Thanks for this.'

'What's going on?'

'Nightmare case.'

'In till almost midnight, out at half five?'

'Nature of the beast sometimes.'

Rob smiled. 'Just take care of yourself, Vicks. Okay?'

'I try to. Every day.' Vicky should tell him about Jamie's fears. Did she have the time? Of course she did. 'Listen, do you think you're maybe being a bit too hard on Jamie?'

Rob nodded. 'Maybe, but how else am I going to get through to him?'

Vicky blew on her tea. 'It's not his fault.'

'No, but we can't afford to lose a grand.'

'Look, I don't know what to do. When I came in last night, Jamie was awake and stressed about it. Rob, he's a good kid. Lots of bad ones out there, we've got at least one good one.'

'Bella's not so bad.'

'She has her moments.' Vicky drank the rest of her tea. 'I really have got to go, but just think about it, okay? You're the expert when it comes to kids, Mr Teacher.'

'Doesn't feel like that sometimes.' He leaned over and kissed her. 'I miss you.'

'I miss you too.'

A SWEATY incident room was the last place Vicky wanted to be at that time of day, feeling that wobbly, especially with that stink of rancid Chinese, Indian and Italian food, shoved in the bins and leaving a minging reek in the air.

A room full of tired cops tapping away at computers. Yawning. Sighing. Checking the clock. Another twenty minutes and they'd be relieved by the next shift.

And no sign of Forrester, here or in his office.

Just perfect.

Vicky stood near a couple of chatting officers, yawning and sipping her tea as she tried to avoid listening to the inanity.

'Aye, I've got ten quid on United this weekend.'

'Brave, brave man.'

So, no progress, then. She sat at a desk and logged in. She opened the case file and a hand grabbed her shoulder.

'Vicks. Morning.' MacDonald, his coffee-stained breath in her ear, looking like he'd fallen down a couple of flights of stairs. Bandages and cuts and bruises.

'Christ, Euan, are you okay?'

MacDonald sucked coffee through the lid. 'Should see the other guy.'

'The concierge, right?'

'Prick didn't go down without a fight.' MacDonald tore the lid off and tipped in a sachet of sugar. 'Still, we arrested him, ran his prints and he's wanted for two rapes in Dunfermline.'

'Good work.' Though Vicky didn't mean it. She just wanted him to clear off and let her get on with it. 'Have you seen Forrester?'

'Not this morning.'

'Sergeant.' Masson was in the doorway, looking their way. 'Need a word about last night.'

MacDonald was already on his feet. 'Thanks, sir. Tough arrest, but we got—'

'Not you.' Masson focused on Vicky. 'You, Sergeant Dodds.'

ENNIS'S EYES looked like someone had stuck used teabags underneath. His skin was no longer a pale white, but now a tired yellow.

A standard trick – keep the suspect up all night, ideally in a cell next to the drunk tank. No sleep, cold room. Or maybe a hot room.

A trick Ryan Ennis would've applied many times over the years as a detective sergeant, but one he clearly couldn't handle himself.

Vicky was standing by the door. 'So, how about you tell us the truth this time, huh?'

Ennis was leaning back in his chair, staring up at the ceiling tiles. His stubble was a patchwork of salt and pepper that aged him even further. 'The truth about what?'

'Last night, you told me Superintendent Brian Masson was working with you.'

'That's right.'

Vicky looked over at Forrester sitting opposite Masson. 'It must've been tough to give us that much.'

'That's the whole truth.' Ennis looked at her now, his eyes bloodstained and raw. 'He approached me. Wanted me to help cover up some crimes. I'm not a detective any more, Vicks. And on admin duties. So. When the boss comes knocking, you've got to answer the door.'

Vicky smiled, laughed. 'See, I remember you telling DCS Soutar to "away and boil your head" when she asked you—'

'I remember.' Ennis shut his eyes. 'But that's all I'm giving you. All I can give you. Masson's bent as a three-pound coin. I just did him some favours in return for staying on.'

That was how he was going to play it, was it? 'Ryan, do you remember that case a few years back, the one where your—'

'Don't.'

'Come on, Ryan. You won't even let me say that your—'

'No.'

'How is she?'

Ennis opened his eyes again but was looking at Vicky's empty chair. 'We're not talking about that.'

'Ryan, you should've been kicked off the force for what you did.' Vicky walked over and sat down. Ennis looked away. 'Happened in this very room. You went way beyond—'

'You don't know what you're talking about.'

'I do.' Vicky nudged Forrester with a playful elbow. 'David here kept you on after all of that.'

Ennis looked over at Forrester. Vicky could see the cogs whirring, wondering if he could finger him with this conspiracy. But he looked back at Vicky, shaking his head. 'He palmed me off onto Masson, didn't he?'

'It's just Masson?'

'Of course it is.'

'Ryan, we know it's not just him. We know there are others. What happened to your daughter – worse happens every week to women in Dundee.'

'How dare you say that?'

'Ryan, I've got a daughter myself. Okay? She might be a lot younger than Teresa, but I know what it feels like. That constant fear and dread. And something really bad happened to Teresa. But whatever they've got on you, Ryan, you're covering up for some very, very bad people who are getting away with some very, very bad crimes. You're doing that, not them. You might not be raping thirteen-year-old girls, but you're helping the men who are.'

Ennis sat there, his chin quivering. 'What?'

'You don't even know who you're protecting, do you?'

'Raping? Kids?'

'That's right.'

'Didn't have a choice. Not really.'

'Ryan, down at Ninewells, there's a girl, not even fourteen, who I dragged from a flat last night. She was raped by a man while another videoed it. They're going away for it. You and Masson can't do anything. And you're going to prison for your part in this. You'll lose your pension.'

'I haven't done any—'

'Her name is Emmy-Kate Mitchell.'

'Shite.'

'You let her go without charge. Fair enough, lot of cops would do that. But you let her go back to a home full of neglect. We found her in an apartment, Ryan, having sex with an abuser.'

Tears formed on his cheeks.

'And Teresa will know her father is the kind of vermin who—'

'Fine.' Ennis sat back, rubbing at his eyes. 'I'll tell you who else there is, but I need something. I'll leave the force. Keep me out of prison, let me keep my pension, and I'll give you the earth.'

Vicky locked eyes with Forrester. He looked as tired as she felt. 'What do you think?'

Forrester sat back with a sigh. 'One of those where we've got to see what's on the table before we buy it.'

Ennis stared at him. 'David, this isn't my first rodeo, okay? I know what happens here. Seen it play out so many times. I spill my guts, you do these people, but you do me.'

'Ryan, I'm genuine. If you agree to testify, and if—'

'Of course I agree to—'

'—and you actually testify, then—'

'Fine. Fine. I get it.' Ennis cracked his elbows off the table and planted his head in his hands. 'Fine, I'll tell you.' He held up his hands. 'I'm not an idiot.' He smirked. 'Back when we worked with her father—' he tilted his head to Vicky, '—that old sod called me "The Rube". You all thought I was a daft wee laddie. Well, I suppose I was. But I learned. Over the years, I learned my lesson, learned how to become a decent cop. Then... Then, I lost my cool. Almost lost my job too. I just need to know you're not playing me here.'

Forrester stared at him for a few seconds. 'Ryan, if what you give us is on the level, then you'll walk free. Keep your pension. Be able to get another job. Obviously, you can't have killed anyone or abused any—'

'Who do you think I am?'

'I don't know. That's the problem. Now, you've got the chance to give us a proffered statement. Everything on the table, and you'll get immunity on the back end. But I need to know who—'

'It's the man who pressured you into keeping me on the payroll.'

Forrester frowned. 'Raven?'

'DCI John Raven.'

Forrester shot to his feet. 'How can—'

'Think about it. Him and Masson have carved up both sides of the divide here in this city. Masson covers operational policing, so any girls picked up on the street can walk free, missing girls cannot be found. But the rapes and abductions, well. Those are Raven's remit, right? He can close them down. Pinned them all to bogus theories. Bounce back to uniform.'

'What did he have on you?'

'Nothing. It was the carrot, rather than the stick.'

'He was paying you?'

'Not directly. Just keeping my salary here. Giving me bags of overtime.'

'And overtime you didn't necessarily work?'

'Don't be daft. I worked every second of it. Didn't want anyone sniffing around my timesheet.'

'Can you prove any of this?'

'I've been doing this game a long time, David. I've got record-ings of meetings. Texts Raven and Masson thought were deleted. Voicemails. All of it.'

'Thanks, Ryan.' Forrester walked over to the door and turned back. 'I know how hard it is to admit to all of that. Thank you.'

Ennis gave the world's smallest nod and Forrester slipped out into the corridor.

Vicky waited behind. 'I'm sorry you felt you had to do all of that.'

'You know, a lot of the time when we had wrong 'uns in here.' Ennis looked around the room. 'Dirty little lying bastards. We'd let them stew long enough to confess. Being on the other side of it, it's...' His shoulders slumped. 'It's such a relief to let it go, Vicky. Such a relief. I haven't slept in *months*. You hit me hard there, all these girls, suffering, just like my Teri... I didn't even consider the full magnitude of it. I didn't ask, just went along with it, selfishly. Now it's out in the open, I want to make sure they go away for it.'

Vicky shivered as she got up. 'I'm glad you're doing the right thing, even though it's way too late for Emmy-Kate Mitchell.'

Ennis slumped back in his chair, tears streaming down his cheeks. A broken man, and a man who'd broken the trust of countless young girls.

Vicky pushed through into the corridor and sucked in the cold air. Her skin felt all clammy.

'...as guilty as a puppy in a puddle, aye.' The door opposite was open and Masson was standing with Forrester in the obs suite.

Vicky shook her revulsion away and joined them. 'How was that?'

'Excellent work, Sergeant.'

'But Raven? Really?'

'He was explicitly named by an Aberdeen cop and we tried to back it all up. I was parachuted in to work alongside Raven, as the two senior cops here, just like Ennis said. And I've been trawling through stuff, online and off. Trouble was, Raven used Ennis to obfuscate things, putting his fingerprints all over these cases. So we couldn't prove any of the allegations. And nobody will go on the record. But if we can get Ennis to back this up, then Raven's going down for a long time.'

'But he's—'

'He's being arrested right now.' Masson nodded thanks at Vicky. 'All down to your tenacity. Want to watch his interview?'

18

The obs suite was cramped at the best of times, but Forrester couldn't sit still, so just made the place feel about half the size, squashing Vicky into a chair in front of the big monitor, next to Masson.

Onscreen, Marcus Ogilvie was prowling the interview room like a lawyer in a trial, all wild gesticulations and posturing, his hair even wilder still. He sat down on the chair, all knees and elbows like a praying mantis, and glanced at his DI next to him, then at the camera in the corner. Despite his skinny frame, his face looked like it had melted, all wobbly folds and crevices. 'John, I don't think you realise the magnitude of the situation you face. As you well know, I head up Police Standards and Ethics for the entire North division. We're investigating you for a number of incredibly serious crimes.'

Bruce Watson sat opposite him, scribbling on a notepad. 'My client acknowledges your CV, Mr Ogilvie. Do you have any questions, or do we just applaud?'

Forrester rested against a chair back and jabbed a finger against the screen. 'Prick doesn't want a Police Federation rep, but a lawyer. I mean, doesn't that scream "guilty" to you?'

Vicky shifted her seat another millimetre away from him. 'This is why we're not in there, sir. We're not impartial like Ogilvie is.'

'Right, right. I'd have torn his face off with my fingers.'

Ogilvie ran a hand over his chin. 'No, but your client should be fuming at being arrested at his home. In front of his wife and children, not to mention his neighbours. At having his electronic equipment taken in as evidence and scoured by a team of forensic specialists. Instead, he's calm and collected.'

'Not a crime.'

'Not the actions of an innocent man, either.'

'Your opinion is immaterial. You've got nothing on my client, so I suggest you let him get on with his job. I gather there's a missing student still not found. And a teenage boy was found murdered yesterday.'

Ogilvie spread his arms on the table and leaned forward, staring at Raven. 'John, let's focus on the facts. Emmy-Kate Mitchell was arrested in December.'

'Not one of my cases.'

'No, that's true. But you helped arrange for her release.'

'You don't have anything, do you? Marcus, let me go and I'll not hold any of this against you.'

'Emmy-Kate was found at a Dundee address last night, where she'd been sexually abused by a man in his forties, while another filmed it.'

Raven was shaking his head. 'We live in troubling times, Marcus, what's this got to do with me?'

'John, I don't have to sit here outlining the case against you, how we got onto you and how much jeopardy you are in.' Ogilvie clapped his colleague on the arm. 'DI Wolfe here will be doing all of that. It'll take hours. Hours and hours. I just want to see if you wish to confess now and spare us all months of misery.'

'No comment.'

'John, your house, your car, your internet and your phones have been wired for sound for two years.'

Raven's mouth fell open. He shut it and swallowed hard. But

didn't say anything. The colour drained from his face and he seemed to age ten years in ten seconds.

'We have plenty to not only convict you but to *bury* you. You'll be in prison for the rest of your life. You'll die there. Your children will grow up with a father in jail. Someone they'll never speak to, except under the supervision of prison guards. Assuming they want anything to do with you. I hope the money you've received is sufficient compensation for that.'

'Superintendent, bullying my client into a conviction isn't going to yield any results. He's an innocent man.'

'No, he's *yet another* corrupt police officer. One last chance, John. Do the right thing. A full, frank confession and a show of remorse, along with an early guilty plea could make all the difference in the world, John, but it's up to you.'

Raven sat back, a grim look on his face.

'So be it.' Ogilvie got up to standing. 'I'll just go and inform Madeline that, given her husband has been arrested and charged, I'm afraid she won't be allowed back into your home for, oh, a week or so, while we make sure we have collected all evidence against you.'

'No comment.'

Masson punched the desk. 'Bastard.'

It snapped Vicky away from staring at the monitor. She craned her neck to look over at him. 'You expected that to work against someone like Raven?'

'Always a chance, Sergeant.' Masson pushed up to standing. 'He's been a cop long enough to develop some kind of conscience.'

Forrester stopped his pacing. 'What's the plan now?'

'Well, David, if you'd listened to his lawyer, you'd have picked up on the fact that you've got a missing student to find. I suggest you focus on her.'

'And me, sir?'

Masson looked at Vicky. 'I've brought in some old colleagues from Edinburgh. People with no link to the locals. Myself and Forrester are speaking with DCI Colin Methven, who—'

'I know him.'

Masson frowned. 'Really?'

'I worked with him on an abduction case in Aberdeenshire about ten years ago.'

'Ah yes. Well. That's good. DCI Methven has experience with this sort of thing. Currently, his team are working a murder in Edinburgh, but we'll draw on his experience to work the disappearance from a strategic angle. We will bring these bastards down.' He checked his watch. 'Sergeant, I'm putting you on lead with the work pertaining to this sex ring. If I was you, I'd get down to forensics swiftly and make sure their evidence trail stands up to scrutiny from our southern cousins.'

One thing Vicky loved was being told how to do her job.

THE FORENSICS LAB was unusually busy for before seven, with more than a few faces Vicky didn't recognise. There was an oasis of calm around Jenny's desk, so she made her way to that.

A big lump bumped into her. 'Oh.' Andrew, looking her up and down with tired eyes. 'Right. You.' Before Vicky could say anything, he darted off through the lab with a taller guy wearing an unfortunate ponytail.

Yesterday... It was going to take a long time to make it up to him.

Then again, Andrew of all people should've known what he was getting up to online, and who with.

Vicky walked off, sadness tugging at her throat.

Jenny was perched on a stool at her workbench, lips twisted up as she focused on a laptop. 'I've never seen anything like it, no.' She looked around the office and focused on Vicky. 'Oh, hey.'

Vicky stayed standing. 'How's it going?'

A thin woman sat on the stool next to Jenny, dark hair in a cute bob, but she had a vicious air about her, like she could cut you. Just like Andrew, she looked Vicky up and down. She stood up tall, a few inches shorter than Vicky, and held out a hand. 'DS Dodds?'

One of those Central Belt accents that could be from anywhere south of mid-Fife.

'How did you know my name?'

'There's this thing called a "camera". It takes "photographs" of people, which lets us recognise people when we meet them.'

Sarcastic cow. Regardless, Vicky shook her hand. 'Sorry, but I don't have any photos of you.'

'DI Sharon McNeill.' She kept holding her hand, like the superior rank wasn't enough. 'I work in the Sexual Offences Unit in the South, based in Bathgate. Brian told me to team up with you, Sergeant.'

'I hadn't been told that much.'

Sharon finally let go. 'Figures.' She sat down with a sigh. 'Well, Ms Morgan here—' she clapped Jenny's arm like they were old friends, '—is trying to unpick your boss's boss's laptop.'

Jenny looked over with an uncharacteristic smile. 'He's a wily old badger, is Raven.' Her voice dropped to a whisper at the mention of his name. 'This machine is encrypted with some stuff even the FBI couldn't crack. Maybe not even the Israelis. There's no way we're getting anything off it.'

'So where does that leave us?' Vicky shot her gaze between them. 'Ma'am?'

'Please, don't call me "ma'am". Sharon's more than fine.' She stared at the laptop. 'Well, we've got a few options here, right? First, there's the flat where you found this girl. Emmy-Kate Mitchell, right?'

'Couple of my guys round there just now.' Jenny tilted her head at her desktop computer's screen. 'Hot damn.'

Sharon jerked forward. 'What's up?'

'Kick ass.' Jenny clicked her fingers a few times. 'That list you gave me? It checks out.'

Vicky got between them, trying to make head or tails of what was going on. 'Care to enlighten me?'

Jenny tapped at the left side of her screen, a spreadsheet of data. 'This is Sharon's list of disappearances from all over northern Scotland in the last ten years.' Her finger tapped on a few names, all marked with "BINGO!" in a column to the right. 'These ones with first names matching those on the site.'

'Wait, the furniture site?'

'Aye. I mean, some of these names are too vanilla. Jane, Anna, Laura. But there's Casey, Millie, Alicia.'

On the right side of the screen was a bed frame called Casey. Special offer.

Vicky looked round at Jenny. 'The thing I don't get is why keep the names? There's an audit trail. Say young Casey McDougall goes missing in Dingwall, then someone uploads a bed on that site called Casey.'

'I know what you mean.' Sharon sat back. 'Our theory is that it's because the girls are abducted to order.'

'So this is...' Vicky didn't have the words, just bile climbing her throat.

'I've been working the Sexual Offences beat for a few years now.' Sharon tucked her hair behind her ear. 'In a lot of cases, the abuser is known to the victim. Say an uncle or a neighbour or a friend of the father's.' She waved a hand at the screen. 'The girls we can't find on the site probably fit into that camp, which is worrying enough. But these ones, the one on the site, someone has scouted them out. They've found young Casey in Dingwall, as you say, and someone has abducted her for them and she's put up for sale. Or he is.'

'Christ. But we found Emmy-Kate on there. Does that mean...'

Sharon thought it through. 'These men, and it's all men, they have a particular target. Emmy-Kate is, what, thirteen?'

'Right.'

'Does she look that age?'

'Pretty much. Wears make-up to make her seem older, but she looks really young.'

'Aye, aye. But the abusers all have a particular look they're going for. An age range. The way it works is one will abuse Emmy-Kate from thirteen to fourteen. When she's gone beyond his target range, he needs to pass her on to someone else, though, which is what this site seems to be for. So someone who wants fourteen-year-olds, he'll get in touch and they start to transition from one abuser to the other.'

'This is horrible.'

'It really is the worst of us. The internet was supposed to set everyone free, but it's just made more and more opportunities for nasty fuckers to be nasty fuckers. And there's both sides of it. The carrot – drugs, clothes, food, hotel rooms, flats even. "I provide all this for you, I love you but I can't afford your lifestyle, you have to help out, baby." We see it is an abduction, right, but it's really more of a *seduction*. And it's only when the victim decides to stop having sex that the threats take place, which is where the stick comes in. "Hey, you owe me ten grand for all the drugs. If you leave now, I'll send your mum and dad videos of all the nasty shit you've done. And I'll share it all over Schoolbook." That's verbatim from a case I'm working just now.' She shook her head. 'The question remains, how did your kid know about it?'

'My kid?' Took Vicky a few seconds to catch the meaning. 'Oh, Noel. Right.' Her frown dipped then came back. 'I haven't got an answer for that. And I've been searching for one. It's how we recovered Emmy-Kate. She was being abused in the flat of our main suspect for Noel's murder.'

Sharon looked right at her. 'You found a physical shop related to this, right?'

'Small Paul's Home Bargains.' Jenny had the street view up on her screen. 'Vicky spoke to the shop owner, who just denied everything, so we think it's a front.'

'And?'

Christ, whoever Sharon McNeill was, she was a nightmare. 'And what?'

'Is it a front?'

'I don't know.' Jenny leaned forward. 'Vicky's been a bit busy, you know? So I dug into it for her. And it is a front business, but it is connected. Remember how there was that thing a few years ago, where tens of thousands of companies were registered in Consett in County Durham? It's an old mining town in the arse end of nowhere, but all these gambling sites and porn sites and God knows what else had their legal addresses there. Paid locals a few grand to do it, some several times over.'

'You think that's what's going on here?'

'Pretty sure. They'll pay him good money for it, and he's got plausible deniability. But it's not beyond the realms of possibility that he's involved.'

'Okay, well, that's good work.' Sharon stood up tall and buttoned up her suit jacket. 'You keep on that, see if you can find anything else. And Raven's laptop, let me know the second you get in.' She looked over at Vicky. 'How about you and me speak to this victim?'

The cleaner's machine thrummed behind Vicky, a deep moan readying the hospital for the horrors of the day to come. Hard to be heard over it, so Vicky tried again. 'We'd appreciate another chance to talk to Emmy-Kate.'

Alison the nurse was smoothing down her eyebrows. 'See, the problem is, she's still in complete denial. We can talk to her about food, meds, her father, all of that, but see when we talk about the ordeal she's suffered?' She zipped up her mouth and tossed the imaginary key away.

Sharon gave her a sympathetic smile. 'I've dealt with many girls in this situation. It's sickening. It's depraved. And what's worse...' She looked over at the room. 'What's worse is the self-denial the girls exhibit.' She stared back at Alison. 'But we can get through to them. So, if you could give us another attempt at Emmy-Kate, maybe it'll help all of us.'

Alison ran a hand through her hair. 'I should run this past Sister.'

'Okay, if that's what you need to do.'

Alison sniffed. 'It might take me a while to track them down. How about you operate on the assumption he okays it. Just don't upset her. She gets a bit scratchy.' She rolled up her right sleeve to show a run of bandages up to her elbow.

Sharon raised her eyebrows. 'We'll be careful. And thanks for this. I appreciate it.' She walked over to the door and opened it to a crack. 'Miss Mitchell?'

Vicky followed her and saw Emmy-Kate sitting on her bed, head slumped. She looked up with violent eyes. 'What do you want?'

'Hey. My name is Sharon.' She stepped into the room. 'I'm a police officer.'

'Another one. Why don't you all just piss off?'

'Can I call you Emmy-Kate?'

'Call me a taxi, bitch. I just want to get home.'

'Right.' Sharon took the seat next to the bed and sat there all casually, like she was a visiting relative. 'To your dad.'

'Aye.' Emmy-Kate was scratching at her arms, her painted nails digging into tanned flesh. 'Just let me go.'

'Hate to say this, but you won't be getting out of hospital into your father's care.'

Emmy-Kate stopped her scratching. 'Why?'

'There's a social worker on her way here. She'll be making arrangements to get you—'

'You can't do this!'

'No, we can. But also, we need to. And have to.' Sharon stepped closer to the girl. 'Your arms are sore because you haven't had your drugs, right?'

She stopped scratching. 'What?'

'Heroin, I'd say.' Sharon reached over and took Emmy-Kate's hand. Vicky expected the girl to act like Tinkle when she wormed her, all flailing arms and legs and teeth, but she just let Sharon examine her wrists. 'Track marks, they call them. Injection sites. How long have you been taking it?'

'Not sure.'

'Less than a year, right?'

'Maybe.'

Sharon let her hand go. 'You're not the first girl this has happened to.'

'You don't know what you're talking about.' The mature adult wannabe was gone, replaced by a child. A scared, lost, lonely child. 'No idea.'

'No, Emmy-Kate, I really do know. Because I've seen many girls in a situation just like yours.' Sharon swept her hair back behind her ear again. 'I work in a place called Bathgate, it's between Edinburgh and Glasgow. There's a couple of motorways nearby. At one, there's a truckers' service station, okay? Guys driving from, say, Belgium to Inverness with, say, chocolate and beer. Doesn't matter. But they take a rest at this place. And there's a cafe there, place called Gav's. Go in, have a meal, get a shower. Most of these guys sleep in their lorries, but sometimes they need a bit of excitement in their lives. There are rooms through the back that most truckers won't know about, but maybe in time they'll hear about them. And what goes on there. And who with. We raided this place two months ago. You know what we found?'

Emmy-Kate swallowed hard. 'No.'

'We found four young girls living there. Older than you. The youngest was sixteen, but the oldest was seventeen.' Sharon pointed at Emmy-Kate's arm. 'They were addicted to heroin too. I interviewed the youngest one. Young girl from Aberdeen, but she'd been abused by her mother's boyfriend since she was twelve. He passed her on to a string of men, all pretending to take care of her, treating her like a princess, but all the time she got deeper and deeper into her addiction. By the time she was sixteen, all she wanted was more heroin. She'd do anything to get it. Nobody had to treat her like a princess any more. They just treated her like... Well, however they wanted. No holds barred.' She stared hard at the girl. 'That's what's going to happen to you, Emmy-Kate.'

'No.'

'Believe me. It is. That man you were with? Mark?'

Emmy-Kate nodded.

'He won't be able to help you. And the other man, nope. No chance.'

'You don't know anything.'

'I know everything.' Sharon leaned in closer. 'We've got your birth certificate, Emmy-Kate. We've got the video of Mark abusing you. You're only thirteen, Emmy-Kate. And your screams were real. You didn't like being there, didn't like them doing that to you. Emmy-Kate, you know you're going to end up in a backroom where old lorry drivers are paying next to nothing to have sex with you, or you're going to end up dead. This is your chance to change that. Talk to us and—'

'Fuck off, bitch.'

'CAN'T DO YOUR JOB, love, ain't my fault.' The interview room tasted of Phil the Mancunian gangster's sweat, his supermarket deodorant a distant memory. 'Know what I mean?'

He was still repped by Fergus Duncan. The smug little shit was at least wearing a full business suit rather than his hunting gear. And he smelled of an oceanic cologne rather than dead pheasant and single malt whisky. 'Sergeant, are you really that feeble? I have already told you my client is innocent of any crimes you put to him. He has nothing to say to you or your new colleague here, so please stop wasting our time. I have much better things to do, and my client wishes to return to his wife and children. They're really missing him.'

Vicky focused on Phil. 'Do they know you're party to the sexual abuse of a minor, Mr Rourke?'

Phil jabbed a finger at Vicky. 'That never happened.'

'But you are Philip Rourke, correct?'

He snorted.

'Sure you wouldn't rather admit it and ask the judge for leniency at the trial?'

'Fuck you and fuck her.'

'You like that word, right? Like watching people doing that, don't you? To children, aye?'

'Fuck off, bitch.'

'You know that filming a man having sex with a child is a criminal offence, right?'

'Shut up.'

'We've got your phone. We've got the footage.'

Duncan sat back, pinching his nose. 'Idiot.' Muttered under his breath.

'Ain't me, love.'

'It is.' Vicky focused on the gangster. 'Your face is on it at the start and the end.'

'Must've been my mate Tony.'

'We all know there's no Tony. So, do you want to admit to this?'

'Nah, you're alright, love.'

Vicky leaned forward. 'Interview terminated at seven forty-five.' She stopped the recorder and stood up.

But Sharon didn't join her. She sat there, staring at the two men opposite. 'You were right. He is an idiot.'

'I never said that.'

'It's on the recording, you daft bastard. Your client is guilty. He's a co-conspirator in the sexual abuse of a minor. He'll be in prison for a long time.'

'This won't even see court.'

'Only chance of that is if he starts talking and he testifies against the people he's working with.'

'You want me to smack some sense into you?'

Duncan put a hand across his client's chest. 'Shut up.'

Sharon laughed. 'I've got some solid contacts in Greater Manchester Police. Won't take them long to speak to Mr Rourke's wife and children, tell them exactly what he's been up to in bonny Dundee. Assuming they even exist.'

Phil pointed at her. 'You keep away from them.'

'What kind of father can work in the sexual trading of children?'

'You want me to show you, bitch?'

'No, just admit to what you've been doing. Tell me who with. And it'll all go away. You can go back home, see your wife and kids. It'll all be fine.'

'Ain't saying nothing to you, bitch.' Phil looked over at Vicky. 'Or to her. Pair of dykes.'

Sharon sat back and grinned. 'Well, we'll see you in court.' She got up and left the room.

Vicky got to her feet. 'Mr Duncan, thanks for helping your client keep quiet. I expect nothing less of you. A colleague will be along to show you out.' With a final nod, she left the room, casually like she didn't care about it.

But this case, it cut her deep. Christ.

Down the corridor, Sharon was checking her phone. 'Emmy-Kate, Phil. Someone's got them well organised. Well coached.'

'You think you'll be able to get a full name for Phil?'

'Hopefully. Should be easy if he's ever been printed. Just in the hands of the internet gods.' Sharon put her phone away. 'Just have to wait and see, don't we?'

'Guess so. What now? Interview Agnew?'

Sharon thought it through for a few seconds. 'No, not yet. I want to see where she was being abused.'

20

Vicky was driving, but it was more like being in a very long, straight car park. She opened her window and let in the cold air, along with a few tons of diesel stink, but she couldn't see anything. No idea what was holding them up, or how long they'd be stuck here.

And she could see the flat from here.

'Supposed to be settling into my new house today.' Sharon was looking across the bridge at the grim Tayside morning. 'Instead, I've driven up here to deal with people like Phil. Child molesters. Makes me feel like my skin's being boiled off.'

'Where have you moved to?'

Sharon looked over at Vicky. 'Bathgate. New house there.'

'That's where you work, isn't?'

'Other side of town, but aye. Two minutes door-to-door. It's not ideal. Just moved from the Royal Mile in Edinburgh. The High Street, if you're local.'

'And are you?'

'My dad would say no. I grew up in Leith, and he's the sort that still insists it's separate from Edinburgh.' She dragged her hand through her hair and fanned it out. 'But it's a house five minutes from where I work. It's got fields nearby for walking. I might even get a dog, but it'd be tough on it being on its own all day.'

'You're single?'

'Right.'

Vicky put the car in gear and let it inch a bit further along the road. It was one of those stretches where she couldn't even pull in and do the rest on foot. 'When he called us "dykes", that seemed to make you smile.'

'I knew I had him.' Sharon smirked. 'Relax, Sergeant, you're not my type.'

'But you are gay?'

Sharon looked around at her. 'That's a bit much for a first date, isn't it?'

'Tell me it's none of my business if you want, but it seemed to resonate with you, that's all. Just like to know what levers people are going to pull.'

'No, it's fine. You're a better judge of character than I gave you credit for.' Sharon tilted her head to the side. 'I have dabbled. And not just at college. But I'm currently just fed up with both men and women.'

'I get that.'

'Do you.' Sharon shook her head. 'I've been working these cases for years now. Lost track of how many. Became a DI through it, thought I was doing good work, but it's hard not to see it when you sleep and worse still when you're awake and miles away from a case. This has been brewing a while. And... I lost my last relationship to it.'

'Sounds tough.'

'It is. But it's the small things, like the track marks on Emmy-Kate's arms. That's what gets to you. Sexual abuse is a crime of infinitesimally small increments. A tiny bit of neglect turns into a lot of abuse.'

'And dealing with that poisons you to people?'

'Completely. Men, because. Well. It's ninety-nine point nine percent men doing it. And women... Not the victims, really. It's usually mothers who, I don't know. They're responsible for the neglect or party to it. Or it's sisters and friends who should've intervened.'

'I've seen that a few times.'

'Have you really?'

'We might not be Edinburgh or Glasgow up here, but we see more than our fair share of cases like that. And there have been a few things in this one that... Hope this is it moving.' Vicky stuck the car back into gear and inched forward. 'The thing is, I just don't understand the psychology.'

'They're sexual predators.'

'No, of the girls. Emmy-Kate, for instance.'

'Right.' Sharon turned to look at Vicky. 'You ever have an older boyfriend at school?'

'Aye. A couple.'

'Any idea why?'

'Don't know. Seemed more mature, maybe?'

'Seemed. They made you feel special. Like you were good enough to go out with them. And what these vermin are doing to these girls is pretty much that, but weaponised. Girls like Emmy-Kate have nothing. The world gives them nothing, especially their parents. So when someone shows them attention, it elevates their esteem. It gives them something. Maybe a purpose, a secret, maybe even love they never had. And that's how they get them. And it's how they keep them in it. That, or it's drugs, or just keeping them in love with someone. It's their need for love, that basic human need for belonging, and then being caught up in their own complicity...'

'Tragic doesn't do it justice.'

'Before you popped down to the forensics lab, I had a look through the case file so far. One thing I didn't quite get.' Sharon looked around at Vicky. 'How did you track down Agnew?'

Vicky winced. 'Through an old case. One run by my sort of ex.'

Sharon sat back with a deep sigh. 'Scott Cullen?'

'How did you know?'

'Because you're that Vicky.'

'You know him?'

'We lived together for years.'

'Shit. Sorry.'

'Well, if you were shagging him behind my back, then I'll consider that apology. Otherwise...'

'I haven't seen him in like ten years.'

'The best way, trust me.'

'Did things get bad?'

'Not really. Look, Scott's a complex man. But we just drifted apart. We had our ups and downs. More downs than ups, to be honest.'

'But he talked about me?'

'He only mentioned you a couple of times. How long did you go out for?'

'A year.'

'A *year*?' Sharon's eyebrows were so high they were almost lost under her hair. 'It sounded to me like a couple of one-night stands.'

'Well, there was that.' Christ, Vicky hated being interrogated like this, especially over her private life. And by someone she'd just met. The traffic wasn't moving at all, either. Just trapping her there. 'When we were seventeen, Scott's parents lived in Carnoustie for a year. It's where I'm from, then they moved back to Dalhousie. We stayed in touch after. Both became cops. And met up at Tulliallan on basic training. A few too many in that pub in Kincardine and...'

'Thanks for being so honest with me.'

Vicky smiled. 'I can understand how poor Phil felt back there. You're a shark tasting blood in the water.'

Sharon laughed. 'I saw Scott yesterday. He's a DI now, would you believe?'

'I remember him being stuck as a PC. A DI? Christ.'

'Meanwhile, you're a DS. You never thought of taking inspector's exams?'

'Got a kid, not got the time. Now I've got two.'

Sharon winced again. Another rabbit hole Vicky could dive down.

But the traffic was moving now and the interrogation was over.

~

VICKY WALKED THROUGH THE FLAT, her crime scene suit crinkling with each step. 'Hard to be back here.'

Sharon walked alongside her down the corridor. 'You rescued her, right?'

'Hard to return to the scene of the crime. It's all theoretical until you see it with your own eyes. Hear it, *smell* it. I know I was good interviewing children and could compartmentalise child pornography, but when I had to interview a victim when I had viewed the video, it was...' Vicky stepped into the living room. Two CSIs worked away, both lost in their own bubbles, even though the place looked completely marked and catalogued. But that sofa in the middle had most of the attention.

The CSI working at it looked up. 'Oh, hey, Sarge.' Zoey stood up with grace and raised a hand. 'Can you just stay over there, please? This place is a jungle and we're not even five percent through it.'

'Define jungle.'

'Let's just say there's no shortage of DNA of all varieties here. Hairs, sweat crystals, skin flakes, semen, vaginal fluids, blood. You name it, it's here.' Zoey shone a black light torch on the sofa and it glowed with a million different stains and particles.

Vicky had to look elsewhere. 'Will you be able to identify anyone else from it?'

'Like I said, we're just finding and cataloguing. Being thorough, you know?'

'I know full well. Anything unusual?'

'Well, there are textbooks here and neither of those two men seem to be the type to study.'

Vicky frowned. 'Textbooks?'

'Uni stuff too.' Zoey pointed to the first box, the lid hanging off. 'Criminal psychology.'

Vicky got out her phone and called MacDonald.

He answered immediately. 'Sup, sweet cheeks?'

'Euan, what course was Ashlynn doing at uni?'

MacDonald paused. 'Why?'

Vicky never had time for his games, but especially not now. 'Just tell me what it was. Please.'

Sharon was tiptoeing through the crime scene towards the box.

'Have to check.' Sounded like MacDonald was flicking through his notebook. 'Eh, I need to speak to young Considine on that one.'

'Euan, for Christ's sake, this is your job. You're searching for a missing student and you don't even know what course she was studying?'

'Vicky, back off. Okay? Been in Cupar since four a.m. following leads on her whereabouts. Means I haven't had the time to see how the boy wonder is doing at the uni. That's it.'

'Thanks.' Vicky snapped the call shut and searched for Considine's number.

'Vicky.' In the middle of the room, Sharon was holding up a textbook. *Criminology* by Stephen Jones. 'It's Ashlynn's.'

'How do you know that?'

'She wrote her name inside the cover.'

21

B ack at Bell Street, the light outside the room was on.

"Interview in Progress"

'Superb.' Vicky opened the door to the obs suite, expecting to see Masson, but finding nobody.

Onscreen, Forrester and Masson were interviewing Mark Agnew.

Vicky held the door for Sharon. 'Let's see if they're getting anywhere.'

Agnew looked like he had slept even less than Ennis had first thing. His hair was slicked with sweat and he looked a broken man. Still, he was fighting. And without a lawyer this time. 'That's not me.'

'You were having sex with a *child*.'

'She's not a child.'

'Emmy-Kate Mitchell is *thirteen*. Thirteen! She's a child!'

Agnew shook his head. 'I didn't have sex with her.' His voice was calm and level, like he believed he was telling the truth.

'Why did you say "she's not a child"?'

'I didn't.'

Masson gave an exasperated yelp. 'You just did!'

'Nope.'

'You said "she's not a child". Therefore you either think Emmy-Kate is over sixteen, or you think that, while she's under sixteen, she seems mentally mature, at least to you.'

'Nope.'

'But you know Emmy-Kate, don't you?'

'Nope.'

Vicky couldn't look at the screen any longer. 'He's delusional.'

'No.' Sharon was staring at the interview. 'He's going down big time. At least ten years, I'd say. And his whole life will be ruined by this, thankfully.'

'But he's keeping quiet. And if Ashlynn has been to his flat, we need to get him talking.'

Sharon stared at the screen. 'They're bulling him. *That's* the problem.'

'You got an alternative idea?'

'Let him bully us.' Sharon opened the door and stepped out into the corridor. 'Your sole job in there is to look sympathetic and nod in agreement with everything I say, even if you want to throw up.'

'What are you going to—'

'Just let me lead, okay? Back me up, okay? That's it.'

Vicky gave her a nod. 'Okay.'

Sharon walked back out, then knocked on the door.

The door snapped open and Forrester popped his head out. 'Can I help you?'

'Get Masson out here.'

'Who are you?'

'She's with me, sir.' Vicky got between them. 'Can we speak to Masson?'

'Right.' Forrester slipped back inside.

Sharon snorted. 'He's a charmer.'

'This is him at his best too. And you didn't exactly introduce yourself to him.'

'Fair comment.'

The door opened again and Masson strolled out like he was

heading to the golf course for a relaxing round. 'Hey, Shaz. What's up?'

'Just thinking you might need a feminine touch in there.'

Masson looked at her, then at Forrester, then back at Sharon. 'I could argue, but I think I'm getting very close to swinging for that creep.' He shrugged. 'Fine. On you go.'

'Cheers.' Sharon messed up her hair so it lost the organisation and hit chaos perfectly, then straightened it all out again. Gave her the look of a bookish type. 'Okay, let's go.' She opened the door and held it for Vicky. 'You first.'

Vicky took her seat opposite Agnew.

He looked up at her and nodded like they were in the supermarket.

Sharon sat on the adjacent chair, her pose erect and tall. 'Mr Agnew, my name is Sharon McNeill. I'm a police officer, just like Vicky here.' She nodded at Vicky. 'Go on.'

Thrown into the deep end. Great.

Vicky looked at Agnew and just knew exactly how Masson had felt. She wanted to slam his face against the table, against the wall, the door, the floor, stamp on it. 'I want to ask you about your attraction to young girls.'

'There is no attraction.'

'Come on. Of course there is.'

'Seriously. This is offensive, by the way. I've got two young daughters.'

'Huh.'

Agnew twisted both index fingers around the middles. 'You got kids?'

Vicky glanced at Sharon and caught a nod. She looked back at Agnew. She didn't want to open up to this guy, but... Maybe this was how she'd get bullied. So she nodded. 'Got two kids.'

'Boys?'

'Boy and a girl. Both nine.'

'Twins?'

'No. My stepson.'

'Right.'

Agnew focused on Sharon. 'What about you?'

'What about me?'

'Any children you want to exploit in a vain attempt to get me to talk?'

'No.' Sharon sat forward. 'I can't have kids.'

Agnew frowned at her. 'Shit. I'm sorry.'

'Thank you for your kindness. I was pregnant once. With a girl. But I lost her.' Sharon sniffed. 'It's been a difficult time for me.'

'Must be tough on you.'

'You have no idea.'

'I can imagine.'

'It's tough on childless women, even in this day and age, you know?'

'Right.'

'Being slave to your biology like that.'

'What do you mean?'

'Well, it's the same for you, isn't it? Agnew, you're a preferential child molester. You can't help it. Slave to your own biology.'

'No, I'm not.'

'And you don't want just anyone, do you? No, you have a type. Someone like Emmy-Kate. Her age. Her look. Her innocence. And it's all about the seduction for you. You love these girls and you want them to love you. You're a rich man, you pay for things. Make her feel special. Make her feel loved.'

'Not me, no.'

Vicky focused on him, wanting to stick his sick face under the table and drive the leg down into his skull.

But Sharon kept going. 'Mark, I understand you. Okay? You aren't a bad person. You're not evil. You're just a product of biology in conflict with today's standards. You have your thing, it's totally okay. I mean, it's okay for gay people or trans people these days. I mean it's not like you have a choice, it's who you are, it's how you are.'

'Exactly.' Agnew was nodding. 'I mean, they shove it all in your face.'

'Completely. It's only society's rules that make what you do illegal, isn't it? Back in the Middle Ages, Emmy-Kate would be married by fourteen. Maybe younger. Maybe even have a few kids of her own already.'

Agnew stared down at the table, eyes clamped shut. Sharon's tender broadside was having some impact. 'I'm not doing anything other than treating them like princesses.'

'And if anyone's being exploited here, it's you.'

'Oh God yeah.'

'I bet you could tell me a few tales, right?'

'You have no idea.'

'Constant demands for clothes, phones, shoes, computers, right?'

'Right. And it's *constant*.'

'And drugs and booze, right?'

'Right. I never take drugs myself. And I don't drink. But, like, if they use my money to buy that sort of stuff, it's not my fault. I'm trying to help them.'

'Completely. You're just trying to give them love they need. These are kids in desperate situations, right? Kids of alcoholics or drug addicts. Kids who have nothing. You treat them as adults, and they enjoy the attention. And maybe they get enough love from you, right? Maybe you're the one person in their life who does love them, if even for a moment. Maybe they'll move on, but maybe they get too old for you, right? And it's no fault of theirs. But you don't want to be trapped with someone who no longer turns you on, right?'

'Right.'

'So you get them to help someone else in return for the latest phones and clothes. It's the kindest way, right? And soon enough they're enjoying *their* attention and not yours. Actually, they've forgotten about you. It's sad, of course, but it's natural. And you've got someone new, who loves you and who you adore. And these girls, they move on to the next guy and so on. But one day, they're too old for anyone, right? So then what?'

Agnew was looking away now.

'I mean, many are hooked on drugs by age sixteen, which is

beyond your preferences. So you pass these girls on to other opportunities where others can help them. Keep it neutral, no judgement here. The whole thing is the circle of life, Mark. The circle of love. You think you treat them well, and they'll do anything for you, but you have to take care of your needs, and if a brothel is the only place that can take care of theirs, that's hardly your fault is it? Emmy-Kate was only fourteen, wasn't she? She still had time. But Ashlynn's nineteen. Tell me about her.'

'Ashlynn?'

'She was one of yours, wasn't she? Five, six years ago, you found her, you loved her. Or maybe someone else found her and just moved her along when the time was right, but she is nineteen now. She clearly isn't your type. How does she tie back to you, Mark?'

'Why are you talking about her?'

'You don't know an Ashlynn?'

'No.'

'You do.'

'I just said I don't.'

'And yet I don't believe you.'

'That's your prerogative. You know, you almost had me going with all that sympathy stuff.'

'Got you admitting to sexual abuse of minors.'

'So? You've got me on video. I could hardly deny it, right?'

'Look, Ashlynn was kidnapped yesterday. She's out there, at risk. Help us find her.'

'I don't know what you're talking about.'

'Come on, Mark. What happened to her?'

'I don't know.'

'Does your mate? Phil?'

'No idea who that is.'

'The man who filmed you having sex with Emmy-Kate.'

Agnew shrugged. 'That his name?'

'Mark, we found Ashlynn's textbooks in your apartment.'

'I don't know anything about that.'

'What do you mean?'

'I don't know.'

'But you do know her?'

Agnew looked at Sharon, then Vicky, then back to Sharon. 'Right.'

'You abused her?'

'Yes.' His voice was shrill and tiny. 'Yes.'

'Like I said?'

'Pretty much.'

'Then she got too old?'

'Right.'

'Here's the thing. With your MO, I'd have expected Ashlynn to have headed elsewhere, but she seems to have hung around. Got to go to uni. But that leaves the mystery of why her textbooks are in your flat.'

'It's not my—'

'What?'

Agnew shook his head. 'Nothing.'

'What I don't get is why kidnap her now. What's she got on you?'

'Nothing!'

'Or is it on Phil?'

Agnew sat back, eyes clamped shut. 'This isn't my fault. I... I thought I was happy. Married with kids, but I've got a thing for young girls. Thirteen-year-olds. I ... It's... I was abused as a kid.'

'I'm sorry to hear that.'

'A neighbour. I thought he was a friend, but his sister, she... She...'

'How old were you?'

'Nine. She was thirteen. Used to... I... You're right, Ashlynn loved the attention and I loved the control. She was so pretty, and I couldn't get enough of her. But then, she started to mature. And my friend had another girl, a year younger. And he had a man and a woman who wanted to be with Ashlynn.'

'A man and a woman?'

'The next one in the chain were a couple.'

'You ever meet them?'

'Once.'

'With Ashlynn?'

'Okay, twice. Juliana was scared of them too. I had to reassure her it would be okay.'

'Who is Juliana?'

Agnew emptied his lungs. 'This is about three years ago? Juliana was a good kid. She wasn't on drugs. A bit older than the others, but she... she looked so pure.'

Vicky got out her phone and pulled up the list of victims. There. Juliana was a coffee table. Sold out. She gave Sharon a curt nod.

Sharon leaned forward. 'What happened to Ashlynn?'

'I don't know.'

'So why were her textbooks in your flat?'

'You'd need to ask Phil.'

'Why's that?'

'I don't know.'

'Come on, Mark. What does Phil know?'

'Look, there's no hope for Ashlynn. She's long gone.'

'That's the trick, isn't it? Once they've stopped being useful to the last man on your chain, men like Phil take them south, don't they? Glasgow, Manchester, Birmingham, London. Lots of illegal brothels there, right? Who cares about them? They're useless to you now and you didn't touch them last, did you? What was Phil there for? Emmy-Kate's too young, isn't she? Was he there for Ashlynn?'

Agnew shook his head. 'He was going to take Emmy-Kate away from me.' Tears flooded down his cheeks. 'One last time.'

'Where was he taking her, Mark? To this couple?'

'Right.'

'And Ashlynn?'

He looked at them with the eyes of a grieving father, not a child molester who had lost his latest victim. 'I have no idea.'

22

Vicky struggled to keep pace with Sharon. Not many people could out-stomp her, but here she was a stride ahead, head down and charging on, the distance growing and growing.

But just like Vicky, it wasn't immediately apparent that Sharon had a plan.

'Hey.' Vicky grabbed her arm and stopped her getting too far away, just like Bella at a play park. 'You okay?'

Sharon didn't turn to look at Vicky, just stood there, head bowed. 'It took everything I had to not smash that creep's face into the wall.'

'I had the exact same thoughts, you know.' Vicky coughed out a laugh. 'A lot of cases I deal with, it's open and shut. Or it's pretty twisted, but it's fairly obvious. With this... Every part of it makes my stomach churn.'

Sharon looked around at her now. 'I've been doing this since January 2014. Over six years on this beat, and it doesn't get any easier. Every day, it's the same shit. Some arsehole who can't keep it in his pants, forcing it into somebody else's pants, against their will. Against their consent.'

'Sounds tough.'

'Most of my remit is against adults. While that girl we picked up at that lorry park was over the age of consent, she led us to what these people are doing. Men like Phil, whoever he is, he's clearly a ringleader. Getting money from men like Mark Agnew.' She looked close to losing it, whatever it was that she clung to so she could stay sane. 'It all just makes me sick to the core.'

Vicky pointed down at the floor, in the loose direction of the interview rooms. 'You were brave in there.'

'Brave?' Sharon barked out a laugh. 'Brave would've been killing him, or torturing him until he told us everything he knew. Anything to help us free other girls.'

'Forrester and Masson could've done that, but they couldn't have done what you did. What you said to get him talking.'

'Unfortunately, I have learned to think the way these bastards think and say the things that make them believe I am the only person who understands them.' Sharon shut her eyes. 'While I die a little inside each time.'

'It worked, though. He opened up to you. He told us the truth. He just doesn't know anything else.'

Sharon opened her eyes again. 'I hate having to bare my soul to animals like him.'

'I've done it myself. It makes you feel all slimy, right? Like they're inside your head as much as you're inside theirs.'

Sharon stared straight at Vicky with glistening eyes. 'Right. Exactly right. "He who fights with monsters might take care lest he thereby becomes a monster. And if you gaze for long into the abyss, the abyss gazes also into you." Nietzsche has a saying for most of the darker sides of policing.'

'Was it true?'

'Every word. It's hard to fake.'

'So you lost a child?'

'It was just an embryo. That's what I've told myself. But if I hadn't... If I hadn't lost her, she'd be seven years old now.'

'Was Scott the father?'

'He might be a clown, but he'd probably have made a good

dad.' She looked off down the long corridor. 'I've no idea whether I'd have made a good mother or not.'

'I think you'd have been a great one.' Vicky gave her a broad smile. 'You care. And that's all you can do.'

Sharon returned the smile. 'Thanks.' She stepped aside to let two people past, lugging a big crate. 'So, did we get anything out of me giving up my deepest truths?'

'Well, Agnew definitely abused Ashlynn. Her university books were there because he'd been abusing her.'

'But she's an adult.'

'She's still around, she has to be fulfilling some role. Maybe she holds the camera for him sometimes.'

'Jesus.' Sharon rubbed at her eyes, streaking her mascara. 'Okay, so we need a plan here.'

'You're the DI.'

Sharon gave a humourless laugh. 'I'm all ears.'

Vicky patted her arm. 'Get yourself cleaned up. I'll see you in forensics.'

~

'FOR THE LOVE OF SATAN.' Jenny thumped the laptop down on the workbench. 'Why does everything have to be—' She spotted Vicky and rolled her eyes. 'You.'

'Charming.' Vicky took the stool opposite Jenny. 'What's up?'

'That Manc guy's phone is what. The one Phil, or whatever his name is, had been recording that video on.'

'Why is it a problem?'

'It's locked, for starters. And I can't get in.'

'Sure you or Andrew will manage.'

'Maybe. The bigger problem is that it's not his.'

'What do you mean?'

'Neither the handset nor the SIM are burners, but...' She held up the phone in an evidence bag. 'This thing is showing up as being bought in Bulgaria three years ago. We can't trace it back to Agnew or Phil.'

'It being Agnew's makes sense to me. Phil's just the cameraman while he...'

'Right.' Jenny was frowning so hard it looked like her forehead might crush in on itself. 'Oh, I'm in.'

'How?'

'There's a backdoor to these models and I just— Ah shite!' She threw it down on the bench again.

'What's up now?'

'Bastard thing's drive is encrypted.' Jenny shook her head. 'We need another password to access any files on it.'

'How many goes do you get?'

'That's not the problem. I'm in, so I can copy the entire drive and try to decrypt it in perpetuity, but that's the amount of time it would actually take. Three. And I've no idea what it could be. If it's Phil's or if it's Agnew's, could be a whole world of anything.'

That hit Vicky like a sledgehammer in the knee. 'So we'll lose the video?'

'Right. And I bet you and Forrester have been in interviews, giving it all that chat about the fact you've got a video and a birth certificate. Well, it'll all fall apart.'

'There's no way to decrypt it?'

'An infinite number of monkeys and typewriters. That or the encryption key.'

Vicky sat there, the room swimming around her, making her feel close to falling off the stool. Losing the conviction... Christ. With Agnew, Phil and Emmy-Kate on the other side, it'd all come down to persuading a jury, and beyond a 'not proven' guilty. And Vicky didn't fancy the odds swinging in their direction.

She looked over the desk at Jenny. 'There's no other option?'

'Look, there's one but it's experimental. Not a great success rate.'

'Well, I don't fancy the chances of us getting the password out of that Phil guy.'

'And Agnew?'

'That's the thing. We won't get either of them to give us their password, will we? I mean, the obvious thing to do is to wait for

Agnew's computers to come in, then we can see what passwords he has set up on that. If he's got a password manager installed, it might give us clues.' Vicky checked her watch. 'But I've got a missing teenager I need to find. And it's all tying together and…'

'And it feels like a film where someone's looking around a villain's desk and trying the name of their dog to get in.' Jenny ran a hand down her face. 'Trouble is, we've had a couple of phones like this over the last few years, but have never been able to get in.'

Sharon was standing at the end of the table, looking like she'd had a shower, dried and applied fresh make-up. And hadn't been crying about her lost child. 'Is there a but here?'

'Aye.' Jenny looked her up and down. 'Andrew's been working with the Met to use their new decryption algorithm.'

'And has it worked?'

'A couple of times. But it needs to be done on the source device, not a copy. There's hardware coupling going on, so it's not like we can clone the device.'

'Out of?'

'About twenty.'

'So a one in ten chance?'

'Right.'

Vicky scanned the room for her brother. Daft sod was over by the window, sipping on a can of WakeyWakey, no matter how many times Vicky had told him to cut out the caffeine, let alone get stuck into the high-strength stuff. 'It feels like we don't have a choice here.'

Sharon nodded. 'Do it.'

Jenny held up the phone. 'This thing will zero. Might even catch fire like in a *Mission Impossible* film.'

'I know. But we've got a missing girl to find. That phone might give us a whole treasure trove of evidence.'

'Might?'

'That's my risk to take.'

Jenny held up her hands. 'Be my guest, then.' She stood up. 'Andrew!'

He hooked out an earbud and looked back over with a smile

that faded when he spotted his sister. He put his earbud back in and went back to work.

'See what I have to deal with?' Jenny set off across the office.

Vicky stopped her. 'Look, this is on me. He's being a child because I thought he'd been involved in the abuse. Let me speak to him.' She got nods from Jenny and Sharon, then walked over to Andrew's bench. 'Hey.'

He unhooked both earbuds this time. 'What do you want?'

'Well, I want to start by saying I'm sorry.'

'What for?'

'For unearthing evidence that linked you to a murder, then questioning you about it.'

'You didn't need to be a dick about it.'

'I had no choice, Andrew.'

'You could've asked me.'

'And if I did that with everyone connected to a case, then we'd never convict anyone ever. And we'd get stuck with a million lawsuits. I had to do this by the book, Andrew. There are people's lives at stake here.'

'Trying to persuade me you had no choice. I know the drill. Just so I decrypt that phone for you. You never change, Victoria. Never.'

'Andrew. This isn't a game. If you can get into that phone, a child abuser will go to prison. If you don't, then he might go free.'

'Don't do that. This isn't on me.' He looked at her, but there was deep hurt in his eyes. Betrayal. No matter that the stupid sod had been playing online games with kids half his age. Closer to a third of his age. And he was taking it out on her.

'Andrew, I had to go through procedure. It can't be one rule for us, okay? But when you threatened to come over the table after MacDonald and "belt his jaw"? Well, I saw Dad in you. That's exactly what he'd have said and done.'

Andrew laughed. He held out a hand. 'Let me see it.'

Vicky slid it over the desk. 'Thank you.'

'This is for the girl, not for you.'

'Even so, I appreciate it.'

Andrew slipped on some goggles like he was doing a chemistry experiment, then slid the phone out of the packet. He snapped the back off and pulled out the battery, then attached a cable to a port hidden inside. The screen lit up, super bright, with some Chinese company's logo. 'Did my lead at least give you something?'

'Turns out there was someone inside the company taking you down.'

'I *knew* it. Scumbag.'

'He's the one abusing the girls.'

Andrew's eyebrows shot up. 'Well, I better not screw this up, then.' He switched to his laptop and hit the keyboard like their dad doing some steering wheel drumming to Lynyrd Skynyrd. 'Bingo.'

'You're in?'

'I'm in.' He leaned to the side so Vicky could see the screen. A progress bar appeared, sticking at 1% for thirty seconds before ticking up to 2%. 'Well, well, well. It's almost full. This is going to take a good while to copy over.'

'Any idea what's on there?'

Andrew switched to a different screen. 'Well, it's mostly photos and... lots of videos.'

'That figures. Child molesters love to collect and relive their abuse.'

Andrew nodded slowly. 'This is really that guy who was killing us on *Indignity*?'

'No comment, but yes.'

'Sick bastard.'

'Is there anything you can get from the videos that might help us track down Ashlynn Thomas?'

Andrew tapped at the keyboard. 'Well, I've got all the metadata on each and every photo. Date, time, GPS location. Daft sod didn't turn any of that off. And I've got the phone owner's location history.'

～

SMALL PAUL'S Home Bargains looked exactly the same as the previous day. The only difference being that the owner of that phone had visited the shop twice since their last visit. And Vicky wanted to know why. And if it was Mark Agnew or Phil.

She looked around the street again. Quiet now, all of the traffic held back upstream in all three directions. She put her radio to her mouth. 'Front entrance secured. Over.'

The radio crackled with static. 'Rear secured. Over.' Karen was down the side street, giving a big thumbs up in case the message hadn't been clear.

Vicky looked around at Sharon, Considine and their three uniforms, Masson's finest. 'Let's do this. Serial Alpha entering the premises now. Over.' She put her radio in her pocket, then led them all inside.

This time, she didn't have to pretend to be Considine's wife or girlfriend. She was a cop, warrant card out. 'Is Mr Johnson here?'

The guy behind the counter had the heavy movements of someone who was seriously stoned. A bear of a man, but with soft eyes. No threat to anyone, especially in his condition. He thumbed up the stairs. 'Showing a customer our new bed range, madam.' His voice was clean and crisp, like he should be on the radio.

Vicky pointed at two of the uniforms. 'Stay here.' She led Sharon and Considine up the creaking stairs towards the fruity tang of furniture polish.

The first floor was all sideboards and coffee tables. No nooks or crannies to hide in, just a big open space. And empty.

'Constable, stay here.' Vicky gave him a final nod, then led Sharon up the next set of stairs, gripping her baton tight.

Sure enough, Small Paul was sitting on an armchair in the middle of a posh living room display.

A woman sat at a dining table, her mouth hanging open. Young, blonde-haired, athletic and looking ready to run.

Vicky dashed over the floor and grabbed her by the arms. She was so light Vicky could lift her off her feet, not that she needed to.

Sharon was towering over the armchair. 'Mr Johnson?'

He seemed to be trying to hide in the fabric, but she wouldn't let him.

Vicky sat the girl down. She did look young, fifteen maybe. Another victim of the chain. 'What's your name?'

She spat in Vicky's face.

'Charming.' Vicky wiped it clear. 'I need your name.'

'Piss off.'

Vicky got out her phone and found the shot MacDonald had sent her. It looked a lot like the girl in front of her, but without the heavy makeup. 'Ashlynn Thomas?'

That got her attention. 'Told you to piss off.'

'It's okay, Ashlynn, we've got you.'

A toilet flushed behind Vicky.

She turned just as the door opened. A big bastard stood there, sharp eyes scanning the terrain, clocking two cops, at the same time as he went for a gun. His face was all scratched and scarred, like he made a point of getting into a fistfight every day.

Vicky let go of Ashlynn and swung with her baton, cracking it off his forearm. He dropped the gun and it landed on his shoe.

Vicky didn't have time to brace herself for an accidental explosion. Instead, she drove her head into his nose and brought her baton up directly into his testicles.

He went down in the doorway and his head cracked off the toilet pan. Blood trickled out of his burst nose down to his chin and his white tracksuit. He was breathing, just.

Vicky dashed over and grabbed Ashlynn by the wrist, then shouted down the stairs, 'Stephen! I need an ambulance up here!'

Sharon had Small Paul on his feet and cuffed already. She frog-marched him across the room. 'That was *brutal*.'

Vicky shrugged. 'Learned some tricks from my dad.'

'Remind me to never cross your brother.' Sharon pointed at the unconscious gangster. 'Now, Paul, are you going to tell me who that is?'

The owner shook his head.

Still holding Ashlynn by the wrist, Vicky got in his face. 'You're probably thinking you can spin some story about how you've been coerced into this. Probably thinking how a decent lawyer like Bruce Watson could maybe cut you a deal. Well, there's no deal at all, until you tell us who he is and who this is.'

Paul looked between them, like he knew the jig was up. 'His name is Sid.'

Ashlynn was shaking her head at him.

'And she's Ashlynn.' Paul let his head go. 'I was keeping her here. Sid and his mate were going to take her away somewhere, but his mate never showed.'

'You get his name?'

'Phil, I think. Sid kept saying he was going to run, but he didn't. Kept on looking outside, waiting for his mate.'

Vicky swung Ashlynn round. The girl was lighter than her gran in her final days. 'Where were they taking you?'

Ashlynn just shrugged.

Sharon reached over and examined her wrists and forearms. 'Where do you inject?'

'Inject?' Ashlynn scowled at her. 'Nowhere, you sick weirdo. I'm not a junkie.'

Sharon frowned at Vicky, but doubled down on Ashlynn. 'So how did they coerce you?'

'Coerce me? Into doing what?'

'Into being abused and keeping quiet.'

'Get over yourself, you dyke bitch. Nobody's abused me.' Ashlynn spat at Sharon. 'Best thing that ever happened to my dull existence.'

Sharon took out a hankie and cleaned off her cheek. 'Stop. Gobbing. On. People.'

'Closest you'll get to kissing me.'

Sharon snapped forward, grabbed her by the shoulders and pinned her down against the sofa. 'You think you've got it all sorted, don't you? Think you know all the answers. I've seen where girls like you end up. Those men were going to take you to a lorry park in the south of Scotland. You'll spend the last remaining years of your youth sucking and screwing fat old men. In exchange for drugs.'

'You want a go on me, you just have to ask.'

'I'm. Not. Gay.'

Ashlynn laughed. 'Keep telling yourself that. I see the way you look at me.'

'Ashlynn, if you give up the names of the men who abducted you, we can cut a deal. Probably no jail time, maybe a chance to reconnect with your mother.'

Ashlynn laughed again. 'Like I told that creepy journalist who's been hounding me, there's nothing to tell.'

Vicky felt like someone was prodding a knitting needle into her gut. 'What journalist?'

'Sick bastard kept following me at uni. Thought it was him who abducted me.'

'Back in a sec.' Vicky walked off towards the stairs.

Considine finally met her by the stairs. He took one look at the unconscious man in the toilet. 'Sarge, remind me never to try it on with you.'

Vicky wasn't even in the mood for putting him in his place. 'Just get the ambulance here.' She skipped down the stairs, the phone ringing in her ears like a drill.

'Hey, Vicks, how you doing?'

'Alan, you're going to meet me at our usual place. Fifteen minutes.'

'Woah, woah, woah. What's this about?'

'I want the truth about Ashlynn.'

'Oh.'

23

The Auld Cludgie Café was busy. Morning coffee drinkers filled the other tables, laughing and joking like everything was normal.

'Here you are, hen.' The waitress rested the coffee in front of Vicky. 'Gave you a wee biscotti, too.'

Vicky nodded, but couldn't muster a smile. She held the cup but her hand was shaking with rage. 'Thank you.'

Alan slumped into the chair opposite Vicky. 'Sorry I'm late. Got held back.' He looked exhausted, like he'd pulled another of his all-nighters, but she couldn't tell if that was writing stories or bumping coke in the worst nightclub in Dundee. How did she ever fall for his bullshit? How did she get pregnant by him? How did she not notice how much of a train wreck he was? Or maybe he wasn't that far gone?

The waitress smiled at him. 'Look like you need a coffee.'

'Please.' Alan dug the heels of his palms into his eye sockets. 'You got any cans of Red Bull?'

'Just got WakeyWakey.'

'Okay, the rhubarb and custard flavour, if you've got it, otherwise the apple strudel. And a coffee. And a bacon roll. With haggis and a tattie scone. Cheers.'

'Coming right up.' She giggled and walked off.

Vicky sipped her coffee and examined Alan. 'You look tired. Night on the charlie, was it?'

'Well, that's a nice way to greet me.'

'Just booze, then?'

'I wish.' He coughed into his fist. 'Night on the crapper. My guts were an absolute disgrace yesterday.'

Vicky raised her eyebrows. 'Wonder what caused that.'

'Aye. Hope it's not this coronavirus thing in China and Italy.'

'It's more likely to be the second-hand pizza you were eating yesterday.' She crunched the biscuit and took another sip. 'Why didn't you go to the police?'

'About taking pizza from—?'

'Alan, I'm not in the mood. You've spoken to Ashlynn Thomas. Didn't think to come to the cops?'

'Does that mean you've found her?'

The waitress put a glass in front of Alan and held out a can. 'Sorry, we've only got liquorice flavour left.'

'Didn't know who thought that was a good idea, but thanks.' He took the can from her and opened it as she walked away. 'Look, I was going to but... Well.'

'So you're still an arsehole.'

'I'll always be an arsehole, Vicks.'

'Because you're more likely to chase a story than a commitment.'

Alan shrugged. 'Still trying to psychoanalyse me, eh?'

'No, I can read you like a book.'

Alan downed his can in one go. 'You have no idea how hard it's been for me, do you?'

'Probably nowhere near as hard as raising our child on my own.'

'Your choice to do that. Not that my behaviour gave you one, I suppose.' He smirked, then ran his hand over his nostrils. God, he was still doing coke. 'You want to know the truth? It's been really hard dealing with all the shit I've investigated over the years. Honestly, I'm trying to make the world a better place. Like you are,

I suppose, but I've worked the people trafficking beat for eight years now. I mean, when I started as a journalist, there wasn't such a thing. What kind of world do we live in where you need two full-time writers just devoted to covering people trafficking?'

Vicky had heard similar words from Sharon, about her stint investigating sex crimes. She had only just met her, but Sharon didn't seem to need to resort to Class As to cope. Still, she kept quiet. Alan was in the flow and coke loosened his lips.

He shook his head. 'I covered this story about a London cop's missing daughter. Heartrending. Then one about a sex farm in the arse end of England. And I worked that case with the kid who went missing from Alnwick who everyone thought was in Portugal. Loads of others. And it all takes a toll.'

'You know that coping by numbing yourself with drink and drugs isn't actually coping.'

'Right.' Alan ran his hand through his hair. 'And the truth of it is that I really can't cope with having a daughter.'

'It's not like you're in her life. Yesterday, you thought it was *her* birthday, not mine.'

'Right. Look, all I know is that I can't handle having a kid.'

'So the court case against me is just petty revenge?'

Alan swallowed hard. 'Pretty much.'

'So withdraw it. Stop. Please.'

'It's not that simple.'

'No, it really is. You're the one suing me. Call your lawyer, tell them to withdraw the lawsuit. End of story.'

'Vicks, the thing is... It's my mother. She wants to meet her only granddaughter.'

Vicky was gritting her teeth tight, almost grinding them.

'You never met her, eh?'

'No. You didn't let me.'

'Well, she lived in Spain for a bit, but split from that arsehole she was bunking with. Back in Crail now.'

'Crail. I keep forgetting you're a Fifer.'

'Can't change my spots, Vicks.' Alan sat back and let the waitress put his plate down. 'Thanks.'

'Sauces are in the corner.'

'Cheers.' He leaned forward and grabbed his roll with both hands.

'Okay, here's the deal. Pay me all of the support money you owe, the amount we agreed last month but backdated to Bella's birth, then monthly support until she's eighteen. Do that, and your mum can look in on Bella from time to time. If she's a nice woman.'

'Thank you.'

'So you'll do that?'

'Aye.' Alan bit into his roll and chewed. 'So why are we meeting?' At least, that's what Vicky thought he'd said.

Vicky finished her coffee and wished she still had the biscuit. 'You're lucky we're in here and you can eat your roll, but I want to take you into the police station to interrogate you.'

He just chewed, slapping his lips together. A dod of haggis tumbled to the plate and he scooped it up on his finger.

'Here's the deal, Alan. We did find Ashlynn, but I want to know why you've been hounding her.'

'Why do you think I've been doing that?'

'*Alan.*'

'Fine.' He rested his roll on the table and finished chewing. Then clawed at his teeth with his pinky nail. 'Right, you know how I've been sniffing around this story.' He sucked at his pinky. 'Ashlynn's name came up from a few girls I spoke to near Edinburgh.'

'You didn't think to tell me?'

'Come on, Vicks. Thing was, I didn't know it was her until—' He burped into his fist. 'Oh Lordy, that roll's repeating on me something rotten. I spoke to one of the lassies last night. Called her up, and she told me about Ashlynn. Another one backed it up.'

'And you didn't connect it with Ashlynn going missing?'

'Of course I did, but I was spraying out—'

'Aye, aye, I get the picture.'

'Look, I've had Ashlynn on my radar for a few weeks from

another source I can't divulge. And I found her last week at the uni, tried to speak to her. No dice. But I know her type.'

'And what type is that?'

'Feels like I'm giving you quite a lot here, Vicks.'

'Do you mean the type who won't speak to the police, but will maybe trust a good, honest journalist like you?'

'No, Vicks. If it was that simple, I'd have just passed the info on to a friendly cop.'

'So what type is she?'

'Ashlynn is a "groomer" for this sex ring.'

It all slotted into place. A perfect fit.

Men like Mark Agnew had a lust for certain girls, but the supply was harder to get, certainly without putting themselves at extreme risk. Having a groomer made perfect sense, meet the next wave of victims, bring them in.

'Go on.'

'Ashlynn was one of the first victims. Way she told it to my source, a friend of her uncle's abused her. She saw it as treating her like a princess, but he passed her to a mate, then another. When she hit sixteen, she found them a new girl. Juliana.'

Another name on the list. A shiver crawled up Vicky's spine. 'Go on.'

'Well, Ashlynn's now nineteen and studying at university, but she's been recruiting girls for this gang. Picking them from the worst parts of Dundee.' Alan pushed his plate away. 'These girls come from difficult backgrounds. Starved of parental affection. Even negative interest elevates them, but these men treat them like queens.'

'And they're treated like adults, and enjoy the attention the men give them.' Sharon's words ran through Vicky's head. 'And the attention they get from helping people in return for the latest phones and clothes.'

'Mr Jones?'

'The next one on the ladder.'

'Right, it's a ladder. And these girls get trapped in it. Drugs too.'

Alan rubbed at his nose again. 'Loss of their income or lifestyle is a big threat, too, so it keeps them quiet.'

'Who's your source, Alan?'

He picked up his roll again but thought twice about it, so dropped it back onto the plate. 'Girl called Juliana put me on to this boy who—'

'A *boy*?'

'Exactly. Turns out Ashlynn started out as a victim, but she ended up getting off on the abuse herself. Young teenage boys are her thing.'

'Christ.'

'Aye. You never think about that side, do you? Boys don't tell. And she certainly didn't. And there's a market for the pretty ones. The men pay double, so it's pretty lucrative, Vicks.'

'Why kidnap her?'

'Well, it could be because I've been hounding her. Or it could've been retribution for failing to put out. But it was probably because her latest victim started talking.'

Vicky shut her eyes. 'This boy was Noel.'

Alan gave her a round of applause. A couple of old ladies looked over at them. 'Got it in one.'

'What did Noel tell you?'

'A bit. Not a lot, but a bit. Didn't name Ashlynn, just explained that she was... How she was abusing him. Thing is, he loved it. Loved feeling like a man, but still, she was four years older than him. So it's abuse, whatever wolf-whistling builders think of it. And he told me about this girl that he knew. Poor thing was walking streets, right? Only thirteen.'

Emmy-Kate. Vicky folded her arms. 'Go on.'

'He said she got arrested and he was relieved.'

'Relieved?'

'Right. He thought she'd get help from a social worker or something.'

'Seems pretty wise for a fifteen-year-old.'

'Some kids, Vicky, they're forty before they're ten. Especially these. But.'

'But?'

'This girl got released without charge.' Alan slurped at his coffee. Way he was going, he'd need a bag of ketamine to bring himself down from all the uppers in his system. 'And I know the cop who signed it off.'

'Name?'

'I know he's been arrested and charged, Vicks.'

'Christ.'

'I'll keep quiet. Don't want to compromise the case against Ryan Ennis.'

Vicky shut her eyes. 'How did you know that?'

'Because he's connected to a doctor doing backstreet abortions for the girls. In deep himself.'

'Shite.'

Alan took out his vape stick and sucked on it. 'Aye.' His words mixed with his pluming exhalation.

'This sex ring Ashlynn's working for. Do you know who's involved?'

'Got a lead on the identity of the Mr Big.'

'Mr Big?'

'Not just that American hair metal band.' Alan took another suck of vape. 'Right, but I could never verify it.'

'Excuse me, sir.' The waitress was back, but her expression could curdle cream. 'Can you do that outside, please?'

'Aye, aye.' Alan got to his feet.

Vicky grabbed his wrist and stopped him. 'Give me the name first.'

'And where would be the suspense in that?' Alan smirked. 'No, I need to run this by my editor. Been a bit too loose-lipped here.' He shook his hand free, then sauntered off out of the café.

Vicky sat back, arms folded, watching him talking on the phone as he covered every square millimetre of the pavement.

It all made perfect sense.

The ladder of abuse, funnelling desperate kids of both sexes through the worst ordeal imaginable.

And one of their own grooming others to repeat it.

All for a Mr Big.

It just got worse and worse.

What she didn't know was whether Alan's decision to delay telling Vicky had any bearing on Noel's fate. Or if it was sealed by virtue of talking to Alan.

A van bumped up onto the pavement, just along from Alan. The door slid open and two big guys in balaclavas got out.

They shoved a hood over Alan's head, lifted him clean off his feet and hauled him into the van, his legs flailing.

The door wasn't even shut by the time the van shot off again.

24

Vicky stood on the pavement, phone pressed against her ear, looking up and down the Marketgait. The traffic was hitting that mid-morning flow, busy but still moving and not yet jammed. Nearby, two pairs of uniforms were interviewing passers-by, but Vicky knew it'd be a wasted effort. She'd been watching Alan and had seen nothing that could identify his abductors. 'Sir, I can't—'

'Step back!'

'What?'

'Just do it!'

Vicky pushed herself back against the wall of the café.

A white sports car slid up onto the pavement and stopped. It barely made a sound, like it had beamed down from orbit.

Forrester jumped out of the passenger seat, right in front of her. 'You okay?'

Vicky put her phone away. 'I'm fine.'

'Aye, that'll be shining bright.' Forrester patted Vicky on the arm. 'It's okay to admit—'

'I'm *fine*.' Vicky shook his hand off.

The driver door opened and Masson hopped out onto the

carriageway. 'I've got six teams scouring for that van. They won't get far.'

'You got plates?'

Masson grimaced. 'Same trick as on the bridge yesterday morning.'

'Same van?'

'No, that was a Mercedes, this is a Citroën.' Masson had his phone out. 'Same deal, white. Probably a rental like the Merc. Probably already dumped and torched, like the last one.'

'I hadn't heard.'

'No, well, you've been busy.' Masson looked over to the side. 'Inspector.'

'Hey.' Sharon tilted her head to the side, her forehead creasing. 'You okay, Vicky?'

'I'm fine.' Vicky held up a phone. 'I found this. Not that we'll be able to get into it, or that it'll help us any.'

'Get that to Jenny ASAP, aye?' Forrester was frowning at Vicky like she wasn't in any shape to be on duty. 'Listen, good work in finding Ashlynn. You two make a good team.'

'Thanks, sir.' Vicky felt the air dig through her clothes and flesh, right down to her bones. 'Alan had been speaking to someone who said that Ashlynn's a groomer for this sex ring.'

Forrester looked at Masson. 'That make sense to you?'

'Perfect sense, aye. Just... Did you get anything out of him?'

'Said she works for a Mr Big in Dundee. He was going to check with his editor whether he could share it. And that's when he was taken.'

Masson stared at the café. 'You think they targeted him?'

'Definitely. He's been getting close to them. Got a few contacts in Sharon's patch who named Ashlynn. Young girls who said she encouraged them into that world. And who said that Ashlynn groomed Noel.'

'You believe him?'

Vicky shrugged. 'Trust but verify, right?'

'Ain't that the truth.' Masson blew air up his face. 'Okay, gang.

We need a plan here. Ashlynn knows something. Can you ladies speak to her again? See if she'll talk to you.'

Sharon folded her arms. 'I was going to lead that, but we're waiting on her lawyer. Someone called Fergus Duncan.'

Forrester winced. 'Sure you've got some absolute wankers in Edinburgh, but I'd love to know if they come close to that wee prick.'

'They've all got their own special moves.' Sharon patted Vicky's arm. 'We'll head back and interview her. See if she can name names.'

'Cool beans.' Forrester opened the space car's passenger door. 'We'll head out and lead the hunt for Alan.' He gave Vicky a hard look. 'We'll do our best.'

'Thanks, sir.' Vicky watched the car swoosh off into traffic. She felt hollow. It wasn't like they'd taken Rob, just her ex. A total dickhead who was suing her for—

Shite! Rob!

She got out her phone and called him. Straight to voicemail.

'This is Rob. I'm probably teaching, so leave a message or drop me a text and I'll get back when I can. Cheers!'

'Rob, it's Vicky. Just checking you're okay.' Vicky ended the call, but instead of putting it away, she went online. No signs of any abductions in Arbroath, but sometimes news travelled slowly, especially from there. Nothing on Bella and Jamie's school in Carnoustie.

'You're not okay, are you?'

'I'm not, no.'

'Shock is a killer. You weren't close to him, were you?'

'Nope. He's just my daughter's father. Estranged as hell. He's such a knob.'

'Poor you. Alan Lyall *is* a knob'

'You know him?'

'Had some run-ins, aye. He was a bit of a prick at a case in Portugal a few years ago. Him and his mate from the *London Post*. There's only so many times you can kick that one arse, eh?'

~

DOWN IN HOLDING, someone was singing from one of the cells. At this time, he must've been seriously blootered last night to still be that far gone. And he was getting the words wrong.

Vicky's phone thrummed in her pocket.

Rob calling...

She answered it and looked around at Sharon, but she was talking to someone on her own mobile. 'Hey.'

'Hey, babe. I just got your VM. You okay?'

'I'm fine. Are you?'

'Aye?'

'And the kids?'

'At school. What's going on?'

'Nothing, really. Just having a paranoid day. That's all.'

'Right. Well, I don't quite believe you. Listen, I can get away from school this afternoon if you need me?'

'I'm fine. Seriously.'

'Okay.'

'Love you. Bye.' Vicky ended the call.

At the desk, Martin was hammering away at a report on his computer. He looked up at Vicky with the eyes of a man used to whiling away the hours with solitaire having to switch to a sudden spike of activity. 'Morning, Doddsy.'

Vicky splayed her hands on the counter. 'Here to take Ashlynn Thomas up for her interview.'

'Aye, you never were an early bird. Wee Considine took her up about ten minutes ago.'

Great. Vicky sighed. 'Right, cheers.'

'Some laddie, isn't he?'

'Daft sod is what he is.'

'The boy's keen, that's all.' Martin sat back down. 'Her brief still hasn't showed up yet, so you can get yourselves a bite to eat. I'll send him up to the canteen.'

'Cheers, Martin.' Vicky looked around. Aside from Sharon tapping away at her mobile, the custody suite seemed a bit empty. She looked back at Martin. 'Everything okay down here?'

Martin sat back and scowled. 'Everything's peachy, aye.' He yawned into his fist. 'Just about to collect the plates after dinner.' He stood up tall and set off across to the cells. 'Come on, Ry, give us your— OH MY FUCK!'

Vicky shot over.

Through the bars, Ennis lay on his side in the middle of the cell, convulsing like he was plugged into the mains.

Martin's hand shook as he got out his keys. 'Come on, come on, come on.' He managed to unlock the door.

But Vicky was first in, pressing her hand to Ennis's neck. 'Still alive.' But he was going to bite his tongue if she didn't act, so she held him down. 'Ryan, it's Vicky. We're going to save you, okay?'

'I'll call this in.' Martin darted back over to his desk.

Vicky cradled Ennis by the head to stop him smashing it off the floor. 'Get me a blanket!' But he was looking too far gone. Eyes rolling back in his head, spasms rocking his torso, arms and legs punching and kicking.

'Out the way!' The duty doctor barged Vicky against the wall.

Two of Martin's team joined him, crowding the tiny space.

Vicky felt like a spare part in there, so she left them to it. In the corridor, she shivered like she'd swallowed a bag of ice cubes.

Sharon narrowed her eyes. 'Someone's got to him.' She put her phone to her ear, then put it away. 'I heard of a case in London a few years back, where someone died in custody. The access records had been fudged.'

Vicky walked over to Martin's desk. 'Who was here?'

'Don't know.'

'You don't know? Your *one job* is to look after suspects!'

'No, I mean, it was just me and the lad here. And the lad's not going to poison someone, is he?'

'That means it's you, Martin.'

'Shite.'

'Is Raven here?'

'Aye. Cell two.' Martin pulled out his giant jailor's keyring and led them past the hubbub to Raven's cell.

Raven lay on his bunk, deadly still.

'Oh, piss it to shite!' Martin twisted a key into the lock and pulled the door open.

Vicky raced in, her heart fluttering.

Raven swung up to a sitting position. 'Are you letting me go?'

Vicky stopped dead. 'You're okay?'

'I'm in a jail cell in my own station, what the hell do you think? Of course not!'

Vicky clenched her fists. 'What did you do to Ennis?'

'Ennis? Eh?'

'He was in the cell next door. Someone's poisoned him!'

'You think I've any idea? I was sitting here, listening to someone trying to sing a couple of Climie Fisher numbers next door. That song was not called "Love Changes Anything" for crying out loud.'

'One of your lot got to him.'

'My lot. Right.' Raven flashed a wide grin. 'Sergeant, you should watch what you're saying to me. That mouth of yours will get you into deep trouble.'

'I don't know if you're confusing yourself with someone who's still a serving officer.'

'Sergeant.' Raven sighed. 'You'll pay for this. Mark my words.'

'You'll get your men to kidnap me?'

'Of course not.'

Vicky leaned back against the bars. 'See, I'm just back from meeting a source in a café. He was about to tell me who you're working for, but some guys in balaclavas abducted him.'

'I'm not—' Raven looked over to the side. 'Well, well. Masson's brought his favourite hatchet woman in.'

Vicky stepped aside to let Sharon into the cell.

'I overheard that, John. As slippery tongued as ever. You're keeping quiet, even about Alan Lyall being abducted.'

'Alan Lyall?'

'You know him, don't you?' Sharon smiled at Raven. 'The weird thing is, he gave us a lead on Ennis and now Ennis is on his way to hospital. Looks like he was poisoned. I presume it was someone working for you or with you. Which was it?'

'Get out of here.'

Sharon leaned in close. 'We found Ashlynn.'

'Who?' Raven was scowling at her. 'Oh, the lassie who was kidnapped. Do you want a round of applause? A slow clap? Well done.'

'She's talking.'

'Well, that's good. I imagine it's just a matter of seconds until you're letting me go and licking my boots, begging forgiveness.'

'No, you're not going anywhere except Perth prison. And Ennis has been talking too.'

'Stop lying, Inspector, it doesn't suit you.'

'You're the one who's lying, John. People are dying here. Kids are being sexually abused.' Vicky ducked her head, getting Sharon to drop out. 'We know about the doctor.'

Raven swallowed hard. 'What doctor?'

'The one who was signing Ennis off for a couple of years until you palmed him onto Masson. Is that how you got him to work for you?'

'You don't know what the hell you're talking about.'

'But you do, John. You know what else he's been doing? Performing abortions on some of the girls, right?'

'Shit.' Raven let his head go. 'Shit.'

'John, this is your only chance. We're not recording this, so you can deny it if you want. These men kidnap *children* and they abuse them. And you sit there, denying everything. Covering up these crimes. You'll never get out again.'

Raven sat back against the tiles and smoothed down his suit trousers. 'What's my way out of this?'

'Talk.'

'Sharon, I've walked this road many times. I know there's always a way out. Please, do me the courtesy.'

'Well, if you speak, and if it leads to convictions, you'll be doing your bit for society.'

'You know what I mean.' Raven licked his lips. 'Are you able to offer me some kind of enticement?'

'Aye, you stand up in court, admit what you've done, testify against people.'

'I'll get off?'

'You know it depends on what you give us.'

'Don't milk this, Sharon. Please.'

'Okay, so you tell us who the Mr Big is here? The boss.'

'It's all lads from Manchester. That's all I know.'

'So far you've only told us stuff we already know. For a DCI, you really don't know how this works, do you?'

'That's it.'

'What have they got on you?'

'Nothing.'

'So, you're abusing girls too?'

'No!'

'Right, so it's boys you're into?'

'What? God no.'

'What makes you—'

'They've cornered me into it.'

'How?'

Raven leaned back against the tiled wall. 'You wouldn't understand.'

'Try us.'

'No. But I'll give you a name.' Raven looked at Sharon, then at Vicky, then at his socked feet. 'Fergus Duncan.'

'The lawyer?'

'Him.'

'He's the Mr Big?'

'Not sure. But he's involved in the ring. Keeps good records too.'

25

Ornate lettering on a hanging sign read "Gray and Leech, Solicitors". Back in the glory days of Dundee, the office would've been one among many on Whitehall Street, but now it was just stuck in amongst generic high street stores. The place looked empty, but it wasn't even lunchtime.

Forrester was waiting outside, like he was just a punter checking the board for houses to buy. Or just idly wasting time.

Vicky stepped out onto the pavement and slammed the door. 'Sir.'

Forrester looked over, shaking his head. 'See how much they're charging for a three-bed in the Ferry?'

'Shouldn't be a surprise.' Vicky joined him by the door.

The lights were on inside, but it seemed painfully quiet. Then again, the firm had a few specialities, so stuff like estate planning and criminal defence would happen through the back, away from the glitzy high-money world of property law.

Sharon joined them on the pavement. 'I'm deferring to you two here.'

'Cool beans.' Forrester stood up tall. 'Still no sign of Alan, by the way.'

Vicky nodded, then pushed the door open.

Before she'd stepped in, a smiling secretary appeared like a genie, clutching her hands together. Her daffodil-yellow dress almost matched the paint on the walls. 'Can I help you?'

Vicky showed her warrant card. 'DS Vicky Dodds. Here to speak to Mr Duncan.'

'Ah, I think he was due on your patch today.'

'Mary, it's fine. I haven't left yet.' Duncan was standing in the doorway behind her. 'Come on through.'

Vicky stood her ground. 'We'd rather do this down the station.'

'Ah, yes. Ashlynn Thomas. The girl all over the news. Her mother called an hour ago. I'll be there as soon as I can.' And he slipped away through his doorway.

'Christ.' Vicky stormed off after him.

Duncan was standing in a kitchen area, pouring coffee from a filter jug into a mug, with a cartoon of a toff and a rifle, "Shooting Peasants". And Duncan was dressed like he was going shooting again, Vicky couldn't decide whether it was birds or poor people. 'Can I get you guys anything? This Colombian roast from Braithwaite's is to die for.'

'Just get your arse into the back of my car.'

Duncan laughed. 'You've always got a way with words, Sergeant.'

Vicky thumbed behind her. 'Let's go.'

Duncan raised his cup. 'I'm just having a coffee.'

'Do you want me to slap some cuffs on you?'

'You'd love that, wouldn't you?' Duncan glugged his coffee. 'Which client is this about, again?'

'No client.'

'So why are you here with your boss and—'

'I suggest you come with us.'

'I'm going nowhere.'

'Fergus Duncan, I'm arresting you for—'

'Christ.' Duncan finished his coffee and tossed the mug into the sink, where it clattered off something. 'This is where I threaten to call up the chief constable and you back down, isn't it?'

'You keep mentioning a relationship with her. Keep trying to use it to get your clients out of deep shit with it. But you really better hope she can get you out of this pickle you're in.'

'Right.' Duncan sighed. 'I'm going nowhere unless you tell me what this is about.'

'Let's start with where Alan Lyall is.'

'Never heard of him. Why should I?'

'Mr Lyall has been investigating a paedophile ring operating across much of northern Scotland.' Vicky waited for any reaction, but got none. 'Seems centred around Dundee. They're taking girls off the streets, abusing them, then shipping them south when they're over the age matching the predilections of their members.'

'That right?'

'Completely. We know about Raven, about Ennis, about the doctor.'

Duncan swallowed hard. 'Shit.' And his guts exploded with a violent fart. Then a damper sound. 'Oh no.' He clutched his trousers, at the back. 'Oh fuck me.'

Vicky snapped out her cuffs and wrapped them around his wrists. He absolutely stank, way worse than opening one of Bella's nappies way back when.

Duncan stood there, with the same calm demeanour, all arrogant and smug, even with soiled breeks. 'If you do me the favour of allowing me to change my trousers, I will go quietly. Please, don't make me beg for my dignity.'

'You really think a child abuser deserves dignity?'

'I've never touched anyone who didn't consent to it.' He clutched his trousers. 'Seriously, I need to clean this up.' He moved to waddle off.

Vicky grabbed his arm and stopped him. 'Why are you working with them?'

'It's just a financial arrangement. Seriously.' He let his head go, the shame and humiliation hitting him. 'The truth of it is, I have a permanent erectile dysfunction as a result of prostate cancer surgery. Everything's still there, it just doesn't work. No amount of Viagra can raise the flag. The only pleasure I can get is punishing young women. All above age and consenting.'

'Sounds like what you smell of.'

'Seriously, I'm laying my soul bare here. Please. Let me clean myself up, then I'll sing for my supper.'

Forrester raised his eyebrows. 'Come on, then.' He led him along the corridor towards the bathroom.

Vicky stood there with Sharon, both shaking their heads. 'What a mess.'

'Literally.' Sharon twisted her nose up. 'We need to get a cleaner in here to sort this out.'

'You think he's the top of the ladder?'

'What, the Mr Big?' Sharon pinched her nose. 'Probably. If what he says is true, he doesn't abuse the girls, but he makes the money. Probably has connections down south, gets the girls shunted off to the brothels and truck stops.'

A loud explosion rang out from down the corridor.

A gunshot, a big loud one.

Forrester!

26

Sharon handed Vicky a Styrofoam cup. 'You okay?'

Vicky cradled the cup in her hands and looked back along Whitehall Street, now filled with police cars and vans. A few journalists were lurking around, and a TV camera crew. She sipped the too-sweet tea and still shivered. 'I'm fine.'

'It's okay if you're not.'

'I'm shocked by his death.' Vicky raised a finger. 'Not *shocked* shocked, but... Stunned. Surprised.'

'It's an extreme thing to happen.'

'How the hell did he get a shotgun in there?'

Sharon slowly shook her head. 'All that hunting he's doing, right? Stands to reason he had his own. Brought it into work.'

'Right. I've dealt with him a few times. He had this way of getting under your skin. Really creepy. And he was always threatening us with going to the chief constable.'

'Anything in that?'

'Never really called him on it, but I suspect not. Then again, you don't want to get into that, do you?'

'No. I've seen people lose days to stupid meetings down in Tulliallan for that kind of nonsense. Scott a few times, obviously.'

'Obviously.'

'We're trying to make this country a safer place, but...' Sharon exhaled. 'Anyway. What did you—'

A car screeched to a halt in the middle of the road and Zoey jumped out. She grabbed a box from the back seat then slammed the door. The car shot off just as fast as it had arrived. She stopped with a sigh. 'Sorry.'

Vicky held her gaze. 'What are you sorry for?'

'Just... Never mind.' Zoey put on a brave smile and lugged her box onto the pavement. 'I'm here to work on the crime scene. Jenny asked me to tell you that Arbuthnott's on her way.'

'Well, it's a formality.' Vicky took another sip of scalding tea, but still shivered. Wasn't even windy, wasn't even that cold. 'Can you focus on the office?'

'Sure, sure.' Zoey set off towards the crime scene.

Sharon watched her go. 'You're lucky you've got such good CSIs. Our lot are all wankers.'

'All of them?'

'Well, not *all* of them, but most.'

'My brother works there.'

'Is he a wanker?'

'Not all of the time.'

Sharon finished her tea. 'I worked with Jenny back in her Lothian and Borders days.'

'Were you close?'

Sharon looked away. 'I know what happened to her boyfriend, put it that way.'

Vicky exhaled slowly. She finished her tea and looked around for a bin.

Forrester stood in the middle of the road, shaking his hands. Eyes shut, he was wearing a tracksuit a few sizes too big for him, covered with a dressing gown. His face was splattered red.

'Come on.' Vicky walked over and dumped her empty cup into a bin. 'Sir. How are you doing?'

'Should've bloody stopped it, Vicky.' Forrester ran his bottom teeth over his top lip. 'Daft sod shat himself and had this tracksuit to change into.' He shook his head. 'He's in there, passing me his soiled breeks and... I *heard* it. He had his shotgun in there with him. He got it stuck, thing was clunking, like he'd hit it off the side of the cubicle. Then I tried talking to him, tried getting him out, but he'd locked the door. So I kicked it open, just as he was swallowing the barrel. Pulled the trigger right in front of me.'

'There was nothing you could've done, sir.'

'Bollocks, Vicky. Don't give me that. Of course I could've stopped it. It happened right in front of me. I'm covered in his brains! Christ, I almost shat my own pants! That prick almost killed me. Just lucky he took his own life rather than going postal in there. He must've stuck the gun inside the folds of this tracksuit in his office. Bastard thing must've been hidden in there. When you play with fire like he was doing, you must know it's going to catch up with you, so you prepare. And when we got in here, he must've thought his days were numbered. Then he shot himself. Actually, keeching his breeks first was probably part of the plan. Maybe allergic to coffee. Means he needs to get a change of clothes. Still. Being involved with that gang, taking their money. Stands to reason he'd want to kill himself.'

'You believe what he said about his erectile dysfunction?'

Forrester shrugged. 'Who knows? Some lawyers can be slippery buggers, others are pillars of the community. Fergus Duncan was a bit of both, wasn't he?'

'Maybe.' Vicky looked inside the office, much busier than it was when they arrived. 'Raven said he kept good records. Did he mention anything to you?'

'He was talking about it, aye.' Forrester rubbed at his fingernails. 'Said something about how he'd documented everything we'd need. It's in a locked box in his office.'

'He give you the key?'

'No.' Forrester grinned. 'But he gave me the code.'

VICKY FOUND Zoey in Duncan's office.

Fergus Duncan was a Dundee United fan. He must've been

thirties at most, but he had signed shirts from the early eighties glory years before his birth. Muddied tangerine and black covered in random squiggles, and signed photos of the main players, action shots at pitchside, scoring goals and celebrating on pitches swarming with fans. In the middle was a photo of a man on the pitch, dancing for joy, wearing a replica shirt and cradling a baby in a tangerine top. Presumably Fergus Duncan and his father, so not before he was born.

A life snuffed out just like that.

Zoey was on her hands and knees poking and prodding at something. She looked around at them, her scowl visible through her crime scene mask. 'I've found a paper file box, but I can't get it open.'

Vicky's own suit crinkled as she walked over and crouched next to her. 'I've got the code.'

'Oh, well. That'll help.'

Vicky reached out a gloved hand and tapped it in. 2868. The light blinked red twice then green. Something clicked and Vicky eased it open.

The box was filed with cantilever layers, all containing paper files. She took out the nearest one and flicked through. Photographs, all timestamped and annotated. Notes from meetings. Transcripts of recordings. Some USB thumb drives.

Zoey had her tablet open, starting to catalogue the contents. 'What is it?'

'It's evidence against a paedophile ring in case he was caught.'

Zoey dropped her tablet onto the floor. 'He's a paedo?'

'Correct. We were onto him, but he took his own life. Chose the easy way out.'

'Blimey.' Zoey looked like she was going to fill her mask.

Vicky fixed her with a hard stare. 'It's *crucial* that you do this by the book, okay?'

'Okay.' Zoey picked up her tablet. It slipped again, but she caught it. 'No pressure, eh?'

Vicky gave her a smile. 'None.' She took another file and started sifting through it.

A dull thud came from the door. Sharon was standing there, her mask misted with condensation. 'Getting anywhere?'

'Sort of.' Vicky flicked through the document. 'You even heard of a Sidney Morecambe or a Philip Rourke.'

'Those are our Manc gangsters.' Sharon joined her in a crouch. 'And I know all about them. But we can do Mr Rourke for distributing child pornography, amongst many other crimes.'

Vicky turned the page. Photos of Fergus Duncan with John Raven and Ryan Ennis, together and apart, all taken from a distance, like they were being surveilled. 'Someone else has been taking these.'

'Mark Agnew?'

'Doubt it.'

'Think that's important?'

'Maybe.' Vicky found one of Fergus Duncan holding hands with a young girl. 'I mean, did you watch that *Spider-Man* cartoon when we were kids?'

'And his Amazing Friends? Ice Man and... Firestar?'

'Right, right. I mean, Ice Man was in those X-Men films, but whatever became of Firestar?'

Sharon laughed. 'You are a real geek.'

'It's my brother's fault.'

'So are a lot of things.' Zoey was shaking her head. 'Firestar was in the X-Men, just hasn't been in the comics for ages.'

'Spot another geek.'

'I've got two brothers who are even worse than Vicky's. And my ex is obsessed.'

'Euan?'

Zoey just rolled her eyes.

'Anyway.' Vicky pointed at the photos. 'In that cartoon, Spider-Man was a photographer, right? He'd set up his camera on a timer to take photos of him, then as Peter Parker, he'd sell them to the paper. The *Daily Planet*.'

'*Bugle*.' Zoey was shaking her head. 'The *Planet* was Superman's.'

'Right.' Sharon grinned. 'So you think Duncan's maybe done that?'

Vicky squinted at the shots. 'The focus is a bit off, so maybe.'

'But we should be looking for someone else who took these, right?'

'Right. Can't harm our case.' Vicky turned the page. 'Bingo.'

Another four shots of Mark Agnew, two solo, two with Emmy-Kate Mitchell. One holding hands in a park, another kissing her across a table set for dinner. Maybe in a restaurant, or maybe it was in a flat, Vicky couldn't tell. Still, there was at least one where they were out in public. So he was brazen with his predation. Like he was begging to be caught, even with his aviator shades and baseball cap.

Another page detailed Agnew's movements and all of his liaisons with Emmy-Kate.

Vicky looked up at Sharon, reading over her shoulder. 'This is very thorough. Maybe there's a PI who works for the firm, someone who Duncan got to tail Agnew.'

'Whoever it is, they're doing a good job of it.'

'Right.' Vicky rifled through more pages of photos, all of Mark Agnew. Six months earlier, the photos changed to another girl, similar age and appearance to Emmy-Kate but with a longer nose and rounder cheeks. Another few pages and there was a girl marked as "Juliana". 'Shit.'

'Yep. It all checks out.' Sharon grabbed another file from the bottom and opened it. Then frowned. 'That's Ashlynn Thomas.'

Vicky took the page. And it was her. A few years younger, her face puffed out with puppy fat before her current lean look, but definitely her. Those eyes. That crease in her forehead.

Vicky flicked through the pages, watching the girl grow up into the young adult she was now. 'There aren't any men here.'

Sharon crouched again. 'Because she's an abuser, like Alan told you. She's a victim of this, sure, but she's become a central part of it. There are no girls to abuse without her acting as the benevolent aunt.'

'You're right. Christ.' Vicky pulled out another file and opened it. More of Ashlynn, back as a young girl. 'Well, this is a double.' She made to shut it.

'Wait.' Sharon took the file and pointed at the side. 'There's a man's hand there.'

Vicky looked at it, but it was just a blurry shape. Could be anything.

Sharon turned the page and there was just one photo. Through a window, Ashlynn was standing in an apartment, wearing expensive lingerie, her arms and legs angled like she was dancing for someone.

On the sofa, a man sat with his top off, leaning forward, hands on his hips.

Vicky gasped.

'You recognise him?'

It was Jason Kellas. Agnew's boss.

27

The *Indignity* office foyer was flooded with light. Hard dance music pounded Vicky's ears. Adverts played on tall screens either side of the reception desk. She glanced behind her, where Considine and Karen were ready in two cars, then nodded at Sharon to take lead as the senior officer.

Sharon powered up to the desk and leaned on the front. 'Looking for Jason Kellas.'

The receptionist wouldn't have been in the target range of Kellas or Agnew for a good twenty years. And her bright-red hair didn't give her that All-American prom queen cheerleader look they seemed to want in their Dundee girls. 'I'm sorry, but Mr Kellas isn't here.'

'So where is he?'

'He left for lunch about twenty minutes ago.'

'You mind checking with his PA?'

'Of course.'

Vicky joined Sharon by the desk and faced away, keeping an ear on the call for any warning signals. 'Twenty minutes ago might've been when Kellas heard of Fergus Duncan's suicide. There could be other cops on his payroll.'

'Right. Someone to poison Ennis.'

'Shite. Aye.'

Keyboard clicking came from the other side of the desk.

Vicky swung around to check the receptionist wasn't warning Kellas.

She was looking up. 'I spoke to Ben, who works for Mr Kellas. He said Mr Kellas has meetings all afternoon and probably won't be back today.'

Vicky smiled. 'You won't mind if we look for ourselves?'

'Of course I mind. Who—'

'Police.' Vicky showed her warrant card. 'DS Dodds. DI McNeill. So, if you've got any CCTV footage?'

'Course we do.' The receptionist twisted her screen around and it showed a four-up display in full colour, timestamped at just before noon.

On the top left, Kellas walked through the reception area, then appeared on the top right just outside, where he slipped off the side of the screen. A few seconds later and in the bottom left screen, a Tesla SUV shot out of a space and made for the Kingsway.

Vicky leaned forward. 'Go back a few frames.' She got out her phone while the receptionist wrestled with the controls and hit dial. 'Jenny, it's Vicky. Need you to run a plate for me.'

JASON KELLAS LIVED in a plot that seemed to take up half of Broughty Ferry. A huge mansion, presumably belonging to a jute baron back in the day, living a life out here while his workers toiled in one of Dundee's many factories. Times had changed, but Kellas had a similar sweatshop up on the Kingsway, making digital goods instead of real ones. And a lot more money.

Vicky parked opposite the address and scanned the area as her seatbelt slid up. 'Some place, eh?'

Sharon was checking her phone. 'Right enough. Still no sightings or ANPR hits.'

'He *has* to have come here.' But Vicky knew it was a hope at best. 'Come on.' She opened her door and got out. The wind had picked up and dragged a bitter claw across her face.

Sharon marched across the road, at a pace Vicky needed to run to catch up. The gate was open and there were signs of life inside the huge house. Lights strobing in the room at the front, a muted din cutting through the windows.

Vicky followed Sharon across the pebbles, clutching her baton tight, then pressed the bell and stepped back, arms folded. They waited in silence, listening to the sounds coming from inside, behind the pale-grey double-sized front door. The kind of cartoons Bella watched, that level of inane din, even worse than the Spider-Man, Scooby-Doo and She-Ra cartoons she watched as a kid. Right?

The deep thuds stopped and the door opened. A woman peered out, mid-thirties with blonde hair thrown back in a pony-tail. 'Can I help?'

'Police, ma'am.' Vicky showed her warrant card. 'DS Dodds. This is DI McNeill. Can we speak to your husband?'

'What's he done?'

'Just need a quick work, ma'am. Is he here?'

'No, he's not. What's going on?'

Behind her was a blur of motion, a small girl chasing after a smaller girl, both blonde haired just like their mother. And very young.

'We need to speak to him in connection with an inquiry. Has he been here today?'

'Not since first thing. Jason leaves about eight o'clock, just after breakfast.'

'And he hasn't been home since?'

'That's what I said, yes.' She put her hands on her hips.

'We understand his car came back here approximately twenty minutes ago.'

'Well, if he did, I didn't see him. I've been busy clearing up after my children. And we've got guests this weekend, so I've had to make up the spare rooms.'

'Are you sure you didn't see him?'

'Look, this is a big property, as I'm sure you can see. There are a couple of entrances. Maybe Jason popped in and I didn't hear him. I don't know.'

'Does your husband own any other properties? Or any friends or family he could—'

'No. You need to tell what this is all about. Now.'

How the hell did you tell a woman her husband was molesting teenage girls behind her back?

Vicky smiled at her, trying to disarm her. 'It's a pressing matter, that's all. We just need to speak to him.' She handed over a business card. 'Get him to call me if you hear from him.'

'Of course.' She shut the door, and a thunk indicated that she'd bolted it too.

'Dead end.' Sharon let out a deep sigh. 'Where next?'

'I've got an idea.'

VICKY PLACED the document on the table and slid it so the top of the page sat at the halfway mark.

Ashlynn had to stand up to reach far enough to pick it up. She recoiled like it was on fire, and glowered at Vicky, but her eyes were bulging. 'Where did you get that?'

'You know the man in that photo?'

Ashlynn looked at her lawyer.

A Legal Aid suit in his fifties with the scar tissue on his cheeks of someone serious about their drinking. He gave a tight nod, which made his jowls wobble. 'You don't have to answer that.'

'Ashlynn, this man's name is Jason Kellas.' Vicky gestured at the page. 'You seem pretty close to him in that photo.'

'How do you figure that?'

'He's holding your hand.'

'My mum had left me in a café in the Overgate. He was helping me find her. I didn't know his name.'

'See, you should've listened to your lawyer.' Vicky put a page down on the table. 'This is you and him from two weeks ago.'

Ashlynn sat back and swallowed hard.

'You want to admit you know him?'

She shook her head.

'Time was, I'd have to say to the tape what your reaction was, but these days, it's all on video.' Vicky pointed at the camera. 'Next item, do you know this man?' She put a copy of a photo on the table. 'You know his name, don't you?'

Ashlynn took a brief glimpse of it, then looked over at the wall, away from the camera. 'What are you trying to achieve here?'

'Get to the truth, Ashlynn. Because of you, young girls and boys are being abused. Some are being killed.'

She looked back at Vicky. 'You have no idea what you're talking about.'

'No? Because we have every idea what you've been doing, Ashlynn. You're the centrepiece of this whole organisation. You were abused at the start, no doubt about it.' Vicky held up the photo of Kellas with her. 'These show how long it's been going on.' She added one of Agnew. 'They show what happened to you. The abuse you endured. These older men having sex with you when you were still a child. Forcing themselves on you. But then, they get tired of you, right? You're too old for them.' She tapped the page with Agnew hugging her. 'So Mr Kellas passed you on to Mr Agnew. He abused you for a while, then he passed you on to someone else. Am I right?'

'This is such shit.'

'You're one of the lucky ones. You're nineteen and you seem to have your freedom. Don't seem too traumatised by your ordeal, right? Because you knew what'd happen, didn't you? They'd spit you out, so you lucked out when you met a girl who looked like you. Younger, similar background to you. Hated her parents. Maybe just one of them. Maybe just a grandparent. Who knows. But you saw something that these men wanted. And you introduced her to Mr Kellas. He took her virginity just like he'd taken yours.'

Ashlynn was shaking her head. 'Shut up.'

'And they rewarded you for it. Paid you? Gave you stuff, maybe?'

'Shut up.'

'And you found another. Then another. Juliana, Emmy-Kate. Others.'

'Shut up.'

'And you started finding boys, right? Boys like Noel.'

'Noel?'

'Or Dax, whatever he chose to call himself. We know about you and him. That you were abusing him, sexually. That's right, isn't it?'

'It wasn't abuse. He's a boy.' But something was breaking inside her. Her lip was quivering.

'Ashlynn, there's no doubt that you have been abusing boys. It's the same scam, just in reverse. You pick up girls for these men, then you find boys for yourself. Do you have sex with them, or do you just hurt them?'

'Shut up!' Ashlynn slumped back in her chair. 'Shut the fuck up!'

'I'm not going to stop until you tell us what you did. Everything. What you did to these girls. To these boys. To Noel.'

'Shut the fuck up!'

'Noel is downstairs in the mortuary. He's dead. Frozen solid until your defence lawyer can do their own independent autopsy.'

'What?' She looked at her lawyer, who didn't seem to even be awake, then back to Vicky. 'What are you talking about?'

'You're complicit in the murder of Noel Russell.'

'No! They kidnapped me!'

'Same time they kidnapped Noel?'

'Yes! We were supposed to be meeting!'

'Right.'

'I swear. I was in the flat, studying. I went to meet him by the Caird Hall, but they took him.'

'Who did?'

'I don't know.'

'And I don't believe you. Because Noel got petrol poured over him and threatened. He tumbled out of the back of a moving van. Meanwhile you got to have cups of tea in a furniture shop. Doesn't seem the same to me.'

Ashlynn stared at the desk, scratching at the wood. Her scent wafted across the room, that sweat mingled with chemicals bleeding from her body. Coke or ecstasy or speed. 'They were just going to scare him.'

'Noel?'

'Right.'

'Who was?'

'I don't know their names. Our Kid. Sid, maybe. They just said they were going to scare him. The plan was to take him to Tentsmuir Forest, pour petrol over him, threaten him, give him a scare or an arse kicking. Then leave him deep in Fife, reeking of petrol, minus a few teeth, and he had to walk back home across the bridge contemplating his life. But he must've got away.'

'Petrol is a slippery substance. Sounds like he tumbled over the side. The way he landed, Ashlynn, it broke his neck. He was dead when he entered the water.'

'Shit.'

'Why did they do it?'

'Because he was saying he was going to speak to that journalist.'

'You know his name?'

'Alan Lyall. I told them about him.'

'They've abducted him too.'

Ashlynn shrugged. 'So?'

'What was he going to say?'

'I can't.'

'Ashlynn, not speaking to us isn't an option here, okay?'

'I can't!'

'You don't have a choice. None at all.'

'It wasn't just me abusing Dax.'

'Go on?'

'Jason was too.'

'Jason Kellas?'

Ashlynn nodded.

Vicky frowned at Sharon next to her. That didn't match their understanding of his MO. Vicky sat back and tried to act calm, but her heart was racing. 'That jars with what we know about him.'

'Jason swings both ways, as my mum would say. It's an either/or thing with him. Sometimes boys on their own, sometimes both at the same time.'

'Were you involved?'

She nodded. 'A few times.'

'With Noel?'

'Aye.'

'And when you were young?'

'Sometimes these kids needed their Auntie Ash to help them out.' She shook her head again. 'Jason paid them well to keep quiet. Thing is.' She nibbled at a painted nail. 'He didn't know that Dax had sussed out who he really was.'

'Wait, he did this anonymously?'

'Right. He's a rich man but he's not famous. I mean, he was always honest with me because he loved me. To all the others, he was called Fred. And they believed it. But Dax... He knew who Jason really was. He worked at that company. Not officially. Jason didn't know, he was just being coached by Mark. Kid was obsessed with that game and knew more than anyone else about it.'

'Is that how you found Noel?'

'No.' Ashlynn bit a big chunk of thumbnail off and spat it onto the table. 'One day, I was waiting on Jason at his flat. And Dax just walked in. This beautiful boy. Like an angel. He had an attitude, but I liked that in a boy. And Jason did too.'

'Wait, you said Jason's flat?'

Ashlynn scowled at her. 'Are you stupid or something?' She shook her head. 'Jason isn't going to be meeting us at home. Or in a hotel.'

'So he has a flat?'

'Honey, he's got a whole block.'

And it hit Vicky. Where she'd caught Mark Agnew abusing Emmy-Kate.

Expensive apartments.

A discreet concierge.

Privacy. Luxury. A place to put up the girls and boys.

28

'Shit.' Vicky stopped and jumped out of the car, leaving the engine running.

Kellas's Tesla was here, wedged between a Lexus and an Audi. No sign of him inside.

Vicky looked over at the building. The place they rescued Emmy-Kate and arrested Mark Agnew and Phil Rourke. She set off and her phone rang.

Forrester calling...

Vicky stabbed her phone and hit answer. 'We're there. Any update on his movements?'

'Phone hasn't been on since, so hard to get a read. You know the drill.'

'Sure do. Okay. Thanks. And Alan?'

'Nope. Sorry.'

'Okay. Cheers.' Vicky ended the call and pocketed her phone. 'I'm heading in.' She set off across the car park, anger thudding in her ears as she stepped into the reception area. And she stopped dead.

Noel Russell's route into the world of sin and degradation, the path to his death, was laid bare in front of her.

Behind the desk, Jim Russell beamed at them, his teeth catching the light. Dressed up in a stupid uniform. 'Alrighty, guys!' Then he frowned, lost to something. 'Wait. You. I know you.'

Vicky walked right up to the desk. 'You're back at work pretty soon.' Too soon. Way too soon.

'Got no choice.' Russell folded his arms. 'Behind on my rent, you know? Get chucked out, so I'm working double shifts. Besides, it takes my mind off what happened to my boy.' He plastered his smile back on. 'I take it you've got a lead for me?'

'Not quite.' Vicky waited for Sharon to join her. 'Is Mr Kellas here?'

'Mr Kellas?'

'Jason Kellas. Your boss. He owns this block of flats.'

'I, eh, haven't seen him.'

'Well, his car's outside.'

'Ah. Okay. So I had to go for a jobbie about ten minutes ago, so—'

'Where is he?'

'I swear, I've not seen him.'

Vicky let out a sigh. 'I wish people would stop lying to us.'

'I swear, I've not—'

'His car's outside!'

'And I went for a dump!'

Vicky stood up tall. 'We know what goes on here. Us finding Mark Agnew here with a thirteen-year-old girl wasn't an isolated incident, was it? We know Kellas uses it for his sex games.'

Russell stared down at the desk. 'This is a load of shite.'

'No.' Vicky grabbed his lapel. 'Children are being abused here. And you turn a blind eye to it.'

'*Children?*' Russell's forehead was twitching. 'No way.'

'They're all under sixteen!'

Russell was lost to something. 'But they seem older.'

'And Kellas is paying you to keep it quiet. While your local fame distracts people from it. And your son's death is related to what's going on upstairs.'

Russell swallowed, his eyes tearing up, with the disgust of a guilty man, or just a complicit one. 'What?'

'Noel met a girl called Ashlynn here. She was abusing him.'

'Fuck.' Russell picked up his computer screen and hurled it at the wall behind him, denting the plasterboard. 'Fuck!'

Sharon hopped over the desk and grabbed him. 'Come on, sir. This is evidence.'

Russell was shaking his head and wouldn't move. 'He told me he was seeing a girl, but I didn't know it was *her*. He said she was older. His mate, that Hayden kid, he was all, "go on, son". When I was that age, I'd have given my right nut to shag an older bird. My mates were all trying it on with younger birds, but I wanted someone with maturity.' He was crying, tears streaming down his cheeks. 'Can't believe I've... Noel... Shite. Wee Noel.'

'Sir, we need to speak to Mr Kellas. He's behind this. He's behind what happened to your son.'

'I've no idea.' Russell sucked in breath. 'And I've just smashed up my computer. Shite and onions.'

Sharon crouched down and picked up the monitor, cradling it like a newborn, then set it back on the desk. 'It's still working.'

'Huh.' Russell tapped at his keyboard. 'I'll check the CCTV for you.' Then he looked like he was going to punch the monitor again. 'No, sorry. He's not been here.'

'You're sure?'

'Aye. Fancy system here. Cameras trigger automatically. Don't ask me how it works, but if he's been here, he's done that whole switching footage thing, you know? Like in films?'

'Right.' Sharon looked at Vicky. 'You got any ideas?'

That fluttering in her gut, that dread that crushed her skull that a child molester was going to get away with it. 'I'm all out.'

Russell frowned and started searching a drawer under his desk. 'Wait, I've got a mobile number. Mr Kellas told me to dial in the direst emergency?' His fingers were dancing across the keypad of his phone.

'Hold on, soldier.' Sharon gripped his wrist. 'Let's not be too hasty here, okay?'

Vicky snatched the card out of his wrist and snapped it, then texted it to Jenny and hit dial.

'Hey, Vicks, I'm kind of snowed under here.'

'Need you to check this number. Just texted you a photo.'

'That's... You can't text a photo.'

'Pretty please.'

'Running it now.' Tap tap tap. Sigh. 'It's off, Vicks.'

'Great.' Vicky looked back at the reception desk. They were going to have to scour this whole building, searching for clues. Which would take weeks. Maybe Kellas hadn't been as careless as Agnew. Maybe he'd run away.

But where?

Manchester? Maybe those goons he was working with would help him escape.

'Vicks?'

She clutched her mobile tighter. 'What's up?'

'Well, you're in luck. That phone's just gone online. Not that I'm a betting girl, but I'd say it's at the V&A.'

29

V icky ducked her head and powered on, running like she was still at school, still able to sprint.

The V&A museum was up ahead, off to the side, the stacked latticework that didn't quite look stable enough to stand freely. Cars and buses swept past, bunching up at the traffic lights.

Vicky put her phone to her ear. 'You got him?'

Sharon sighed down the line. 'Traffic in this place is worse than Edinburgh. I'll be *hours* getting out.'

Vicky took a glance to the right, no cars, and bounced across the road. She slowed to walking pace, breathing like she'd just run a marathon rather than a few hundred yards and joined a coachload of students. They sounded like Glasgow, looked like Glasgow. Big enough to let Vicky blend in, at least height-wise, unlike the school kids up ahead, who were primary age. Bella's age, Jamie's age.

She stopped by the small pond, that had so bewitched Bella when they visited yesterday, and looked through the tunnel. No sign of Jason Kellas over by the river.

The traffic was bumper to bumper. No sign of him over the other side, by the hotels and apartments springing up.

Up ahead, the *Discovery* sat in its dock next to the visitor centre, the masts standing proud over the city. Beyond was the twin supermarkets, Tesco and Ashworth's, or she could head right and into the city centre.

Wait.

A blue Tesla sat in the small loading bay up ahead.

A white van pulled in as traffic piled past.

Kellas got out of the car, looking like a man on the run. He banged the back of the van and the door slid open. Two men inside, looking back the way.

Right at Vicky.

One of them pointed towards her.

Kellas followed their look, then back at them. He tried to jump up, but they pushed him back. He landed on the pavement and something was flung out of the van at him. The wheels spun and the van shot off away from them, weaving in and out of the Perth-bound traffic.

Kellas wrestled the object off him and stood up, dusting himself down.

Alan got to his feet, gagged and bloody. A fresh scar lined his cheek.

Vicky ran towards them, her feet rattling off the pavement, phone against her cheek. 'Sir, get units to outside the *Discovery*. An ambulance! Now!' She pocketed her phone and launched herself shoulder-first at Kellas, driving him into his car with a sickening thud.

She landed on him, wrestling for his hand.

But he was too quick for her. He grabbed her wrist and flipped her over, almost under his car. Something bit into her chin, something cold and metal.

A knife.

She lay prone. 'Jason Kellas, I'm arresting you—'

'What?'

'—child abuse, multiple counts, you sick bastard. My colleagues are on their way. Give it up now.'

Kellas was looking around. At her, at the road, at Alan lying on the pavement, then back towards the museum, then towards the supermarkets.

Karen and Considine were barrelling towards them, eating up the asphalt.

'Shite!' Kellas pushed up to standing and raced away from them, head bowed, knees pumping hard.

Vicky rolled over and kicked up to standing. 'Alan, stay here!' She shot off after Kellas.

'Mmf mmmf!'

Vicky followed Kellas's path towards the museum, back towards his flat. She was narrowing the gap, but he was close to the queue. Easy to lose himself in there, cause enough confusion that he could get away.

Forrester and Sharon were running towards them.

Kellas spotted them and stopped, looking behind at Vicky, then over the road.

As she closed on him, she could follow his thinking, all the paths closed off.

Except one.

Kellas powered on towards the museum, hitting the narrow tramline running through the wedge taken out of the building, over the small lochs.

Vicky kicked on, closing in on him by each step.

Kellas took the turn along the waterfront. The Tay was all grey in the noon sunlight, dark clouds against the blue sky.

Vicky snapped out her baton and threw it, cracking it off the back of his knee.

Kellas went down in a heap and Vicky took three giant strides then launched herself through the air. She landed on him, breathing hard, and pressed her knee into his back. No getting away this time.

'Jason Kellas, I'm arresting you for several counts of sexual abuse of a minor.' She hauled him up to standing, arm twisted behind his back. 'Do you understand?'

He jerked around, slashing his knife through the air between them.

Vicky jumped back, but caught the blade on her wrist. Her whole arm screamed out. She lashed out with her baton and cracked it off his wrist. 'Would you just *stop*?' She slapped her cuffs on him and pushed him over to the bench and sat him down.

But it was too easy. Far too easy. All the police corruption she'd uncovered, all because of his abuse. All the lives ruined.

'How much?'

Vicky frowned. 'What?'

'How much to let me jump over the side?'

'You haven't got enough.'

'A hundred million.'

'Still nowhere near enough.'

'Come on. You were complaining about a grand's worth of in-app purchases. Just a million would change your life. A hundred times that. You'd be a lottery winner.'

'No thanks.'

'Come on. I know how much cops earn. Do it.'

'You know how much Mancunian gangsters earn too.'

'They're friends.'

'Phil Rourke? Sid Morecambe?'

'Right. I was at university with Phil. He got in with a bad crowd. Almost dragged me down with him. Took me on a drug deal with him to this port near Liverpool. What a rush, but I needed to get out. That seeded the idea for *Indignity*, though.'

'It's a stupid name for a game.'

'You say that, but I'm the one who can buy you.'

'Is it some gang code?'

Kellas shook his head. 'My old man was a huge fan of Deacon Blue. That Dundee connection. It's the inverse of their song, *Dignity*.'

'Seriously?'

'Nobody else knows that.' Kellas looked right at her with his doe eyes. 'Seriously, we can save everyone a lot of hassle here. Let me go, I'll pay you two hundred million quid.'

The truth was Kellas had more money than Police Scotland. Forget fannies like Fergus Duncan, Kellas could afford high-end

London lawyers. He could crush any prosecution and buy his freedom.

Vicky could see it all so vividly. Kellas getting off with Noel's murder, with what he did to Ashlynn, to Juliana, to Emmy-Kate. Walking away a free man. Maybe suing Police Scotland, ruining Vicky's career.

And maybe more people would die.

Vicky snapped on a glove and picked up the knife by the handle. 'Come on.' She grabbed Kellas by the arm. 'Let's get you down to the station.'

'Seriously, I can give you three hundred million.'

Pocket change to a man like him.

'I'm not taking your money.'

'That's how you're playing it, huh? Very noble. Thing is, if you won't take my money, hundreds will. I'll be out before dawn and my lawyers will see that none of it sticks.'

Vicky looked around. No sign of Sharon or Forrester. And nobody was watching, no eager eyes inside the museum. She held the knife tight in her hand.

'Maybe I'll sue you, Vicky. Abuse of process or something. Maybe show your wee boy some more of my video games. What was his name again? Jam—ugh!'

Vicky impaled Kellas right through the genitals.

Kellas stared at her for a few seconds before he screamed, loud and high. He collapsed back against the bench and blood trickled all over his pale jeans, soaking them a deep red.

Vicky had gone too far. He was bleeding out. She'd hit the femoral artery.

Shit.

What had she done?

Sharon stepped between them, pinching Kellas's neck. 'He'll be dead within a minute.'

'You saw that?'

Sharon nodded.

'I didn't do that just because he was a child molester. He was coming after my children next.'

'You need to be quick.' Sharon gestured with the knife still in Vicky's hands, dripping with blood. 'Right now, you need to cover this up as an accidental death. You need to prove it was a fight to the death. You acted in self-defence.'

Vicky took one look at the knife and knew she had no choice here. That bastard had poked the bear. She turned the blade around and stabbed herself in the abdomen.

30

T he lights were way too bright. Something beeped next to her. She was lying in a bed. A hospital bed. At least she had her own room.

'You've been operated on, Vicky.' Forrester was standing by the window, bleached by the bright lights in the courtyard outside. Must be Ninewells. 'You're in recovery, though.'

'What happened?'

'What do you remember?'

Vicky woke up and it felt like someone had stabbed her.

Shit. Someone had.

Herself.

'Don't remember anything.'

'Well, it was touch and go for a bit.' Forrester stepped forward and she could make out his face in the dim room. 'He got you good, though. But not as good as you got him.'

'Where's Rob?'

'He's getting a coffee. You scared him half to death.' Forrester laughed. 'Which is less than Kellas.'

'What happened?'

'He won't be abusing any more kids.' Sharon was there too,

sitting by the bed, hands clasped together. 'He died. Bled out by the museum.'

Vicky shut her eyes and felt the room swim around her. 'His poor wife and kids.'

'Well, I've spoken to Mrs Kellas. She didn't know about his... extracurricular activities. Now wasn't the time. I expect she'll keep the company going until she can sell it to someone. Anyone. Maybe she'll make a substantial donation to some charities to help fight against human trafficking and rehabilitate victims like Emmy-Kate. Oh, she's now talking big time. Going to be a lot of convictions, Vicky. Thanks to you.'

'Look, his death, it's—'

'Nobody needs Kellas hanging around. Not his wife, not his kids. Nobody.'

'But I—'

'Shh. It wasn't your fault, Vicky.' Sharon was staring hard at her. 'I was there, I saw the whole thing. You were brave. He could've got away. He pulled a knife on you, for crying out loud.' She smiled. 'If only I'd been a few seconds sooner. But, whatever happened, you did the right thing. You acted in self-defence. Someone was going to die either way.'

Vicky had to look away. She had no choice. That bastard was coming after her kids.

Forrester was nodding along with it, emphasising every beat. 'Ennis died too. Poisoning. Someone got to him. Someone on the inside. Sharon here and Masson have got their work cut out unearthing the full extent of it.'

'Will you find them?'

Sharon shrugged. 'I don't know. But it's good seeing you back amongst the living. Keep it that way.' She pushed up to standing. 'Now, I've got a hungry cat to feed back in Bathgate, so I'll be in touch.'

'I'd say it's been a pleasure.' Vicky winced. 'But my guts feel like a Forfar bridie.'

Sharon smiled. 'Keep out of trouble, you hear?'

'You too.' Vicky watched her go, then switched her focus to Forrester. 'Sir, I need to—'

'Rest. You've been through a hell of an ordeal.'

'No, I mean, I—

'Vicky, you've taken down a sex ring. Take this as a victory. Oh, and when you're back on duty, you'll be an Acting DI.'

'What?'

'Raven's singing his heart out. Soutar's asked me to step up to Acting DCI. I can give you MacDonald or get one of Considine or Woods to act up too?'

'Woods.'

'Done.'

'Hey, Vicks.' Alan stood in the doorway, resting on his drip. 'You look as bad as I feel.'

'Charming.'

Forrester stepped over to the door. 'I'll give you guys some space.' He left them to it.

Alan took Sharon's seat, resting against his drip. 'Thanks, by the way. You saved my life.'

'I'm sure you irritated them to the point where they'd rather kick you out of a van than listen to your rancid chat.'

He laughed. 'I'm injured, badly. Nothing like your surgery and all that, but I'll be on this drip for a few days. They fed me shite.'

'What, crisps?'

'No, actual shite. Dung. Cow shite. And some dog shite too. Said I've been spouting enough of it, that it's time I got a taste for it. I'm on so many drugs, it'll be all over my system for a week.' He scowled. 'Look, this whole thing has been a turning point for me. Made me think a lot about us.'

'What, you want to be a father figure to Bella?'

'The opposite.' He shook his head. 'I love the rush of the story, even being force fed dung. And I'm going to make a mint off this experience. Books, Vicks. I'll be an actual author. Keep the kid, Vicky, I'll send you a cheque each month.' He paused, licking his lips. 'If she is mine.'

If Vicky could've moved, she would have thrown the little

creep out of the window. 'How dare you? Trying to weasel out of child support by—'

'Come on, Vicks, we weren't exactly exclusive, were we?'

'I was!'

'Aye, aye.'

'Look, Alan. You owe me money for Bella. A lot of money. If it takes a paternity test to get you to man up then so be it...'

'Excellent.' He took his time getting to his feet. 'I just want to dot the I's and cross the T's. That's all. Be sure I'm paying my own debts and not Scott Cullen's.'

'*Scott Cullen?*'

'Come on, Vicks. Big sexy guy like that. Heard all about it from his old flatmate. Rich.'

'That's complete bullshit, Alan. As much as it pains me to admit, Bella's your daughter.'

'Get the test done, you'll get your money.' Alan hobbled off out of the room with his saline drip.

Vicky lay back in the bed, wishing she could go after him, scream in his ear.

Scott Cullen being Bella's father? Christ.

Hardly.

Guy might've thought he was a Grade-A shagger, but he was always too pissed to get it up.

The door flipped in, shrouded by the familiar tang of machine coffee.

Rob was in the doorway, eyebrows up. 'You're awake!' He set his cup down and rushed over, grabbing her and burying her in a cuddle.

'Hey, you'll burst my stitches!'

Rob let her go and stood up, hands in pockets like he didn't know what the hell to do. 'I've been so worried about you. I thought you were going to die.'

'I'm made of tough stuff. Where—'

'Kids are with your parents. I left school as soon as I heard.'

He touched the bandages on her stomach. 'Are you okay?'

'I'll live.' Vicky winced. 'You should see the other guy.'

AFTERWORD

Hey,

I hope you enjoyed ready that!

These books have been such a strange thing for me. Writing about my hometown and area.

I initially outlined this as FALLEN, the sequel to SNARED way back in 2015, but I reused most of that story for the Fenchurch book, KILL WITH KINDNESS. The idea was based on the characters from the second novel I wrote — relax, it was rubbish and I have no intention of republishing it. It's weird how ideas go round and round like that — the fifth Cullen novel was based on the first one I wrote, which was even worse, but it also featured the video games company in this book as Cullen ventured north to his hometown of Dalhousie (I really wish I'd not invented a town and actually gone with Carnoustie, but hey ho). Anyway, for this one I kept the boy falling off the Tay Bridge and went with a very different story. It's been a brutal experience researching and writing it, I have to say, but I hope it's an eye-opener for you and that you enjoyed it.

My gran and my Great-Uncle Syd (he really is great, honest) both went to Rockwell High back in the thirties and forties. The school itself closed down in 1997 when it merged with Kirkton

High to form Baldragon Academy, and the site itself has been used as a further education centre, but Dundee City Council are trying to sell it off just now. There was a school song, "Rockwell and Right", that I remember my Gran singing to me when I was a wee fat laddie, but I can't find on the internet. Uncle Syd doesn't remember and nor does Alistair, a friend of my mum's who found a vague reference in a poem. I seem to be the only person my gran told me about it. Very strange and shows the fragility of history. If you do remember it or know someone who does, please let me know!

Whether there's a third book depends on how sales go for this one. I'll keep an eye on it and let you know if I do another one.

Thanks to **Kitty** for helping with the initial idea, alpha reading and moral support throughout; to **James Mackay** for the procedural analysis, development editing work and so much more; to **John Rickards** for the fantastic copy editing; to **Vicki Goldman** for the sterling job proofing; and to the many beta readers, thanks for all your help and support.

Thanks to Colin Scott, you know who you are and what you do for the mental health of me and my friends, though you're to blame for our livers being worse.

If you spot any typographical errors, please email me at ed@edjames.co.uk. Thanks! In fact, you can email me about anything, if you want.

If you've got a moment, I'd appreciate it if you could leave a review on Amazon:

https://geni.us/EJD3back

Ed James,
Scottish Borders, April 2021

ABOUT ED JAMES

Ed James writes crime-fiction novels, primarily the DI Simon Fenchurch series, set on the gritty streets of East London featuring a detective with little to lose. His Scott Cullen series features a young Edinburgh detective constable investigating crimes from the bottom rung of the career ladder he's desperate to climb.

Formerly an IT project manager, Ed began writing on planes, trains and automobiles to fill his weekly commute to London. He now writes full-time and lives in the Scottish Borders, with his girlfriend and a menagerie of rescued animals.

OTHER BOOKS BY ED JAMES

SCOTT CULLEN MYSTERIES SERIES

Eight novels featuring a detective eager to climb the career ladder, covering Edinburgh and its surrounding counties, and further across Scotland.

1. GHOST IN THE MACHINE
2. DEVIL IN THE DETAIL
3. FIRE IN THE BLOOD
4. STAB IN THE DARK
5. COPS & ROBBERS
6. LIARS & THIEVES
7. COWBOYS & INDIANS
8. HEROES & VILLAINS

CULLEN & BAIN SERIES

Four novellas spinning off from the main Cullen series covering the events of the global pandemic in 2020.

1. CITY OF THE DEAD
2. WORLD'S END
3. HELL'S KITCHEN
4. GORE GLEN

CRAIG HUNTER SERIES

A spin-off series from the Cullen series, with Hunter first featuring in the fifth book, starring an ex-squaddie cop struggling with PTSD, investigating crimes in Scotland and further afield.

1. MISSING

2. HUNTED
3. THE BLACK ISLE

DS VICKY DODDS SERIES

Gritty crime novels set in Dundee and Tayside, featuring a DS juggling being a cop and a single mother.

1. BLOOD & GUTS (a new prequel coming soon)
2. TOOTH & CLAW
3. FLESH & BLOOD
4. SKIN & BONE (coming 1st May 2021)

DI SIMON FENCHURCH SERIES

Set in East London, will Fenchurch ever find what happened to his daughter, missing for the last ten years?

1. THE HOPE THAT KILLS
2. WORTH KILLING FOR
3. WHAT DOESN'T KILL YOU
4. IN FOR THE KILL
5. KILL WITH KINDNESS
6. KILL THE MESSENGER
7. DEAD MAN'S SHOES

Other Books

Other crime novels, with Senseless set in southern England, and the other three set in Seattle, Washington.

- SENSELESS
- TELL ME LIES
- GONE IN SECONDS
- BEFORE SHE WAKES

ED JAMES READERS CLUB

By signing up to my mailing list, you'll get access to **free, exclusive** content and be up-to-speed with all of my releases:

And, in case you missed it, I published a Vicky Dodds prequel novella in April 2021. Get it in paperback or for FREE on Kindle here:

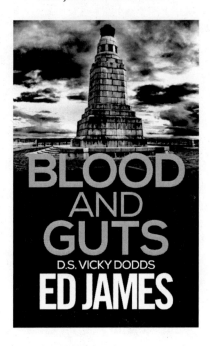

https://geni.us/EJDoback